From Hackerville with Love

by Megan Carney

Learn more about Megan Carney at

megancarney.com.

ISBN-13: 978-1734759006

To everyone in desperate circumstances trying to do
the right thing.

Chapter 1

The perfect bar was hard to find.

A kitchen that was open late was nice. A place with booths in dark corners where she could hide was good too. There should be enough regulars that it was never quiet—that was, after all, the point. But not so many people she would get looks for taking up space for a couple hours. More importantly, the regulars had to be aloof. Navy Trent didn't want to talk.

The waiter (also the bartender) slid her plate in front of her. A thick burger with a side of fries.

"Anything stronger than water?" he asked.

Drink would not combine well with her nerves tonight. "No. Thanks."

Like a good bartender, he sensed her mood and didn't tarry. "Settle up at the counter when you're ready," he called over his shoulder.

1:40 a.m. The bar would close in twenty minutes and then she would be back where she started the night—alone in Jackson's apartment wishing he was home. The burger was too large to hold in one hand. Navy unwrapped the paper napkin holding a set of cutlery and took out the steak knife. A spot of dried food tarnished the metal. She picked it off with her fingernail. She had to force herself to eat. Sometimes the mundane necessities of life escaped her. Barbecue sauce dripped from the burger to the table, and she searched for the napkin to clean it up.

"You know what they say."

The man who had sat down on the bench across from her carried a cloud of aroma – beer and sweat and cigarettes. His eyes were bloodshot, and his left eyelid drooped slightly lower than his right. The small detail was enough. What little appetite she had deserted her and she clenched her fists under the table. He wasn't a large man and being drunk would make him clumsy. An elbow to his nose and a kick to his shin would be enough.

"Closing time," he continued. He wasn't slurring his words as much as his breath would suggest. Perhaps she shouldn't underestimate him. He looked her up and down. "You don't have to go home, but you can't stay here."

She had chosen her privacy too well. The high walls of the booth kept her hidden from everyone in the bar but her unwanted suitor and two men who must be his friends. They were slightly less drunk, leaning on a wall a few yards away. They seemed embarrassed. It was time to go, before she followed through on the moves her muscles were already planning. She pulled money out of her wallet—too much to pay for a half-eaten burger—and dropped the bills on the table. "Sorry, I'm not interested."

He looked hurt. He had no idea how close he was to being hurt for real.

"Don't be like that. It's just a line."

She slid out of the booth and stood up. His two friends – also in rumpled business shirts and jeans – were coming over.

Not to corner her, she reminded herself. This wasn't Amsterdam, where she had been abducted. It was just a neighborhood bar in DC. They were just collecting their friend. They mumbled something apologetic.

The one in the blue-striped shirt tapped her unwanted suitor on the shoulder. "You made your play, Charlie. She's not interested. Let's go."

Navy didn't know whether it was stubbornness or pride that made Charlie grab her wrist. He was stronger than she expected. Not the strongest man she'd fought by far. But strong enough. If only she had known then what she knew now.

"Hey!"

The yell made her freeze. It wasn't Charlie—he was on his back, moaning. Navy was straddling his chest. She didn't know the sequence of moves she'd used. The yell must have been from the man in the blue-striped shirt. He was scared now instead of embarrassed. His eyes were following her hand; she was reaching for something near the edge of the table. She was reaching for the steak knife.

She scrambled to her feet and backed away from the trio. Blue-striped shirt was helping Charlie into a chair. The few patrons left at the bar stared at her, wide-eyed. It could have been pity or surprise. The bartender hovered near the edge of the wood counter, ready to intervene. She had to get outside before anyone noticed she was shaking. Before someone called the police. The muggy summer air clogged her lungs. Find the car, she told herself. Find the car and get back to Jackson's apartment.

When she tried to unlock the door, the keys slipped from her hand and into the shadow beneath the car. She swiped at the glimmer of metal. Grit from the parking lot dug under her nails. Slow down, she told herself. The calmer she was, the faster she would get out of here. She wiped the keys on her jeans and opened the car door. Tiny, sharp rocks pricked her skin when she gripped the steering wheel. She had nearly pulled a knife on a man named Charlie for being a bad pickup artist. She hated herself for that almost as much as she hated herself for the feeling that right now, more than anything in the world, she wanted Jackson.

Chapter 2

Byron hated the sound of that giggle. Insomnia had forced him out of bed and down to the kitchen for a midnight snack. Instead, he found his daughter, Clara, caught in the blue glow of her laptop screen in the living room. The girl who had brought home crayon drawings of their house. The girl who had cried the first day they dropped her off at kindergarten. Now she was a freshman at college, home for summer break, sitting on the couch and flirting with a man over Skype.

The man was Andrei Radu and he lived in Romania. Clara didn't know, but Andrei was a man with criminal ties to very dangerous people. Byron couldn't tell her because everything he knew about Operation Quicksand was classified. He wasn't supposed to know about the operation at all; he'd only run across the file because he'd been checking up on Andrei. Clara also didn't know her dad was an analyst at the CIA. She didn't know that he used to be an undercover officer. He was tempted to tell her, even though it broke several rules, but at this point it wouldn't help.

Byron had never liked any of Clara's boyfriends. She wouldn't believe his reasons for disliking this one. At least he knew how to end the call.

"Clara, sweetie, is that you? I didn't know you were still up. Do you want some hot chocolate?" He took two mugs out of the cupboard. Clara never said no to hot chocolate.

"In a second, Dad." Then more softly, "Andrei, I have to go. It's my dad."

Byron couldn't hear Andrei's reply. Clara used headphones with a mic. That damn giggle again.

"No, you really shouldn't ask him," she said. "Trust me on this."

Then, a heavy sigh and the snap of plastic as she pulled her headphones off. She walked into the kitchen holding her laptop out like a sacrifice, the screen facing Byron. He looked into the face of the man he had, more than once, imagined murdering. Andrei was handsome like a statue. His chiseled jawline framed dark blue eyes and black hair that fell across his face. He had lost some weight since the last photos from Interpol. Byron wondered what Andrei thought of the middle-aged man with a receding hairline. Andrei might think Byron was an easy target.

"Dad, this is Andrei," Clara said. "Andrei, this is my dad, Byron."

"Mr. Macalester," Andrei said. "I have looked forward to meeting you." The only way Byron could tell English was Andrei's second language was the overly formal tone.

"I've heard a lot about you." Byron forced a smile. "It's nice to finally meet you."

"Clara says she is coming to Bucharest for a study abroad program next semester," Andrei said.

Not if you're still in Romania, Byron thought. "Yeah, she's really excited about it."

"Clara didn't want me to ask you, but my mother is old fashioned," Andrei said.

According to Interpol, Andrei's mother was dead.

"I would like to invite Clara down to stay with my family in Râmnicu Vâlcea for a weekend when she is in Bucharest. With your permission, of course."

Râmnicu Vâlcea was less formally known around Byron's office as Hackerville, a sleepy Romanian town with a reputation for cybercrime. And Andrei's "family" was Dragomir Pirvu's organized crime ring. Byron didn't want to imagine what a Romanian cybercrime ring would want with his daughter. "I expect she'll be busy with her studies." Byron's refusal actually seemed to cheer the bastard.

"Yes, of course," Andrei said. "It's too far away. I should have realized."

"I told you," Clara said to the screen. "I'll call you tomorrow." She closed the laptop forcefully and turned to Byron with a familiar glare.

"That's an expensive laptop," he said. He dropped two squares of the special chocolate he'd bought for Clara into a pan of milk. The burner glowed orange when he turned the knob.

"You met him for two seconds, Dad. What could you possibly have against him?"

Byron concentrated on stirring the milk to keep a skin from forming. "He's bad news, Clara."

"You always say that."

It was true. This time he had facts, though. Facts he

couldn't share with her. "Just last week he was complaining about that hospital bill, right?"

"What does that have to do with anything?"

He hoped a plausible lie would work in place of the harsher truth. "It sounds like a scam. I read about it in the news the other day. These people look on dating sites and develop relationships so they can ask for money. They start out with small requests, then bigger and bigger until—"

"I'm a starving college student."

She had a point. "Still," he said. "Didn't he try to ask you for money for an apartment deposit once?"

"He didn't ask me for anything. He was just upset because the apartment he was supposed to move into was cockroach infested and he refused to move in and the landlord kept his deposit so he had to . . ." Clara stopped and collected herself. "Anyway, he never asked."

The chocolate melted into swirls of brown. "Can you trust me on this?" Maybe a joke would lighten the mood. "I didn't earn these wrinkles for nothing, you know."

"You can't stop me from seeing him."

The hell he couldn't. "Tuition's going up next year," he said. "We may not be able to afford study abroad, it'll take you an extra semester to graduate and—"

"Don't you dare!"

He hadn't heard her hit that octave since their legendary battles over curfew in high school. He heard creaks upstairs and knew Clara had woken Nancy.

"You'd take away my tuition money because you can't handle the fact I have a boyfriend." Clara balled her fists. There were spots of red on her cheeks. Such a young face to be so contorted with anger. "God, you're rich." She stormed upstairs, each step pounding in his head. He heard a hushed conversation at the landing, Clara's sharp tones and her mother's calm ones. Clara's bedroom door slammed. His wife padded into the kitchen.

He'd forgotten to stir the milk and it was curdling. He poured the mess down the sink.

"Up to your old tricks, I see," Nancy said.

"He's dangerous. It's not just me this time." Byron hadn't shared details, but Nancy knew where he worked and what kind of contacts he had.

"I believe you. But Clara never will."

"She can't go if we don't pay for it," he insisted.

"She'd never forgive us."

"She's too stubborn."

"Like her father." Nancy tightened the belt on her robe. "Anyway, she can always get student loans to cover the tuition and living costs."

"So what do you think we should do?"

"I know what kind of friends you have. I'm sure you can think of something."

There were a few options he had considered.

Nancy touched his arm. "Something honorable."

That left fewer options. Just one, in fact.

Chapter 3

Navy's arms ached and her knuckles were sore. Even though she was wearing boxing gloves. Most Saturday mornings in DC she was sparring at the gym. The exertion and pain were a welcome distraction. Unlike the bar last night, there were no spectators here. Navy and Logan, her sparring partner, had the gym to themselves. After two matches, Navy had almost forgotten the face of the man with the drooping left eyelid.

Logan fastened his gloves and stepped onto the mat. "Ready, Violet?"

"Whenever you are, Preppy."

Outside of the gym, Logan dressed as if he lived in a mansion on Martha's Vineyard. The nicknames were mostly affectionate. Navy wasn't sure she would call Logan a friend. He was a good sparring partner. Logan was bigger and stronger; she was faster and more technical. They made each other better.

"Trivia round?" Logan asked.

Recently, they'd been playing a trivia game during boxing rounds. Fighting was a mental challenge as much as a physical one. Winning required learning her opponent's tactics and weaknesses, even as her opponent was learning hers. Adding trivia questions to the already complicated calculus increased the mental load, and the challenge, for both of them.

They sparred at fifty percent power by agreement. As the gym owner often said, your sparring partners are your toys. Don't break your toys. Navy started with a combination: jab, cross, uppercut, hook. The last hook landed lightly on Logan's chin.

"How many wives did Henry VIII have?" she asked.

"Six." Logan countered with a jab to Navy's face and, when she blocked with both arms, a lower punch that landed solidly on her stomach. She backed off to catch her breath but kept her feet moving. The boxer's bounce, they called it. A slight rotation of the core on the balls of her feet, a slight shift of weight from right to left with a rhythm as steady as a pendulum's swing.

"Why'd you take a job in DC?" Logan asked.

She stutter-stepped. Logan knew she worked at the CIA. Navy had seen him in the office in passing once. He worked in college recruiting. Outside the office, they only acknowledged each other as fellow gym members. She answered with a mock punch to his liver and swept his leg. "To learn new things," Navy said as Logan regained his balance. A safe answer in public.

Logan countered with a knee and a jab, cross, jab that Navy blocked easily. "You are a fast learner. But I don't think that's why."

Normally, Logan's questions were limited to actual trivia. Navy executed a new combination that brought Logan to the edge of the mat. He threw an uppercut, cross, and when she blocked, stepped to the center of the ring.

"What are the enzymes used in cheese-making called?" Navy asked.

"Rennet." He moved in. His strength temporarily overwhelmed her speed and she found herself panting when they separated.

Navy delivered a flurry of punches. Logan's counterattack didn't land, but it did force her back.

"Hypothetical," Logan said. "You're lost in a hostile urban environment on a cloudy day and you need to find south."

At least this one wasn't personal. "Northern or southern hemisphere?"

"Northern."

"Look for satellite dishes. They're pointed south."

"Correct," Logan said.

The professor-like tone rankled her. As if she were being evaluated for something. Navy moved in to attack with both words and fists. "In network traffic, what does UDP stand for?"

"Cheap shot," Logan answered as he dodged her right hook. "Next question." The sparring match continued like a good conversation; no attack left unanswered.

Navy jumped between literary questions and marine biology and American history. Logan's hypotheticals got more complicated and bizarre. Someone's Facebook page says they love cats, how would you arrange an accidental meeting? You have access to someone's credit card records. How would you build a psychological profile? His questions required answers in paragraphs instead of sentences.

Navy felt the mental strain. She was writing small essays while also focusing on her footwork, her strategy, and the form of her punches. The complicated questions were a bonus.

Last night's encounter was pushed further down in her mind. But the effort tired her more quickly, and Navy hadn't slept well anyway. She stumbled during his next attack and landed hard on her knee.

Logan dropped his fighting stance and held out a hand. "Done for today?"

"I think so," she said reluctantly.

"Good round. Have you ever . . ."

The instructor for the 10:30 class entered the gym. Navy sat down on a chair and took a gulp from her water bottle. Logan took a gulp from his.

"Have you ever considered fieldwork?" His voice was quiet, but his expression was mischievous.

Navy shook her head. The question was ridiculous. Analysts worked under a different directorate than field officers. Plus, she'd had enough of risking her life for principles. She'd had enough of risking her life, period. Hadn't she? Maybe what kept her up last night had been the familiar tinge of excitement she felt. Getting her opponent to the ground had been effortless. She could barely justify last night's actions as self-defense. And yet, something about the moment was comforting. She had felt powerful. But why should she feel powerless?

She was better equipped to handle an attacker now than she had been when she was attacked last year. She was, in theory, safer than she ever had been. Recovery was an elusive concept. Navy went to her job. She hung out with friends. She had Jackson. She functioned. The violence that itched at her was a

16

distraction. Scratching it would only make it worse.

Logan was still watching her.

"Not my thing," Navy said.

"You sure about that?"

Navy ignored him and retrieved her phone. There was a text message from Byron.

"Jackson will be home next Saturday around lunch. Thought you might want to know."

One week. Too long, and somehow, too short. She was impatient to see him, but she didn't want him to see her in her current state. By the time Jackson arrived, how would she feel about the fact she had come close to killing a man without cause? She still felt guilty about the men she had killed who had deserved it. Jackson was too good at reading her, she'd never be able to hide her state of mind. Even if she kept her secrets. She would add last night's adventures to the set of things Jackson didn't know about her and she hoped he never would.

And why was Byron telling her? Normally, she only knew a rough time frame for Jackson's engagements and only learned he was coming home when Jackson texted her from the airport.

"See you next week, Preppy," Navy told Logan.

"Later, Violet."

Navy ignored the jab and headed toward the locker rooms. A nice long, hot shower was just what she needed to forget last night's adventures and Logan's questions.

Chapter 4

Jackson stepped off the gangway and into the muggy Dulles airport. His T-shirt stuck to his sore shoulders. At least in Kandahar's dry climate he could sweat. Even the best air conditioners couldn't make DC comfortable in the summer. Of course, the company was better here. He threw his pack over his shoulder and weaved through the crowd hemmed in by gray pillars punctuating the concourse. Large fans whirred beneath bright ads on the walls.

As operations go, this last one wasn't bad. Mostly politicking with the local warlords. No atrocities he had to force himself to forget. It had been longer than usual, though. Six weeks gone on assignment for the agency. It seemed even longer now that he had someone in his life. He would need a day to catch up on his sleep and let his bruises fade and then he would call in a favor to get a friend to fly him down to Des Moines to see Navy. He took his phone out to check his messages. It would take him a day just to return them all.

The refugee center wanted to know when he could do volunteer counseling again. His dentist was calling to say Jackson was due for a six-month checkup. His sister wanted to know if he was going to make the Fourth of July family reunion. Kevin, his handler, had called in the middle of Jackson's flight and wanted his incident report. Typical. Just one more message, and it wasn't from Navy. It was from Byron. An invitation to dinner, maybe.

Byron held barbecues every few months for close friends and family. As long as the grill wasn't snowed in, the party went on.

"You should be landing soon. Navy's new gig, the cybersecurity analyst thing, has her in DC a couple weeks a month. She needed a place to stay so I gave her a copy of your keys. I figured you wouldn't mind."

He didn't. But when he'd offered Navy a set of his keys before he left, she'd refused. The polite mechanical voice on his phone interrupted his thoughts, asking if he wanted to save the message or delete it. Jackson replayed it.

"You should be landing soon. Navy's new gig, the cybersecurity analyst thing, has her in DC a couple weeks a month. She needed a place to stay so I gave her a copy of your keys. I figured you wouldn't mind. I broke protocol and told her when you'd be home. I need to come by for some business – around sixteen hundred." There was a long pause and then Byron cleared his throat. "Try to have some clothes on when I get there."

Navy was at Jackson's apartment waiting for him. Jackson picked up his pace as he moved toward the taxi stand, brushing past tourists arriving for the weekend and businessmen whose ties floated in the gusts of the fans. Even on Saturday morning, traffic moved sluggishly. In a sky the color of steel, a helicopter flew over the highway, then tilted toward the Pentagon. Jackson tapped his fingers on the seat of the taxi impatiently, stuck in the press of cars. He had the fare ready when the cab stopped in front of his apartment building. Jackson didn't give the cab driver time to count it before grabbing his backpack. A green light blinked on the lock when he swiped his fob at the door. The elevator took too long, so he took the steps two at a time up to his floor.

Pans clanged in his kitchen. The scent of bacon and eggs drifted into the hallway. He stopped, savoring the sounds of his occupied apartment. It could have been their apartment, if Navy had allowed it. He wondered if accepting a set of keys from Byron meant something had changed. In the year since they'd been together, she had carefully avoided the word "love." But she had taken over part of the closet in his bedroom.

One four-letter word she wouldn't say, a ring of keys she wouldn't accept; he knew these things shouldn't bother him. He had her affections in every way that mattered. He turned his key in the lock but the door opened for him.

A smile played on Navy's lips. "How long were you planning on waiting there?" Her chin-length blond hair was still damp from the shower. Her cheeks were flushed – she preferred her showers close to scalding. A tight shirt hugged her curves and a pair of his boxers hung low on her hips. God, he had missed her.

He wrapped one arm around her waist, dropped his pack, and kicked the door shut behind him. She laughed and threw her arms around his neck. Their kiss was hard, slow, and lingering.

"Did you miss me?" he asked.

"Not a bit," she answered—the ritual they'd shared since the first trip that had separated them. She pressed her face into his

20

sweaty shirt. Her wet hair soaked through the cotton. "Long flight?"

She knew he wasn't allowed to give her any details about where he'd been. "Long enough," he said. He studied her face again, this time noticing the shadows under her eyes. "You haven't been sleeping."

"Bad week at work." Her downcast eyes betrayed the lie. "Byron gave me a package for you. It's in the living room. Some special beer he ordered that he said you liked?"

A not-so-subtle change in topic. Jackson decided to let it pass. When she didn't want to talk about something, it was no use trying to force her.

"Anyway, I think Byron's trying to get on your good side."

He pulled her closer and buried his nose in her hair. The smell of her shampoo – peaches and ginger – loosened the knots in his shoulders. "I don't know why he'd be on my bad side."

"He told you he was coming over?"

"In four hours." He nuzzled her neck and tightened his hold on her waist.

She smiled and pushed him away. "Food first, Romeo. I was at the gym sparring all morning. I'm starving."

Almost every drawer and cabinet in his small kitchen was open. The few pans he owned were stacked precariously on the counter. The rest of his counter space was taken up by two paper grocery bags. "When did you start cooking?"

"I didn't," she said. "I found the best deli. Giraldi's? It's only a block away." She stuck her head into another cabinet and her voice echoed. "They do a take-out brunch."

The only restaurant Jackson knew about near his apartment was the Chinese place that was open until two in the morning.

"I just need a cookie sheet to warm up the cinnamon rolls. Best I've ever had." She opened the next cabinet. "You do have a cookie sheet, right?"

He tried to remember if he did and if so, where he would keep it. "Try the oven."

She opened the preheating oven. "Huh. In the oven. Is that a bachelor pad thing or a secret agent thing?"

"I turn it sideways if the Russians are attacking." He snuck a kiss before he went into the bedroom to unpack his bag. Dust sprinkled on the comforter when he emptied the contents. The clothes seemed cleaner when he packed them last night. Now they smelled like cigarette smoke from the fighters, gun oil from the shipments he'd helped broker, and coriander from the rich lamb stews he'd been served. His phone and laptop were near dead. He plugged both of them in but turned off his phone. Kevin's report could wait until tomorrow.

Jackson heard the oven door open and close. The smell of cinnamon and frosting wafted down the hall. He was impatient to get back to Navy, but a gentleman would shower. Thankfully, his drill sergeant at boot camp had been strict. He could shower in two minutes with time to spare. Three minutes later, he was dry and in clean clothes. Cleaner than he'd worn in weeks.

Navy served warmed slices of spinach and bacon quiche. The buttery crust melted in Jackson's mouth. The cinnamon rolls were as large as his hand and as good as Navy promised. Neither spoke. When she reached for seconds, their fingers brushed. While he scraped the last of the frosting off his plate, her toes crept up his leg. She stood up and walked toward the bedroom, hips swaying. He followed.

Her body was familiar to him, but no less thrilling for it. Frowning slightly, she touched each one of his bruises, but asked no questions. Navy knew he couldn't answer them. She had her own bruises. From sparring, he figured. Still, the evidence of her pain made his homecoming bittersweet. What specters was she really fighting at the gym? And yet, the distraction of his questions faded with each kiss, each caress. As always with her, and only her, his passion overwhelmed his instinct to analyze. Knowing she was safe, being close to her, these were the cravings he had pushed into the back of his mind for weeks. Her bare shoulder against his sheets. His hands, her hands twisted together in the stripes of light cast by the blinds. He let himself be carried away in a blur of images and ecstasy.

Afterwards, he stroked her hair until she fell asleep. In ten days he would be gone again. Who could blame her for keeping her distance? Her brow furrowed and he smoothed it with his fingers. He wondered if last year's kidnapping and attempted rape haunted her dreams. They haunted his. Despite his best efforts, he hadn't arrived in time to help her. She refused to talk about any of it. Or to see a therapist. And he didn't want to waste his time stateside arguing. When Navy's breathing was deep and even, he crept out of bed and dressed.

At 15:55 Jackson was at his kitchen table, still littered with dishes, nursing a cup of coffee. As his watch changed from 15:59 to 16:00, there was a knock at the door. Punctuality was a habit Byron had never abandoned, even though it had been years since he'd been undercover.

He let Byron in and gestured toward the table. "Have a seat. Do you want anything? Coffee? Orange juice? Water?"

Byron pinched the corner of a take-out bag. "Coffee. Please." His blond hair was going gray and the hairline was steadily creeping back. A bulldog physique was hidden underneath the doughy figure. Civilian life had added the pounds. He looked the same as the last time Jackson had seen him. But the fidgeting hands, the sloping posture. The subdued, almost apologetic manner. Those weren't the same Byron he knew.

Jackson put sugar and cream into Byron's coffee and cleared a space on the table for it. "Something bothering you?"

"Is Navy around?"

"You have business with Navy?" Byron analyzed intelligence supporting undercover missions. Navy analyzed malicious code found in the wild. Their work rarely intersected.

"Well, probably better to start with you."

Jackson watched Byron stir his coffee.

"There's this mission in Romania – to infiltrate a cybercrime ring. Navy's name has come up as a possible candidate for the undercover work."

"No." As if Jackson's word could kill the possibility. "She's a tech, not a field officer. It's not even her department."

Byron was fidgeting again. "It's an open secret how she escaped her kidnapping. How she evaded capture when she went on the run. She has tactical skills and computer savvy. It's a rare combination." He shifted the cup between his hands. "It wasn't my idea. It's only talk, so far."

"Then kill the talk."

Byron looked at Jackson's expression and flinched. "The thing is, I don't want to."

"You better explain yourself," Jackson said through clenched teeth.

Byron pulled a file out of his briefcase and slid it across the table. Jackson made no move to open it.

"It's this cybercrime ring in Romania," Byron said. "Dragomir Pirvu's crew. I shouldn't even be showing you the file. But I thought it might help explain."

The name was familiar. Dragomir Pirvu greased palms in many areas of the world – occasionally in places where Jackson worked. The people Dragomir funded weren't generally known for their good deeds.

"They need a programmer, someone who can write exploits. We'd like to put someone on the inside."

"We have field officers trained with those skills."

"Not enough. They've delayed the operation twice because they don't have an officer with the right qualifications."

Jackson glanced toward the bedroom, remembering the

fan of Navy's hair against the pillow. "What's the rush?"

Byron spun his coffee cup by the handle. The sound scraped at Jackson's nerves. "Well, you know how it is," Byron said. "Opportunities come and go."

"You're here to ask my permission to get the operations director to recruit Navy."

"Permission? This is professional courtesy." That was the Byron Jackson knew. The diplomatic bully. "It's Navy's permission I need."

"She doesn't want to go." Jackson hoped.

"Doesn't want to go where?" Navy asked. She was dressed in shorts and a tank top now. Her hair was pulled back in a ponytail.

Jackson gripped his coffee cup tighter. He hadn't been able to protect her last year; he wouldn't repeat that mistake again. "Ask Byron." Jackson watched Navy's thoughtful expression and felt the contrast to his anger. He knew she was evaluating the situation and judging them both. As any good officer would.

"Okay. What's this all about, Byron?" Navy rested her fingers on Jackson's neck and despite his anger, his breathing slowed.

"Your name has come up for an undercover mission. You know about Hackerville?"

"Since when is the CIA concerned about some thugs in Romania who do penny stock scams and counterfeit medication?"

"Tip of the iceberg," Byron said.

Jackson shook his head. Byron had just as many scars as Jackson: the puckered skin of healed bullet wounds, bones that ached long after the break mended. Navy hadn't set out to acquire tactical skills. She had been forced to learn them with a gun pointed at her head.

"Don't you have field officers for that sort of thing?" she asked.

"We don't have anyone who could go until October," Byron said.

She frowned. "If timing is such an issue, why hasn't the operations director approached me?"

"Yes, why *is* that?" Jackson echoed.

Byron glared at him. "As undercover work goes, it's pretty light. Dragomir runs a botnet. He sells access to the machines he's taken over. Criminals can rent time on Dragomir's botnet for hiding attacks. And, uh, downloads of things. You would help them program some more exploits to infect machines. And while they're not looking, add some lines of code to the software package Dragomir's clients use. Just so we can trace his clients." He cleared his throat. "You're famous for your coding skills now. And last year's scandal is the perfect cover for wanting to betray your government."

Men above Jackson's pay grade had decided against rescuing Navy after she had been mistaken for a CIA officer and kidnapped by terrorists. A rescue attempt would have risked blowing another officer's cover.

"I know what exploits and botnets are," she said. "You haven't answered my question."

Byron sighed and rubbed his chin. "It's Clara. She's doing this study abroad thing in Bucharest next semester. She posted on her Facebook profile that she was going and somehow this guy – Andrei Radu – found her. They've been Skyping for two months. It's nearly every day now. So I did some checking."

"You used your access as a CIA intelligence analyst to research your daughter's boyfriend," Jackson said.

"I used my access to research a suspicious pattern associated with a phone number," Byron corrected.

"Uh-huh," Jackson said.

"Andrei works for Dragomir. Hackerville is only two hours from Bucharest. I threatened to pull her tuition funding if she went to see him and now she won't talk to me."

Jackson knew how determined Clara could be when she really wanted something. Especially when it came to love. In high school, she had run away for the weekend when Byron had told her she couldn't see her college boyfriend any longer. Over the years, and countless barbecues at Byron's house, Jackson had watched Clara go from a curious toddler to a precocious teenager to a gifted freshman linguist. Clara was the kind of girl who won you over on the first meeting. She had a bright smile, an open heart, and a laugh you couldn't help but echo. Jackson saw Byron's plan. "If Navy goes to Hackerville, you can wrap up the whole operation before Clara gets there. Andrei will be in jail or on the run."

Byron nodded. "Navy's the only person who can go without needing months of training. I can't afford to wait."

Jackson's coffee was cold. He waited for Navy to object. Surely she could see how foolhardy the idea was.

"I'm sorry to ask," Byron said. "But it's my daughter. You understand."

About wanting to protect someone so badly you'd sacrifice anything? Jackson understood. He looked at Navy. "There's no such thing as 'light' undercover work."

Navy pressed her lips together and squeezed his shoulder.

"I'd do it myself," Byron said. "You know I would."

"What about Erin?" Jackson asked.

"Erin hasn't been a programmer for years. And she never wrote exploit code. I don't need someone who knows ten ways to kill someone with a plastic spoon. I need a programmer who can handle herself." Byron turned to Navy. "I'd understand completely if you don't want to. But if you're willing, I'd consider it a personal favor."

Navy looked more sympathetic than afraid. Jackson had a sinking feeling in his stomach. She had been to plenty of dinners at Byron's house over the past year too.

"I'll look at the file," she said.

"You're not seriously considering this." Jackson felt the chip in the handle of his coffee mug dig into his hand. His face was warm.

"Give us a chance to talk," she told Byron.

"It's too dangerous," Jackson said. It was the wrong thing to say and he knew it. There were few things Navy hated more than being told what to do.

She jerked her hand away. "I can handle myself."

Maybe he could convince her not to go for his sake. "It's not about you. I can't handle it. Watching—"

"—the person you love go into a dangerous situation and not knowing when they'll be back? You're right. That wouldn't be fair."

The remark stung. Jackson glared at Byron, who looked away. Before Byron had shown up, everything was going fine. Jackson caught Navy's hand before she could move farther away. "If you go, I go."

Her scowl dissolved into surprise. Was she really so surprised he wanted to protect her?

"I should probably leave," Byron mumbled. "Give you a few days to talk things over."

Jackson waited until Navy had locked the door behind Byron. "Cybercrime is still organized crime. It's no less dangerous."

"I know." She traced a pattern in the crumbs on the table. "I wouldn't even consider it if it didn't involve Clara."

"We can find another way," he said.

"You want to send Erin over there with a plastic spoon."

Better than sending you, Jackson thought.

"Without an official mission, you'd have no logistical support. It's more dangerous and you know it."

He wanted to ask if she woke up needing him when he wasn't there. If she worried while he was gone. But part of him didn't want to know the answer. He loved Navy, even if she wouldn't let him say it. And he loved his job. It was hard to imagine his life without one or the other. Love. She had used the word. "You said 'the person you love.'"

Her eyes widened and she backed toward the fridge. "Do you want some orange juice? I want some orange juice." She stuck her head in the fridge and surveyed the nearly empty shelves. There were exactly three things on the shelf: a very old bottle of ketchup, a jar of olives, and a carton of orange juice.

He got up from the table and leaned on the counter across from her. "You used the word love."

She shook her head without turning around.

"Before Byron left. You said 'the person you love.'"

She stood up and crossed her arms over her stomach. "That doesn't sound like me. I think I said 'the person you care about.'"

"Nope."

"Perhaps deeply care about."

"Nope." He picked her up by the waist and set her on the counter. "You said—"

She kissed him. "I said nothing of the sort."

"I heard—"

She kissed him again and traced the line of his waist. He couldn't make himself pull away.

"I know what you're doing," he mumbled through her

kiss.

"Oh?"

"You're trying to distract me."

She moved her fingers to trace the line of his ribs. "In that case, I should probably stop."

He wrapped her legs around his waist and lifted her up. "No. You should most definitely not stop. But we're going to talk about this later."

Her bubbling laughter filled his ears. "If you say so."

Chapter 5

The dark dream slipped away as soon as Navy woke, leaving her with a vague sense of dread and a heartbeat like the pattering of mouse feet. She knew the dream well enough. A damp basement where her circling footsteps landed on discarded needles. Gunshots and a crowbar whistling by her ear. A hulking man twice her size, intent on killing her slowly. Or that other basement. The one where a man had carefully undressed, preparing to rape her, while another man held her. The basement where she had stabbed one man and shot three others. She wondered if the gunfire would ever stop ricocheting in her head. She closed her eyes, snuggled back against Jackson's chest, but sleep had deserted her for the night.

Navy sat up carefully and hugged her knees. She focused on Jackson. The sight of him kept the shadows in their corners. She held a hand over his chest, wanting to bury her fingers in the dark curly hair. A scar, curved like a sliver of the moon, ran from his neck to his chest. Seeing the scar always reminded her of the risks he took. Love. What did one little word matter anyway?

If it matters so little, she argued with herself, say it just to make him happy. Even imagining saying the word made her throat close up. Some mistakes only needed to be made once.

"Hey," he said. His green eyes seemed to be the only thing with color in the room.

She was glad he was awake. "You should go back to sleep. You must be tired."

He shook his head and pushed himself up, the sheets pooling at his waist. He was, by most measures, a good catch. He had a long straight nose and dimples in his cheeks even when he wasn't smiling. Wrinkles were just starting to fan out from the corners of his eyes. She even liked how the pillow tousled his dark brown hair. "Nightmares again?" he asked.

"Yeah." Normally she didn't have nightmares when they shared a bed. She dropped her hand to the sheets, felt the light dusting of gritty sand that always followed Jackson home. From Afghanistan, most likely. That's where a psychologist with combat training who spoke Pashtun would be the most useful. The cold mountains would account for his pale arms, windburned face, and cracked cuticles.

"We can ta—"

"No." She looked away from his hurt expression. "It's just being in DC more often, I think."

"Or Byron's request."

"You're psychologisting again."

"That's not even a word."

"Sure it is," she said. "Psychologisting, verb, when your psychologist boyfriend overanalyzes—"

He trapped her in a tight hug until she could only smile against his chest. She wriggled free and stood up. The air felt cold after the warm bed.

"I need a walk," she said. It was 4:00 a.m. "How about

you?"

Jackson nodded. "It'll be nicer before the sun comes up."

She dressed in jeans, a short-sleeved shirt, and a jacket – knowing the humidity that was oppressive during the daytime made the air chilly before the sun rose. They walked past the weekend's dishes on the kitchen table, down the beige hallways of closed doors and into the sleeping city. Navy shrugged off the light jacket and let the dew collect on her bare arms. She found it easier to breathe outside the confines of walls and ceilings.

"Which way?" Jackson asked.

Left or right? An inconsequential decision. And yet, with the decision about Byron's request weighing on her, choosing a direction to turn her feet was difficult. Habit took over. She turned toward the strip mall where she often found herself picking up dinner. "This way."

Navy pointed at a closed storefront with a striped green and white awning. "Giraldi's. The take-out place."

Jackson took her hand, forcing her nervous steps to match his slower ones. "Best cinnamon rolls I've ever had."

Apartment buildings gave way to small, neat houses with manicured lawns. Dark windows hid the secrets of their occupants. The hazy air cocooned her as they walked the quiet streets. After her nightmares, a walk outside normally cleared her head. Today she felt as foggy as the air.

"Have you made up your mind?" he asked.

It was Monday. Barely two days since Byron had asked

her about going undercover. "About the cinnamon rolls? Definitely the best ever."

Jackson frowned. "You know what I mean."

A bluish-pink horizon was framed by the end of the street. She had known Clara for only a year, but in that time they had grown close. A typical visit with Jackson in DC included a Saturday evening at Byron's house. Clara had adopted Navy as an older sister, sharing conspiratorial stories about her latest hobbies or love interests. Navy hadn't known the handsome man with blue eyes Clara had been raving about was a Romanian criminal. Byron, unfortunately, was right about Clara being determined to see Andrei. Last time Navy had talked with her, she'd been counting down the days. Sweet, sharp Clara – who had Byron's intelligence without his brooding. A girl who trusted the world too much. Navy had loved a dangerous man once and it cost her dearly.

Plus, it was Byron asking. "I owe him," she said. "I wouldn't have survived last year without his help."

"Part of the job," Jackson snapped.

She pulled them to a stop and raised her eyebrows. "If he'd been doing his job, he would have let the terrorists execute me."

Jackson scuffed his shoes against the sidewalk. "Yeah, I know."

She kissed him on the cheek. The sun had risen slightly and some windows lit up in the houses they passed. Dew sparkled on pink petals in the flowerbeds. Dogs were let out into fenced yards. "I looked at the file. It's like Byron said, all I have to do is sneak in a few lines of code. Easy enough. It's not like what you do."

"You're not supposed to know what I do." He kept his eyes straight ahead.

"I know your skills and I see enough field reports that I can guess."

"You worry about me when I'm gone."

Of course she worried a little – it was only natural. "Would you prefer that I didn't?"

"That's not . . ." He ran a hand through his hair. "If my job is a problem, there are always openings at headquarters." He looked as if he had just taken a gulp of expired milk.

Navy shook her head. "Nobody said anything about you giving up your job. And I don't need babysitting."   "You have a lot to recover from. There's no shame in needing a little help."

Their conversations always seemed to circle back to this. "I already told you I don't want to talk about the nightmares." The red hand on the crosswalk light guarded an empty street. She didn't want to stand still. She heard the speeding car too late. Jackson yanked her back just as she felt the whoosh of air from the car passing. An angry, extended honk disturbed the otherwise peaceful morning.

She brushed his hands away. "I'm fine. Your job is fine. Everything's fine."

"Why don't I believe you?"

She studied his hands with her own. His fingers were

callused; the nails were far from manicured. He had never been anything but gentle with her, but she knew he was a dangerous man. A dangerous man and a good man. "You need your job – I can see that." *Maybe I need to go to Romania*, she thought. *Maybe you don't need to know why.* "I'll be fine, I promise." Her first instinct was to push him away. Instead, she leaned against him. He hesitated, then returned the embrace. The last tendrils of her nightmare faded.

They turned back toward Jackson's apartment. They were almost inside when he said, "Say no to Byron. For me." He tried to make his tone light but she could see the worry in his eyes.

"Jackson, it's not about you."

He cupped her neck and gave her a kiss that left her toes tingling. "I can be very persuasive, you know. And I'm not above using hypnosis on you."

Navy laughed and pushed him away. She already knew her answer, even if she couldn't say it just yet. She had to go. Not just because she owed Byron and she wanted to protect Clara. She needed another enemy. Another fight. A fight she chose rather than a fight that chose her.

Chapter 6

Navy balanced her tray on one hand while she squeezed through the usual lunchtime crowd at the deli near her office. There was only one table left, in the corner. Perfect. This was a working lunch and she wanted the privacy.

The laptop she pulled out was the latest in the MacBook Pro line, part of the bonus for taking the cybersecurity analyst position at the CIA. The CIA recruiter had mistaken the reason for her hesitation and sweetened the pot by adding the laptop. The truth was, she'd been reluctant to leave her old job even though it had been obvious it was time to go. The new job was just a first step. She hadn't told Jackson yet, but she was planning to move to DC. Navy was tired of all the attention she got in Des Moines.

In Des Moines, she was the local girl who had killed a government assassin and written a virus that had dethroned a president. In Washington, she was old news. In this little deli alone, she could spot one senator under investigation for illegal arms deals and a White House intern who was being watched for her ties to the Chinese.

The film she'd installed on her laptop screen ensured it was readable only to the person directly in front of it. The code she was disassembling was some of the least sensitive she worked with – a garden-variety virus found on a State Department laptop that had recently traveled to Hong Kong.

A program could easily translate the binary code into assembly code. Now her task was to figure what the assembly code did. Each line of assembly was one small instruction: push this number into a register, add two registers together, shift the bits to the left. A simple addition and multiplication in a high-level language like C could be several instructions in assembly. Attackers wrote their programs using deliberately complicated routines to make sure the assembly was difficult to interpret. But there was always one clue. And that was enough.

"You shouldn't work over lunch. It's bad for digestion."

The voice was familiar. The face that belonged to it was almost familiar. Sleek black hair framed an oval face with a pointed chin – like her own. The same almond-shaped hazel eyes Navy remembered. But the petite nose that had turned up at the end, like Navy's, was now straight. The line of the cheekbones had changed too.

"Erin?" Navy asked.

"Do you like the new nose?"

"I barely recognized you."

Erin was not the kind of friend Navy had ever imagined having. Erin, like Jackson, worked undercover for the agency. Unlike Jackson, she took a certain amount of joy in the less savory aspects of her job.

"Your infamy was making life difficult," Erin said. Navy's resemblance to Erin had led to Navy's kidnapping last year.

"I'm sorry."

40

Erin shrugged. "I like the new nose better. No offense, of course."

Navy could only nod. Her first lessons in hand-to-hand combat had been from Erin. Erin had been the first to confront Navy's survivor guilt after Navy had escaped. *You don't need to go over all the ways things could have gone worse. You don't need to know why you made it out in better condition than your friends.* In Erin's own clumsy, abrasive way, she had been trying to help. Trying to attach those memories to Erin's new face was disconcerting.

"It's not so uncommon these days. With facial recognition software and surveillance cameras everywhere, plastic surgeons are the CIA's new best friends."

Navy took a bite of her BLT to cover her nerves. Erin never stopped by just to chat. "Did Jackson send you here to talk me out of going to Romania?"

"No. I wouldn't want to."

"If you're attempting reverse psychology, Jackson already tried that."

"I had to see for myself." Erin studied Navy with an impish grin and narrowed eyes. "Navy Trent. Honorary field officer."

"You don't think I can do it." Navy was sure that was why Jackson was set against her going. But he knew better than to come out and say it.

"I didn't say that. I just don't think you know what you're getting into."

"He doesn't think I can."

That same impish grin flashed across Erin's face. "He still thinks you're a civilian." She said "civilian" like it was a swear word. "You stopped being a civilian when you killed that first man. The other four were just a bonus."

"I had no choice. You know that." Navy looked to see if anyone had heard. Not everything she had done was well known. But the low-level din in the crowded deli kept their conversation private.

"Choice. Who cares about choice? They deserved it."

Time with Erin often left Navy feeling like her brain had been scraped out of her skull. "Not that I don't enjoy our little talks, but why are you here?"

"To make sure you know what you're getting into before you say yes."

"It's a few lines of code. I could write it in my sleep."

"Forget about the code. You have to get recruited without looking like you want to be recruited. You need to earn their trust. Then you have to get access to the system. And after your little masterpiece is put in place, you need to get out before they figure out what you've done."

Navy didn't want to admit she hadn't considered all the details. "I survived last year."

"You're clever. You're decent in a fight."

Erin leaned in and Navy felt like an ant under a magnifying glass.

"Going undercover is about more than that. You have to

42

leave yourself behind.”

Navy had no idea what she meant. “I’ll be fine.”

“Prove it.”

“I’m not going to start a fight during my lunch hour.”

Erin laughed and Navy didn’t. “A fight? If you have to fight, something went wrong.”

The sounds of the deli filled the silence between them — conversations between friends, family, coworkers. The White House intern under suspicion ate at the counter with her back hunched over from nerves or guilt or fear. Paper crackled behind the order counter as sandwiches were wrapped. The sting of pickles and fresh-cut onions filled the room. Ice crunched out of the pop dispenser and the sweet whoosh of liquid followed. Navy finally managed to look at Erin.

Erin’s expression, for once, had no trace of mischief. “I’m going to pick a man in this crowd. You will get that man to come to this table in the next five minutes. Without moving from your seat or saying a word.”

Navy thought of Jackson and anger warmed her cheeks. “This is a silly exercise. How will it prove anything?”

“Then don’t do it. Tell Byron you want to go today instead of tomorrow.”

Turning the exercise into a dare was a cheap trick. “Fine. Pick your man.”

Erin pointed to a man in a sky-blue shirt a few tables away. A woman and a child shared the table with him. The woman had her back to Navy. The child stared at Navy with wide eyes. A family man.

Erin tapped her watch. "Four minutes thirty seconds."

Navy gulped down some juice to wet her throat. The only approach that occurred to her was the obvious one. She thought of Jackson, the lazy afternoon they'd spent in bed – sleeping, talking, kissing, making love. She caught the man's eye. She dropped her eyelids slightly and turned the corners of her mouth up. Her face was seducing a stranger. Her body wanted to run in the opposite direction, find Jackson, apologize.

The seduction was working.

The man gathered up his family's napkins and dishes on one tray. He rubbed his wife's shoulder and pointed toward the door. Navy's intense focus meant she heard only his voice over the rest of the conversations in the deli.

"Go get the car," he said to his wife. "I'll clear the table and meet you outside."

When the woman and child left, he walked toward Navy's table. Her stomach was doing somersaults. Sweat pricked at her armpits. Her pulse sped up.

"Keep your cover," Erin warned softly as the man approached. Erin's expression was neutral, as if they were two friends discussing a movie.

The man's eyes skipped over Erin and landed on Navy with bald desire. He had bushy eyebrows and thin lips. "Hi."

She was surprised she had an answer. "Hi, yourself." Like a bad porn film.

He glanced out the window then took her hand. His

wedding ring pressed against her fingers and his breath smelled like tuna. The man wrote a phone number on her palm and closed her hand over it. Navy saw the scene as if she were standing outside herself. *Leave yourself behind.* The man, a shameless cheater, thought he was in control.

"She'll be gone tonight. Call anytime after six." He walked outside. A car pulled up to the curb and he got in. Navy watched him kiss his wife on the cheek.

"Are you happy?" Navy snapped. "I feel sick." And beneath that, an emotion she didn't want to name. An echo of what she'd felt throwing a man to the ground not that many days ago. Satisfaction. Power.

Erin ate one of Navy's potato chips and smiled. "I knew you were a natural."

"You can have the sandwich too. I've lost my appetite."

"Admit it, you had a little fun."

There was no point in denying it, Erin could read Navy too well. "We should leave," Navy said.

"I haven't finished my lunch," Erin said.

"But I just—"

"Look around you." Erin gestured at the rest of the diners. "No one cares."

Erin was right. Navy had invited a man to cheat on his wife and the world had moved on.

"Not bad for a first try," Erin said. "I would have done a little less flirt and gone for the 'do I know you from high school?' Flirting with an asset can get tricky – they end up expecting certain things to happen."

Navy's subterfuge hadn't even been necessary.

"You're thinking about the wife, aren't you?"

And Jackson, Navy thought. But she wouldn't admit to any regret in front of Erin.

Erin finished off Navy's sandwich and licked her fingers. With the still-wet tips, Erin pointed at the phone number written on Navy's hand. "If you're so concerned, go ahead and tell her."

Chapter 7

The blue glow of Andrei's laptop filled the small room he shared with Petru, his nephew. Petru shifted in his sleep, no doubt disturbed by the light. Andrei wished that Dragomir would let Petru have his own room – Nicolae didn't need a separate room for the hookers he hired. Andrei wished that he wasn't forced to work nights as well as days.

He wished for a lot of things.

When he had won Pwn2Own the first year by breaking Chrome, Firefox, and Explorer within five minutes it had been for fun and profit. It was a good way to impress his friends and showcase his skills for future employers. The second year he won, he'd felt like he was on top of the world. When he graduated from the University of Bucharest, he would have his pick of employers. Perhaps working for Rapid7 with their Metasploit scanner or Microsoft or Google, to make their browsers more secure.

But then Dragomir started calling with job offers. At first Dragomir tried to buy Andrei's skills with money—lots of money.

When it became clear Andrei would not be bought, Dragomir turned to threats against him. Andrei knew the next step would be threats against his family. He drained his savings, packed a small bag and decided to disappear. He couldn't leave without saying goodbye, so he'd made one last stop at his sister's house, the only family he had. Dragomir's men had been watching. They could have just kidnapped him. Instead, they waited until Andrei went inside. The last image Andrei had of his brother-in-law was a spray of red arcing from his throat – he had refused to let go of his son, Petru. Andrei's sister, Afina, was beaten until she was unconscious. He still didn't know if she had survived.

Now his payment for working day and night was singular: Petru remained untouched.

Before Petru's kidnapping, Andrei had known Dragomir as the owner of one of the biggest botnets in the world. What Andrei knew now made his stomach turn every morning. Dragomir's gang specialized in the sex trafficking of children. Anonymity was preferred, of course, and Dragomir sold that too. For a small subscription fee paid in a cryptocurrency, you could access Dragomir's network of compromised machines and commit a crime on someone else's IP address.

An icon jiggled at the bottom of Andrei's screen, then a message popped up asking if he wanted to accept a call from Jessica. He didn't, but there were consequences if he didn't meet his quota.

"Jessica, it's so good to hear from you. It's so hard being in different time zones."

Jessica thought he was a college student in Bucharest. She lived somewhere in Idaho – a little town whose name he could never remember. He tried to pick out girls from smaller towns. They tended to be less suspicious.

"It's just been the craziest week," she said. She launched into some story about overtime at work because all the other cashiers were sick. He struggled to keep his eyes open.

"Sounds harsh. It's been pretty quiet here. Just missing you."

"I'm saving up money to come see you."

He hated this part. It was one thing to flirt a little; it was another to ask someone who didn't have a lot of money to give some to you. "I wouldn't want you to see the place I live now." That part was true enough. "Maybe when I move. I found a new place, but I won't be able to afford it until I pay off the hospital bills."

"I've been thinking about it and . . ."

The girls always hesitated here. He could almost hear the litany of their mother's/father's/aunt's/uncle's objections playing in their minds.

"They gave us a little bonus at work this year – just a couple hundred dollars – it's not a lot but I could wire it to you."

All the women. Exactly the same. The first conversations were full of cautious introductions, nervous jokes about all the pyschos or scammers you could find on the internet. Then long conversations full of flirt and revelations – childhood stories, intimate details of her daily life and his fictional one. And then he would make his first complaint. He would start small – a broken appliance in his apartment the landlord wouldn't replace. Or his car was broken and he needed it to get to work. The key was to never ask for money. Just imply that you needed it. When they offered, refuse the first time.

"That wouldn't be fair to you," he said. "There's that purse you wanted, right? You should treat yourself."

"My birthday's coming up. My parents will buy it. I can wire the money today."

Last week she had mentioned her birthday. He wanted to remember all the details. He wanted to treat them all well. But he was supposed to bring in so much money every month. And that meant a lot of women. If he didn't, he was punished. Sometimes he was punished just because Nicolae felt like hitting someone. That was all right. He could handle anything as long as they didn't hurt Petru.

"I'll be fine," he said. "I can dodge the collector's phone calls for a few more weeks."

"That's it. I'm wiring you the money. If you don't pick it up, Western Union will keep it."

Refuse the second time and accept the third. "I'll pay you back, I promise."

"You can just take me out to a nice dinner when I come visit."

She would be profitable for him. A few more small requests and then he would say he wanted to come see her instead. He would say he bought the airline tickets from his cousin's travel agency but his cousin drank the money away. She would be distraught. Her family would be expecting to meet him. She would send him the money to buy new tickets. He would never show up.

All the women. Exactly the same. Except for Clara, of course. Clara would have given him money during their first conversation. He'd found her profile on Facebook. Normally, he avoided women close to major cities but the kindness in her smile attracted him. And the quote on her wall: "Be kind. Everyone you meet is carrying a heavy burden." He hadn't expected her to be a good mark. He just wanted to talk with someone other than his ruthless keepers or Petru, with whom Andrei had to keep up a strong front.

Clara listened with all her heart. She'd already offered him money. He'd refused. He would keep refusing. Because she just might be his ticket out.

Chapter 8

The phone number on Navy's hand wasn't getting any lighter. Of course Erin would pick a man with a fancy ink pen instead of a cheap ballpoint. The hot water stung her palm as she circled the washcloth one last time. It was no use. The phone number would have to fade on its own.

She heard the front door of the apartment open, Jackson's footsteps in the kitchen. Then the heavy clunk of his bag dropping on the kitchen table. She locked the bathroom door and stared at her hand. Maybe he wouldn't notice. No, he noticed everything. She couldn't get away with lying to him; he always knew. She would have to explain what had happened at lunch. She turned the water off and sat down on the closed toilet. Her face felt as warm as her hand.

His footsteps circled the apartment and stopped by the bathroom door. "Navy?" When she didn't answer he tried the door. "Are you all right?"

"One minute." The leaky tap dripped, dripped, dripped.

He tried the door again. "Look, Erin called me. We can talk about it."

Jackson always wanted to talk. She was sure the conversations he wanted to have wouldn't end well.

"Navy, open the door."

"I said one minute." She stared at the doorknob as if it might unlock on its own. What did she have to be ashamed of, really? It was a dress rehearsal. A test. She counted thirty more drips of water before she opened the door.

He looked first at the washcloth, then at the wet bar of soap, then at the steamy mirror. She pressed her hand against her thigh as she stood up.

"Are you planning on keeping your hand like that for the next week?" he asked.

"I suppose Erin told you everything."

Jackson nodded. "She said you passed." His expression was as blank as a stone wall. He picked the washcloth up from the floor and hung it on the towel bar to dry. "Food's getting cold," he said as he walked toward the kitchen.

Navy caught up with him. A bag from his favorite Chinese place sat on the kitchen table. Her mouth watered at the tangy scents of soy sauce and sesame oil. "You're not angry?"

"Standard exercise. It's Erin's way of saying she likes you."

Making Navy feel sick was Erin's way of expressing affection? "I don't understand."

"If Erin thought you'd get yourself hurt, she would have tried to talk you out of going."

"Oh."

"People do care about you, Navy." The remark slapped her across the face. He looked at her, as if trying to figure out something to say, but then turned back to the cupboard and pulled out plates.

"You make it sound like I've decided to go."

"Haven't you?"

"I haven't." She wondered if that was a lie.

He lifted cardboard containers of food out of the bag. She could smell her favorite, orange beef. It was no wonder she was hungry; her lunch had totaled three bites of a sandwich.

"You're meeting Byron tomorrow," he said. "You'll have to make up your mind before then."

She touched his arm and he jerked it away. The mask on his face dropped and she finally saw his anger. The truth both frightened and relieved her. She saw his muscles shift under the cotton shirt. A dangerous man and a good man.

"What do you want from me?" he asked. "You want me to be okay with you going undercover? I'm not. I know it's not fair. But it's how I feel."

Navy wanted the nightmares to stop. She wanted Clara to be safe. Navy wanted things between her and Jackson to go back to the way they'd been. She pressed her hands together and the raw skin on her palm tingled. "How much danger is Clara really in? I mean, if we could keep her here?"

"You're the one she confides in. You think there's a way to keep her here?"

She shook her head. "Maybe if Byron had come to me before threatening to cut off her tuition. She's head over heels in lo—" Love. That word again. "She'll do anything for Andrei."

"I can sympathize with that." His expression was so intense the eye contact seemed physical.

She dropped her forearms to the counter. "And there's

54

no officer who can go?"

"Not in time for Clara's study abroad."

Silently, Navy cursed Erin for whetting her appetite. She wanted to tell Jackson that her skin had crawled at the touch of another man. She wanted to tell him about the dark joy she'd felt to have a man as her puppet – moving to her whims. She wondered if that dark joy meant she wasn't the kind of person Jackson wanted. If she wasn't the civilian he had coaxed back to life after she had clawed her way to survival.

"I don't want to go," she said.

"You're lying." He sat down calmly at the table. He'd set a place for her.

"You don't know that."

He raised his eyebrows. Of course he would know she was lying.

"It's hard to explain." She opened the carton next to her plate and the sweet citrus scent took her back to the first meal she'd shared with Jackson. In a little room in the back of a Chinese restaurant in Amsterdam when her bruises were still fresh and scars were just forming.

"Not so hard," he said. "You want the thrill. The challenge. The adrenaline. The permission to do bad things for a good cause."

Maybe Jackson wasn't so different from Erin after all. Maybe Navy wasn't so different either. "What if I do?"

He dipped a wonton in sweet and sour sauce and held it, dripping, over his plate. "You're wondering what will happen to us."

She couldn't read his expression. "I don't want to change careers. Just this one operation. For Clara. For Byron. For me."

"If you go, I go."

She couldn't make any promises about the future and it was too much to expect that he would. She nodded.

Chapter 9

Jackson had to fill out the expense report three times before he got it right. He gave up on the rest of his paperwork and went to find Kevin, his handler. Early on in their relationship they had come to an agreement: Jackson agreed to follow orders if Kevin agreed to give good ones. It had worked so far. Jackson was lucky that Kevin had been assigned to lead Operation Quicksand – he couldn't have asked this favor of anyone else.

Jackson checked Kevin's office, then the meeting rooms. Kevin must be hiding in his favorite spot: the map room. He pushed open the heavy door and found Kevin, as expected. The third-floor room was a relic of the Cold War. Jackson had a certain fondness for the place. Shelves of heavy tomes lined the walls and deadened outside sound. The air was musty with the smell of old books.

The maps told the stories behind the comic books Jackson had grown up on – a conflict with clear borders and good guys and bad guys and a way to know when you had won. The conflicts that had him circling the globe now were decidedly murkier. The adversary could be anywhere and wasn't beholden to any nation-state. There would be no Malta Summit, no declaration of peace. He would stop finding enemies when he stopped looking for them.

From his seat at the table, Kevin acknowledged Jackson with a nod. Scattered papers fanned out in front of him.

"You're here to talk about the Hackerville op," Kevin said.

"Actually, I wanted to look up the borders of Czechoslovakia in 1941."

Kevin closed his laptop. "You might as well sit."

"Navy's decided to go." Jackson pulled out the chair across from Kevin but couldn't sit. He walked to a shelf and ran a finger down the dusty binding of a book.

"I figured I'd hear the news from Byron."

"She's going to tell him later today."

"And you're here to give me the scoop?"

Jackson sat down and pressed his toe against the chair leg to keep his foot from moving. "You'll be her handler?"

Kevin nodded. "I won't be easy on her."

"I wouldn't want you to be."

Kevin was a ruthless and talented trainer. If Erin was right about Navy having the instincts for undercover work, Kevin would be the one to hone them. Jackson was too upset about the idea of Navy going to be any judge of her talent.

"You want me to scare her off?" Kevin asked.

Jackson heard himself laugh. "Don't bother."

"Then you're here to ask for something else."

"I want to go with you. I speak enough Romanian to help with surveillance duties."

Kevin sighed. "You know that's a terrible idea."

"Probably."

"What did Navy say?"

58

Kevin was right to ask. As her handler, Kevin's job was to make sure she had everything she needed. If she said Jackson was a problem, Jackson wouldn't be allowed to come as part of Navy's team.

"Navy wants me there." Jackson hoped.

"It's my duty as your friend and your handler to talk you out of this."

"You can try."

When Kevin wanted to, he could make his stare feel like an X-ray. "If you come, your role will be observation only. Nothing operational."

Jackson nodded.

"That means if she's in trouble, you're not going to be the one rescuing her."

Jackson clenched his jaw. "I know."

"Can you handle that?"

"I'll be fine," he lied.

"No, you'll be a pain in the ass."

"I can't be in the dark again." A year wasn't enough time to fade the memories of floundering while Navy had been underground. Endless days and nights without sleep, wondering if the next story on the news would include where they found her body.

"You want to watch her go into a dangerous situation where you won't be able to help her. Some people would call that torture."

Jackson kept his eyes fixed on Kevin. "I told you, she

wants me there."

Kevin's smile had no humor in it. "You mean you made her promise to let you come."

"Semantics."

"God, you're stubborn."

"I think you've satisfied your duty now. I still want to go." Jackson would go, with or without Kevin's permission. But this way, they could both pretend it was Kevin's decision.

"Fine. You'll owe me. I don't suppose you can tell me why this operation is being rushed? Or why Byron is so hot to go out in the field again?"

Jackson had no doubt Kevin would eventually figure out that Byron had pushed up the timetable and why. Revealing the facts so easily, however, would be a betrayal. Kevin would never allow Byron on the team if he knew. "How much is it worth to you that I've never told anyone you hang out here?"

Kevin grunted. "Get out of here before I change my mind."

Chapter 10

The slats of the park bench pressed damp rectangles against Byron's back. He'd been waiting for twenty minutes. He checked his watch again – Navy wasn't late, he was early. The light afternoon breeze did nothing to dry the sweat on his neck. He tried to read the paper again but the words swam in front of his eyes, overshadowed by a memory that had been running through his head all morning.

Clara – freshman year of high school – sitting in a boy's car in Byron's driveway. The first time he'd seen her kiss a boy. The boy had been a perfect gentleman when he introduced himself. He'd promised to have Clara home before curfew and it was five minutes to ten when they pulled in the driveway. Byron had wanted to strangle him.

This time it wasn't just a boy from the neighborhood struggling with acne and insecurity. Byron had no choice but to interfere. Still, he wondered if in his desperation he was asking Navy for too much. He knew his judgment was compromised. If he was wrong about Navy's skills, it could cost her her life and him Jackson's friendship. Byron might have lost Jackson's friendship already.

He spotted Navy's aggressive, graceful stride a few meters away. The long steps belied her medium height. The wind caught strands of her light hair and she tucked it behind her ear. She nodded toward the folded paper at his side. "Are we practicing dead drops?"

"Too windy to read."

She leaned back and he saw a line of sweat darkening her hairline. "So this is a nice summer day in the capital."

"A nice day in DC is a day without a meeting," Byron joked wanly. He felt the slats of the park bench dig into his back. Navy's silence added to the guilt already weighing on him. He tapped the newspaper against his leg, both impatient and afraid for her answer.

"Yeah, I'll do it."

He let out a breath he didn't realize he'd been holding. A good person would ask if she was sure, give her a chance to back out. "Thank you," he said. "I'll owe you."

"Not me. Jackson." She checked her watch. "I'm not sure he's going to forgive either of us."

In the field, Jackson was known for his steady nerves. Some even found him cold. "He's a little overprotective when it comes to you."

Her smile wasn't for Byron. "I don't mind. Much."

"Is he insisting on coming?"

"That's nonnegotiable."

"It's a bad idea."

"I know."

Byron tried again. "He can't think straight when you're in trouble."

"Yep."

"Navy . . ."

"Your daughter's involved and you're still planning to go," she said. "Even though you haven't gone undercover for years."

"That's different."

Navy arched her eyebrows. "Really."

"Clara won't be there with me. Do you have any idea how difficult Jackson was when you were playing cat and mouse with that psycho Curt last year?"

"Oh, I can imagine." Her eyes scanned the park and landed on an approaching figure. Jackson.

"If you know it's a bad idea then why—"

Navy tilted her head toward Jackson. "You tell him not to come."

"Shit." Byron saw her point.

"He'll be there whether you invite him or not." She bit her lip and looked down at the dirty sidewalk. "Make sure he comes home. Don't let him do anything stupid."

Easier said than done, Byron thought. "I'll do my best."

Jackson stopped in front of Navy, keeping his back to Byron. "You said we were meeting for lunch."

Navy had her smile back. "Did I say for lunch? I meant before lunch. As in, before you and Byron have lunch."

The last thing Byron wanted to do was sit across from Jackson's flinty eyes for an hour. But a promise was a promise.

Navy kissed Jackson on the cheek. "Time to kiss and make up. Or it's going to be a very long trip to Romania." She walked away before either of them could object.

Jackson took Navy's seat. He kept his eyes fixed on her departing figure. "She's going because she thinks she owes you."

Obligation wasn't the only reason, Byron hoped. "It's a few lines of code. Just enough to track payments to the botnet so we can get Dragomir's clients arrested. Odds are she'll be in and out before they even know."

"It's dangerous."

"Risky," Byron said. "Not dangerous."

"You're splitting hairs."

Both Jackson and Byron watched Navy disappear from view.

"You knew she'd say yes," Jackson said. "Why bother talking to me first?"

"I thought you might settle for punching me in the gut instead of breaking my neck."

"I'm still deciding," Jackson said darkly.

People heading to lunch spilled out of the offices surrounding the park. The scratching of men's dress shoes and the clicking of women's heels filled the sidewalks. "Look, I didn't know she'd say yes. I wasn't really expecting it. But I had to ask – for Clara's sake."

Jackson shook his head and looked away.

"I overheard her talking to Andrei. They're already making plans for her first weekend there. Son of a bitch keeps telling her about his mother's fine cooking."

Jackson's expression didn't change.

"His mother is dead, Jackson. Maybe Dragomir wants

Andrei to bring in—" Byron couldn't even finish the sentence. His daughter, trapped in the sordid flow of human trafficking that sloshed around the globe. "I don't know what Dragomir's gang wants with Clara. But they won't get her."

The anger tightening Jackson's expression faltered. "I want to see Clara safe as much as you do."

Byron risked a hand on Jackson's shoulder. "I know."

"I suppose you tried talking to her again?"

Byron grimaced. "That girl can swear like a sailor. I wonder where she learned that."

"Probably from all the times you described her past boyfriends."

Better to let Jackson get a few jabs in, it would make him feel better. "Was it my imagination or did I hear Navy use that l-word you've been waiting for?"

"It was a slip of the tongue," Jackson said.

"You don't believe that."

Jackson stared morosely at the horizon.

"You know, she doesn't talk much about the years she lived in Cedar City," Byron said. "Didn't she go to college there?"

"Yeah."

"You should ask her about it. Maybe there's an ex. A reason she's so skittish."

Byron often wondered why Jackson was still a field officer. There was no denying Jackson was good at his job, but the costs were high. Long-term relationships were difficult at best with his frequent, long absences. Jackson had never been satisfied with short-term acquaintances, like many of his colleagues. He never talked about wanting a white picket fence or kids, but Jackson had always wanted a partner.

"Navy cares for you. Anyone who's seen you two together can see that."

Byron saw a flicker of hope before Jackson's face hardened again. "If there were something she wanted me to know about Cedar City, she'd tell me."

***

Navy edged past the college student reading "Never Eat Lunch Alone" at the deli counter. She would be eating lunch alone too. But she didn't mind. Dealing with people for the other seven and half hours of the day was enough. Someday, maybe, an introvert would write a book with career advice for other introverts.

"The turkey sandwich and chips, please," Navy told the cashier. "And a cup for water."

Hopefully Byron was making progress with Jackson right now. Navy knew Byron's friendship was important to Jackson. Right now Navy needed to focus on mending a friendship of her own. The free table outside on the patio should work. Navy needed the quiet. She pulled up Sara's number and stared at the screen. Navy hated lying to Sara.

"Are you excited about the trip?" Sara gushed, skipping a greeting.

"I—uh"

"We're going to visit *all* the Smithsonian museums of course. And the Lincoln Memorial. And the International Spy Museum. Are you allowed to go there if you work with spies?"

"I'm really sorry, Sara. But I can't see you when you come to D.C."

In the long silence that followed, Navy heard the sounds of a coffee shop. "You have to cancel," Sara said.

"I know, it sucks. We've been planning this for weeks." Navy didn't know how to soften the news.

"And we haven't seen each other in months, between my schedule and your work trips."

"Something . . . came up," Navy said. "Something I can't reschedule."

"Are you okay?" Sara asked. "Are you in trouble again?"

Navy wondered how close to the truth she should get. "No, nothing like that."

"You sound worried about something."

Navy shook her head and smiled. "You can tell that from a thousand miles away."

"How long have I known you?" Sara asked.

"Too long, apparently." Navy tapped her fingers on the table while she measured her next words. "Everything's fine. Mostly. Just a last minute trip."

"Is this last minute trip dangerous?"

So this is what Jackson meant when he talked about awkward conversations with his parents. "I'll come down to visit you, I promise."

Sara huffed. "You can't tell me anything."

"I can't. I'm sorry. But I do owe you a visit," Navy said.

"When you said everything's mostly fine . . ."

"Jackson and I are arguing. A little. But it's typical relationship stuff." *Because every couple argues about going undercover in a Romanian cybercrime ring.*

"You do owe me," Sara said.

"I do. And Sara?"

"Yes?"

Navy had never considered this part of undercover work. How do you say goodbye without saying goodbye? Just in case? "I miss you. I promise I'll see you soon."

"You will, because if you don't come down to visit me—"

"You'll storm the capital," Navy said.

"And you know that because?"

"I've known you for too long."

"Exactly," Sara said. "Wherever you're going, be careful."

"I will." Navy wished she could reach through the phone and hug her friend. "I'll see you in a couple months." *Probably.* Navy knew she was taking a risk going undercover. Every officer who went into the field knew that. And most of them came back. Most of the time.

Chapter 11

Andrei, huddled under the thin blanket with Petru, heard Nicolae's footsteps in the hallway. Another predawn room search. Still, it was important that Andrei act surprised so Nicolae wouldn't think he was trying to hide anything.

The door swung open and crashed into the wall. There was already a depression in the plaster. The sudden light made Andrei blink as Nicolae flipped the switch.

"Room search," said Nicolae, grinning like an idiot.

Great, Nicolae was drunk. Petru made a sound like a hiccup and started to cry softly. Andrei scooped him up before Nicolae noticed. The only safe place in the small room was the one bare corner that wasn't taken up by the bed or Andrei's desk.

"Just go back to sleep," Andrei told Petru. "We'll be back in bed before you know it."

Petru buried his head in Andrei's shoulder, understanding that Nicolae shouldn't see him crying.

Nicolae threw the blanket down on the floor and tore off the sheets in one sweep of his arm. The mattress flopped heavily against the frame and he swayed, nearly falling. He made a show of flipping the mattress over, looking underneath the bed. It was all a show. A little reminder that even Andrei's dreams weren't safe.

Nicolae searched the desk too, throwing pencils and notebooks on the floor. He flipped through some of the pages –

Andrei kept notes on his marks so he could keep them all straight.

"Clara Macalester," Nicolae read. "Study abroad in Bucharest next fall, likes vanilla cupcakes, birthday May 4, 1994. You've written a lot about this one. Is she special?"

She was, but not in the way Nicolae thought. "Just a difficult mark," Andrei said.

Nicolae stumbled away finally, slamming the door behind him. The room was in shambles. The mattress was upended on the bed frame; the sheets were tangled on the floor and sprinkled with paper clips from his desk. It would take half an hour just to get the room put back together. The sleepless nights. The constant abuse. Andrei's plan had to work soon. He wasn't sure how much more he could take.

Why hadn't Byron Macalester taken the bait yet? Andrei had all but proposed marriage to his daughter. For the first time, Andrei considered the possibility that Byron Macalester wasn't a CIA man like Andrei thought he was. Clara had told him how often her father, Byron, was absent for weeks when she was young. Byron had missed her fifth birthday. He'd missed half of her summer T-ball league when she was going into first grade. She told Andrei about Byron's current long hours at work, supposedly as a librarian for a small law firm downtown. Clara had said her father was just a workaholic. Andrei had suspected otherwise. So Andrei did his own research.

Dragomir's network included corrupt law enforcement officers wherever he operated. Dragomir even had a few Interpol officers on his payroll. Over nearly two decades, Dragomir had collected a lot of intelligence. A man matching Byron's description had been involved in several operations in eastern Europe during the times Clara said her father was gone when she was in elementary school. A few well-chosen marks allowed Andrei to verify that no one named Byron Macalester worked at a small law firm in downtown DC. He had flirted with someone in HR at every single one as Byron Wright, an aspiring artist in his forties in Boston. *I have a second cousin with the same first name, weird right? He works at a law firm in DC – do you know him?* Andrei had been careful never to type "Byron Macalester" in any chat window. Everything he typed was monitored. *Wish I knew his last name, but he changed it for his acting career. A big scandal in the family. No one will talk about it.* Nicolae had never connected Byron Wright the persona with Clara Macalester's stories about her father, Byron.

Andrei thought about meeting Byron over the Skype call several weeks ago. Byron's angry reaction to Clara's trip had confirmed Andrei's suspicions. Byron Macalester had seemed to know exactly who Andrei was. And yet there was no sign the CIA was coming after Andrei. Either Byron Macalester, the ruthless agent who had systematically pursued Russia's spies in Eastern Europe, had chosen to let Clara's relationship with Andrei continue or Andrei was wrong. Byron Macalester was just an overprotective middle-aged suburban dad.

And Clara might just become another casualty weighing down Andrei's conscience. He hugged Petru tightly, comforted by the boy's even breathing. Asleep already, as if Andrei's arms offered a magical sort of protection. Sometimes Andrei was glad Petru still believed in the illusion. Sometimes Andrei resented the effort required to maintain the pretense.

If only Petru knew how powerless Andrei was.

Chapter 12

Navy told her coworkers she was going out for coffee. Her coworkers weren't supposed to know she was attending the mission briefing for Operation Quicksand. As far as they knew, her upcoming absence was for vacation.

The key card reader in the elevator glowed red, waiting. She pressed the button for the fourth floor and slid her card into the slot. A minute later, the door opened onto an eerily quiet floor. No one looked up as she passed the rows of tan cubes on Jackson's floor, but she had the distinct feeling of being watched. She tried, and failed, to imagine him at one of the impersonal desks. Navy rarely saw Jackson at work, and when she did it was always awkward. They didn't try to hide their relationship, but they didn't advertise it either.

Navy knew perfectly well she might be walking into a room full of people who hated her for what she'd done. Depending on whom you asked, the events of last year either made Navy a whistleblower or a traitor. And, as if that wasn't bad enough, she and Jackson had been tiptoeing around each other all week. Now they would have to sit in the same room and act professional.

The briefing was in the Mandarin room. But there were no signs in the hallways to give her directions. She wandered the gray hallways past rooms labeled Punjabi and Urdu and Kurdish. There was even a hallway with rooms labeled Klingon, Sindarin and Gelfling.

A wiry woman with cropped brown hair brushed past her then turned around. "You're Navy Trent." She was as thin as a string bean but her handshake was painfully firm.

It was still disconcerting to Navy that everyone in the building seemed to know her.

"The briefing is this way." The woman pulled on Navy's arm. "Hurry or we'll be late. Kevin hates it when people aren't on time."

Navy hurried behind the woman. "I'm sorry – it's just there are no numbers on the rooms and—"

"Ah, yes, the cursed linguist."

"The what?"

"Fourth floor layout was assigned to a frustrated linguist. He arranged the rooms according to his tree of languages. There's a method to the madness, if you stay around long enough."

Navy began to see it as they rushed down the maze of hallways. One hallway with Latin languages – Spanish, Portuguese, and Italian. Another hallway for dead languages with rooms labeled Latin and Sanskrit. And then, sure enough, a hallway with languages of Asia: Japanese, Korean, and at the very end, Mandarin.

The woman opened the door to a small rectangular room and found a seat at the table. Navy avoided Jackson's eyes and found herself staring into the icy blue eyes of a blond man at the head of the table.

"Try to be early next time." This was Kevin, then. He

74

tapped his fingers impatiently on a pile of folders. He had lanky limbs and hair that refused any part. His expression was as curiously neutral as his accent – as if he had spoken too many languages for too long.

The only free chair was between Jackson and Byron. Across from her were the brown-haired woman and a black man who could have passed for a gymnast.

"You'll need introductions, I suppose," Kevin said. "I'm Kevin Fellows. I'll be your handler. Do you know what that means?"

The only thing she could find in his tone was a hint of irritation. "Like a manager," she said.

"Close enough." Kevin pointed to the gymnast. "Martin Huff." Then to the woman who had showed her the room. "Anna Sharp." They each nodded to her in greeting. Their posture reminded her of Jackson – relaxed but alert. Never completely off duty. "You know Jackson and Byron. Anna and Martin are the rest of your support team." He stared at her like she was supposed to speak.

"Good to meet you," she managed.

"I'm giving you a larger support team than I normally would for an operation like this. Because of your lack of experience."

Kevin didn't want to work with her. She couldn't blame him.

"I don't suppose you want to clear up this mystery for me?" Kevin asked.

She straightened her back. "Mystery?"

"Why Byron wants to do fieldwork all of a sudden. Why Operation Quicksand is being rushed when it means I have to work with an amateur."

Navy had no idea what kind of strings Byron had pulled, but she knew Byron would never be allowed to go if the truth came out. The operation would be delayed until a real field officer was available and Clara would go to Hackerville for love.

"Someone offered. I accepted. No one told me anything was being rushed." She wondered whether she had fooled him.

"Whatever," he said finally. Kevin slid a white folder to everyone in turn. Jackson caught his with a practiced swipe of his hand. Navy's nearly slid off the table. "These are your individual marching orders for Operation Quicksand. Read them, memorize them, and then destroy everything but your plane tickets and cover documents." The folder was thick, enough for a small novel. Kevin pinned her with his eyes again. "Jackson can show you where the shredding room is."

She nodded dumbly, wondering how much Kevin knew about them. Surely Jackson wouldn't be allowed to go if Kevin knew they were together.

"Our target is Dragomir Pirvu. He runs the Bleda botnet. His online activities are funding arms deals for the wrong side. The goal of this operation is to track down Dragomir's clients so we can make sure evidence of their activities reaches local law enforcement and his revenue sources dry up. What's your objective, Navy?"

Finally, an easy question to answer. "Clients use a program called Attila to reserve time on the botnet. I need to modify the code in Attila so Dragomir's clients can be tracked." Dragomir had an admirable sense of history. Bleda was the brother of Attila the Hun. Who better to command the zombie hordes of Bleda than the infamous Attila? It was doubly ironic considering that most historians believed Attila had murdered his brother.

"If you have questions, you come to me first," Kevin said. "Not Jackson. Got it?"

So Kevin did know about them. "Understood." These days, Navy could barely ask Jackson to pass the salt.

"This is what happens when I pull the short straw," Kevin muttered.

Navy looked down at the table to avoid seeing what Anna and Martin thought of her.

"We need your word," Anna said to Navy.

"My word on what?"

"Your distress word," Kevin said. "We'll have a bug on you the whole time. Your distress word is how you tell us you need backup. Pick a word you can work into conversation easily."

"Paradise." It seemed as good as anything else.

"Use it in a sentence."

She knew she would have a few things to learn but she could put together a sentence. "Seriously?"

Kevin's expression didn't change. "You're at lunch and

you need to call us. Use it in a sentence."

She resolved not to fail at anything in front of Kevin. It would give him too much satisfaction. "Do you know where I can buy good oranges around here? I've been spoiled ever since I lived in Florida – citrus paradise."

"Not bad. For the next half hour I want you to practice not using your distress word. Better yet, practice that for the next week. If we have to rescue you, you lose your cover."

Maybe Jackson had been right to tell her not to go. Kevin didn't seem to have any faith in her at all. Erin's compliments over lunch had been lukewarm at best. Kevin opened the folder in front of him and everyone else followed suit.

The first page was a detailed itinerary. Six flights to Bucharest and hers was the last. Six flights leaving Bucharest and hers was the first. She realized she had been expecting to have Jackson beside her the whole time. But, of course, it wouldn't work that way. She was going to play the role of a traitor, and traitors traveled alone.

"We're planning on three weeks," Kevin said. "But I'm hoping we can wrap things up in two. Our base of operations is a house near Dragomir's headquarters. Navy, I've rented an apartment for you that's a ten-minute walk away. The apartment is connected to an old tunnel system that we'll be able to use to get in without being seen once Dragomir starts tailing you."

She would be watched even while she was sleeping.

"Be sure to read the emails the landlord and I exchanged, in case you run into her. As far as she knows, she's been talking to you the whole time."

While she and Jackson had been avoiding each other, Kevin had been pretending to be her. For some reason, the thought made her shiver.

"Tell me your post, Martin."

Martin's folder was closed but he recalled the details without hesitation. "Coffee shop across from Dragomir's headquarters."

"Anna?" Kevin asked.

"Bike messenger," she said.

Kevin pointed at Byron.

"Chess tables in the park outside Dragomir's headquarters," Byron said.

"Jackson?" It sounded more like a challenge than a question.

"In the surveillance van. With you." Jackson's business-like tone was barely recognizable to her.

Kevin reached across the table and closed Navy's folder – interrupting her reading mid-page. "Your cover story. Go."

"I'm making money on the black market by selling exploits found by CIA bug hunters. I allow Dragomir to talk me into being hired as a programmer to put the exploits into their crime pack."

"That's the how. The most important part is the why."

"I'm betraying my agency as revenge for my kidnapping last year." A botched CIA operation had led to a case of mistaken identity, and a group of people in a room very much like this one had decided that rescuing her would make damage control too difficult. Normally she could mention the kidnapping without blinking, but today her thoughts snagged on the filthy, stinking closet where she had awaited execution. Only Jackson seemed to notice her flashback. Those green eyes again, pulling her back from a dark place. Somehow he always knew.

An image appeared on the projector screen when Kevin opened his laptop. The picture was labeled Dragomir Pirvu. He had deep-set eyes and a toothy smile. If she passed him on the street, she would have mistaken him for a grandfather. Maybe he was. Along the left side of the picture was a long list of crimes. Illegal arms deals ranging from machine guns to rocket launchers. Funding terrorist training camps in return for safe passage of his drug shipments. Partial or full responsibility for bombings in several countries. Some of the crimes were blacked out. No one in the room offered to fill her in or seemed surprised by the redactions. The picture changed before she could finish reading.

Nicolae Sas, Dragomir's main lieutenant. Even in the candid surveillance photo, his smile was more of a grimace. His left eyebrow was interrupted by a scar. His list of crimes was no shorter than Dragomir's, but it was less diverse. Enforcement – often lethal – seemed to be his specialty. More faces flashed by and Navy knew she wouldn't remember them all. Finally, they came to the man keeping Byron up at night. Andrei Radu, almost-graduate of the University of Bucharest and winner of Pwn2Own two years in a row.

"Explain to me what this Pwn2Own thing is," Kevin said.

It was the first time he'd said something to her that didn't sound like a test. "It's a contest at CanSecWest, a computer security conference in Canada. People compete to write exploits for all the major browsers. The browser vendors use it as a way to find bugs in their products. There's prize money, but mostly contestants compete for the bragging rights."

Currently, Andrei was the only known programmer for Dragomir's gang. He was classically handsome, with a square jaw, blue eyes, and thick black hair. She could see why Clara had fallen for him. The most recent surveillance photo had caught him with his hand on the door, just entering headquarters. His mouth was turned down slightly and he was looking over his shoulder.

"Is it possible Andrei wanted to make a name for himself on the black market?"

"I suppose so," Navy said. "But lots of legitimate companies hire people with the same skills."

Kevin continued to examine Andrei's picture, larger than life, on the screen.

"You're wondering why his criminal record starts with Dragomir's gang," Navy said.

"Good." Kevin didn't look away from the screen while giving her the bare compliment. "Yes, exactly. What do you think of him, Byron?"

Anna and Martin exchanged a confused look, Navy

focused her eyes straight ahead – she didn't dare look at Jackson.

"Maybe he was just careful," Byron said.

"Sure," Kevin said.

Navy was grateful when Kevin turned off the projector and closed his laptop. Everyone gathered their folders and stood to leave. Her head swam with all the details she was supposed to remember. And that didn't even count everything in the heavy folder.

"Everyone here knows this so I should tell you, Navy," Kevin said. No one moved. "I don't make rules lightly. When I do, I expect them to be followed. No questions, no exceptions."

She tried not to squirm.

"This rule is just for you. You may see someone in trouble. You may see someone about to get hurt. Do not attempt to save anyone but yourself. You will do only what is necessary to keep your cover. No heroics, understand?"

She wondered if she could watch someone suffer just to save her own skin. "I understand."

"You don't have the same training we do. Remember that."

Kevin seemed to relax. He turned to Martin. "I've had this song in my head all day," Kevin said. "That Guns N' Roses one? I can't remember the name of it. Where the grass is green and girls are pretty? You know that one?"

"Yeah, I think I know it," Martin said.

She had one foot out the door when Kevin addressed her again. "You know that song, Navy?" There was an expectant silence in the room.

The name of the song was "Paradise City." Paradise. Her distress word. This was another test. "'Kiss-My-Ass City,' I think," she said.

"Well done. Stay for a second and let's talk."

A private conversation with Kevin was the last thing she wanted right now. She looked at Jackson. He shook his head slightly and gestured with his eyes toward Kevin. What had she done wrong now?

"I'm your handler, remember?" Kevin said. "Jackson can wait outside."

She sat.

Kevin sat backwards in the chair next to her, perching his chin on long, graceful fingers. "Byron tells me you and Jackson aren't that close."

That must have been how Jackson was able to get on the team. "Not really. He's gone a lot."

"You're a good liar. Better than I expected. I'd almost believe you weren't staying in Jackson's one-bedroom apartment."

"Then Byron didn't—"

"No, he knows better than to lie to me." Kevin frowned. "Most of the time. And he wouldn't lie about you. I'm Jackson's handler."

She couldn't hide her surprise. Jackson hadn't ever said who his handler was. Thanks to him, she looked like a fool in front of Kevin.

"He didn't tell you, then. How does that phrase go? Trouble in?"

"Kiss my ass." She wondered what else Kevin knew. Aside from Byron and Erin, Navy knew nothing about the people who inhabited his world away from home. She tried to imagine Jackson in the dusty mountains of Afghanistan with this praying mantis of a man, whose limbs seemed long enough to enfold prey.

Kevin smiled. "You might ruin that boy for me. Used to be I had to force him to take vacation – now he can't get enough."

"I'm sorry?"

"I should hope you're not."

"Why are you allowing him on the support team if you know that Jackson and I are . . ." She couldn't think of the right words to finish the question.

"A favor. For a friend." Friendly wasn't a word she could associate with Kevin. "My turn to ask a question." As if anything about this conversation was even. "Why are you agreeing to go undercover?"

Navy didn't know the right answer. "The hazard pay."

"You don't need money. You have a healthy savings account and no debt. Not even a mortgage. Your hobbies are rock climbing and backpacking and you already own all your equipment. You earn a salary that would make someone comfortable in DC, but you spend most of your time in Iowa. When you're not living in Jackson's apartment, that is. As far as I can tell, the only expensive habit you have is takeout.”

“Maybe I have an illegal gambling problem.”

“You don’t even have a bookie.”

“How would you know?”

“Honey, I know your favorite radio station. You think I don’t do my homework?”

Southern. Rural but upper class. That was the accent hidden in his vowels.

“This isn’t some Nancy Drew mystery with treasure maps and grandfather clocks.”

“I know.”

“I don’t need some bored civilian looking for an adrenaline rush messing up my operation.”

“It’s not about that.”

“Well, that’s not a lie at least.”

Navy waited for the next attack.

“Do you understand who Dragomir is?” Kevin asked.

“A criminal.”

“An asshole. Who needs to be taken out.”

“This is personal for you.” Navy was surprised; Kevin seemed too pragmatic for vendettas.

“Let’s call it enlightened self-interest. He deserves to be taken out.”

“Code is my weapon,” Navy said. “The rest is up to you.”

Kevin nodded slowly. “Fair enough. Given what you’ve been through, I would have expected a preference for the quiet life.”

“Maybe you didn’t do your homework as well as you think.” She was tired of everyone thinking they knew what was best for her.

“So it’s not about adventure. And it’s not about money. Then why take the risk?”

Permission to do bad things for a good cause, Jackson had said. There was a certain thrill that tempted her. But beyond that, a siren’s call from the ghosts that haunted her dreams. She couldn’t explain it to Kevin any more than she could explain it to Jackson.

“You’re not going to tell me? Fine,” Kevin said. “But promise me one thing.”

Whatever will end this meeting, she thought. “Name it.”

“Follow my orders and I’ll keep you safe. I have a reputation to protect.”

“A reputation?”

“I’ve never lost an officer and I don’t intend to start with you.”

Suddenly she was glad he was Jackson’s handler. “I’ll try not to get blood on your merit badge.”

“Good. Send Byron in on your way out.”

In the hallway she found Byron and Jackson leaning against the wall with studied nonchalance. “You two couldn’t eavesdrop, could you?”

“Door’s too thick,” Byron muttered.

She glanced back at the open door. Byron must wonder

if she had spilled his secret. "He had more rules for me," she said. "Now he wants to see Byron."

"I figured." Byron walked into the room and carefully shut the door.

"Do you think Byron will be able to keep Kevin from figuring out why he's going?" she asked.

"I give him fifty-fifty odds." He shuffled his feet. "I know I said I'm not okay with this. And I'm still not. But we don't have to be strangers."

Her hand itched for his. She wondered if personal contact at the office would embarrass him. "A thaw would be nice."

"How about lunch, then?"

She lifted the thick folder. "I can't. I have to memorize this before it self-destructs."

He rubbed the spot between her shoulders that always hurt after a long day. "I can find us a quiet room. Get some food. Everything okay with Kevin?"

She wanted to ask why Jackson hadn't told her about Kevin but she was tired of fighting. "Yeah. Fine. He's . . . um . . . thorough."

Jackson laughed. "That's one word for it."

Chapter 13

Navy knew the sound of that zipper. It was the zipper on the small duffel Jackson took on most of his operations. She reached across the bed, still half-asleep, and found Jackson's side empty. The morning Navy had spent three weeks preparing for had finally come. Her eyes went to the shadow at the periphery of her vision—him standing by the closet, bag in hand. He was ready to leave.

"Why didn't you wake me up?" She rubbed her eyes and read the clock. He didn't need to leave this early to make his flight to Bucharest. The objects of their cohabitation came into focus as her eyes adjusted: her toiletries in the bathroom that could be seen through the open door, her clothes hanging in the closet, her book on the nightstand. Jackson studied her for a long moment, as if he wasn't sure he would find her in his bed again.

"You don't have to get up," he said.

"I want to." She sounded more challenging than affectionate.

Jackson pressed his lips together and nodded. She followed him into the kitchen. He put a filter in the coffee machine and added four scoops of his favorite blend. Sometimes when he was gone she would open up the container just to smell it. It was a strong blend, bitter with just a hint of cinnamon flavor. She never used his coffee when he was away.

The living room looked small and claustrophobic with

the shades down. She opened the curtains, hoping for dawn, but the sun was still nestled below the horizon. Jackson had disappeared again into the bedroom. She took out two coffee cups.

There was a demanding knock on the front door. She padded across the linoleum and peered into the peephole. Kevin stood in the hallway, dressed in a business suit and carrying a briefcase. As if it were perfectly normal to arrive before dawn at someone else's apartment. She looked down at her bare arms and legs. All she was wearing was a T-shirt and a pair of Jackson's boxers. Kevin knocked again, harder this time. "Let me in, Navy," he said.

He couldn't possibly see her. She slid the chain free and unlocked the deadbolt. "You have X-ray vision now?"

Kevin didn't give her state of undress a second look. "Jackson would have let me in already. And you're the only person who's stayed over in a long time."

She wondered if being nosy was part of his job or something he did for fun.

"Jackson still here?"

"Packing." She hugged herself. "In the bedroom."

Kevin didn't ask where the bedroom was before going down the hallway. The two men talked in low, hushed tones for several minutes before Kevin returned to the kitchen. The coffee was nearly done. She took out the cream and sugar for herself. Jackson took his coffee black.

"I have presents," Kevin said. "Sit." The chair at the

kitchen table seemed too short for him. She had imagined that the apartment belonged only to the lazy weekends she and Jackson spent together. Jackson had no doubt shared beers with friends here. And his bed with other women. Perhaps women who didn't ask so much of him.

"It's a bit early for Christmas," she said.

Kevin snapped open his briefcase. "Your phone." It was the kind of phone sold at most truck stops, except a little thicker.

"It looks a little flimsy."

"It's meant to look cheap. A disposable phone looks better for your cover. The bug inside piggybacks on cell phone transmissions to avoid tripping RF bug finders. There's a small delay between when you speak and when we hear you – five seconds maybe." He took the phone from her and popped the main battery out. He pointed to two wires that came out from behind the green circuit board. "These wires go to the auxiliary battery. If you have to take the main battery out – or someone takes it out for you – we'll be able to hear you for a few minutes."

If someone took it out for her, she hoped to be fighting, not talking.

"I'm your aunt."

"You're my what?"

"In your contacts. I'm your Aunt Gertrude. If I text you, don't reply. Just meet me at the base."

She wished she had already had her coffee. "Okay."

"The address of the base is?"

90

One of the many things she was ordered to memorize. "Calea Dorabantilor 302."

"What's the route from your apartment to the base?"

"Three blocks north, one block west."

"Good."

If Kevin stayed much longer she wouldn't have any time alone with Jackson before he left. "Is that it?"

"Almost. Tell me what you're going to do after you land in Bucharest."

"Rent a car and drive to Râmnicu Vâlcea, also known as Hackerville. Go to the apartment you rented. The landlord will leave the keys underneath the statue. Wait twenty minutes then walk to dinner at the bistro across from the base. Go to the alley behind the base when you put the flowerpot in the window."

Kevin had told her the extra delays were necessary so her support team could make sure she wasn't being followed. Another thing they had to do just for her. Jackson came out of the bedroom with his bag swung over his shoulder. He walked past her to set his bag down by the door. He walked past her again to return to the kitchen. Both times he kept his eyes straight ahead. As if Navy weren't there. But when he filled the two mugs by the coffeepot, he poured cream and sugar into hers.

"Another cup for me?" Kevin asked. "I prefer honey."

Jackson gave him a hard look. "If you want your cup to go."

"Fine, fine. I wouldn't want to interrupt anything." Kevin let himself out.

"Should we sit in the living room?" Jackson asked.

They sat on the lumpy couch, avoiding each other's eyes. He drank his coffee in gulps. She covered the ceramic circle with her hand. "Stop. You'll burn yourself."

"I have to get to the airport."

"You have time. I memorized everyone's flight schedule, remember? And everyone's aliases. I'm surprised Kevin didn't make me repeat that too."

Jackson set his coffee down and ran a hand through his hair. "You should listen to him. He's saved me from myself more than once."

"I can't imagine the great Jackson Fletcher needing to be rescued."

"It's easy to lose perspective when you're in the field," he said.

"You mean you start to sympathize with the target?"

He pulled her bare legs into his lap. His hands moved to the soles of her feet. "Not exactly. It's like you forget what the real battle is. It's hard to explain."

"Try."

The coffee pot sputtered over the hum of the refrigerator while she waited for him to answer. "Imagine you're a lifeguard," Jackson said. "And you see a hundred people drowning, but you can't save them all. You have to focus on your objective. On the people you're supposed to rescue. The people you have the power to rescue."

Navy thought of Erin's almost ruthless lack of

attachment. Of how restlessly Jackson slept the first few nights after he came home. Both were reactions to the same pain. A pain that Jackson had wanted to spare her. "I think I understand," Navy said.

Jackson shook his head. He pressed his thumbs into the arches of her feet, then rolled each toe between his fingers.

"Mmmmmhmmm," she mumbled. As she relaxed, she tried to find a part of the worn-out cushion that would support her. "This couch sucks. We need a new one."

His hands stopped. "We?" There was a smile in his voice.

She kept her eyes closed. "You. You need a new couch." She was startled when he stood up.

"My flight," he said. "I have to go."

She walked him to the door. They stood inches apart – afraid to touch, afraid to separate.

"Jackson—"

He cupped one hand behind her neck and the other at her waist. The kiss felt like goodbye. His watch beeped. "I have to go."

"I know." She didn't ask for any reassurances. He didn't offer any. She untangled herself from his arms and stood back, cold again. "Go. I'll see you tonight. At base."

Chapter 14

Andrei started the ToppleWords game on his computer again. He glanced back at Nicolae, lounging in the corner of the office. The beige square was Andrei's daytime prison. Every day he made the five-minute walk with Nicolae from the house where Petru was kept to Dragomir's headquarters.

Andrei rubbed the sleep from his eyes. He hadn't slept well since the day Dragomir had kidnapped him and Petru. Andrei didn't expect to sleep well again.

The blinking flash graphics in the game annoyed even him, and he was the one who coded it. Whenever he worked on the game, he thought of the nights he had played board games at his sister Afina's house. That was where the idea for the game had come to him. Nicolae thought it was just another game laced with viruses to add computers to their botnet. To Andrei, it was his last hope. A way to communicate right under Nicolae's nose.

ToppleWords was a cross between Jenga and Scrabble. Players could choose from randomly selected letter tiles to build their next word. But letters worth more points "weighed" more — play the wrong word and the tower would be unbalanced. The player who made the tower fall lost half their points.

Now he needed a cheat mode. It would be too hard to put together a coherent message with randomly chosen tiles. The cheat mode would be activated by feeding the bouncing monkey a banana from the tree. That was easy enough to code. In cheat mode, both players got to choose from the entire alphabet of tiles. That would satisfy the communication piece. But he needed a way to cut the conversation off quickly, if need be.

A special keystroke. He added a routine that required both players hold down a set of keys during the game. If either player let go, the tower collapsed. That would satisfy the need for secrecy.

The last piece he needed was a way to avoid being caught. Andrei knew Dragomir ran a keylogger on his machine at home and the one at work – everything he typed was recorded. The keylogger recorded everything he clicked on too. He adjusted the display algorithm so that after every play the tiles rearranged themselves. If anyone asked, he could say it was a way to add difficulty to the game.

Dragomir's unmistakable heavy footsteps echoed in the hallway. Andrei's fingers slipped and he accidentally deleted a line of code. No good ever came of a visit from Dragomir.

"I have an assignment for you," Dragomir said to Nicolae.

They spoke with each other as if Andrei were invisible. Like he was too weak to do anything about what he overheard.

"Navy Trent is supposed to fly into Bucharest today," Dragomir continued.

Dragomir owned a crooked agent inside Interpol who sent him a daily list of known CIA employees traveling to Romania. Excitement made Andrei's fingers clumsy – maybe his message had gotten through. Navy Trent, the woman who made headlines by publicizing the CIA operation that nearly killed her and was then hired by the same agency. He gave up trying to type coherent code and pretended to keep testing his game.

"You want her dead?" Nicolae asked.

Andrei suspected Nicolae would kill for fun even if his job didn't require it.

"Not yet. Ask around town," Dragomir said. "See if she's headed here. I need to know if she's meeting with any of my rivals. Or employees."

"And if she is?"

"Take care of her and whoever she's working with. Be creative. I want to be sure everyone understands the consequences of cooperating."

The first few months of life under Dragomir's thumb had been terrifying. Now, even the prospect of a creative death at Nicolae's hands seemed relatively tame. Andrei spent his sleepless nights imagining all the possible endings to his new life and none of them looked good. Right now the threat was that if Andrei didn't work hard enough, Petru would work. Sooner or later they would put Petru to work anyway; Dragomir never left a business opportunity unexploited.

Andrei had spent one year of his life extending the empire of a despicable man. His code being used to write games with Flash exploits that recruited machines to the botnet. His code being used to help Dragomir's clients order denial of service attacks. His code being used by the worst criminals to obscure their tracks in Dragomir's anonymizing proxy service. His code was the reason he had lost a sister and Petru had lost his parents. Andrei would save Petru or he would die trying. Dying would be a small price to pay for redemption.

Chapter 15

All the rooms at the base were barely wider than they were tall. Jackson fidgeted in the leather chair on the second floor. Kevin had kicked him out of the kitchen – on the first floor – for hovering. And upstairs, there was Byron. Despite Navy's order to kiss and make up, he hadn't completely forgiven Byron. It was easier to be angry at Byron for asking than at Navy for saying yes.

He checked his watch again. Then stared at the brick wall the building shared with the wine bar next door. Just two blocks past the wine bar was Dragomir's headquarters. Where Navy would end up if she was successful in getting recruited. He could see Kevin strategizing with Martin downstairs, discussing the best way to storm Dragomir's headquarters if necessary. If Navy's cover was blown or she had to use her distress word or they overheard her getting injured or—he had to focus on something else. There was nothing else in the room but Anna and all the weapons they would need to use if—

Jackson pushed himself out of the chair and walked to the window.

Anna looked up from taking inventory. "She's not due for another hour. Relax."

"Did Kevin say if she made her second flight?"

"I'll bet the flight attendant even gave her a pair of wings." Anna tossed him a pack of cards and the corner cut into his thigh. "Play solitaire or something."

"I'm going for a walk."

"Kevin said to keep you here." Her nonchalant pose was deceiving.

And hadn't he told Navy just this morning to listen to Kevin?

Anna pushed the curved magazine for an assault rifle into the cutout in the foam and shut the heavy plastic case. "Please tell me you're not going to be this useless the whole time."

He'd hoped his instincts would take over once the operation started, but so far he felt the same nerves he had had as a rookie. His thoughts stubbornly circled back to one thing: Navy shouldn't be doing this. Byron should never have asked.

"She'll be fine." Anna stacked the cases in a corner and wiped the gun oil off her hands with a cloth.

Jackson thought of the dreams that furrowed Navy's brow while she slept. "You've only known her for three weeks."

"Three weeks while I helped Kevin train her."

He didn't like where Anna was leading him.

"Erin thinks she's ready. Kevin thinks she's ready. We're all here. She'll be fine."

"Is there some sort of mass conspiracy to get my girlfriend killed?" he snapped.

"That was last year. Byron!"

Byron came downstairs from the bedroom. "Yeah."

"Babysit Romeo for me. I have to get to Navy's

apartment to watch for tails."

Jackson returned to the window.

"You – uh – want to play crazy eights or something?" Byron asked.

"No." Jackson's face warmed. He knew he sounded like a toddler about to throw a tantrum.

"I'll give you one free punch. If it'll make you feel better."

"Don't tempt me." Jackson tried solitaire but he couldn't keep clubs straight from spades.

Byron hid behind the paper he'd picked up at the airport.

Solitaire was the wrong sort of puzzle. Jackson spread out a sheet of newspaper and took out his handgun. The magazine disconnected with a satisfying click. He double-checked the barrel to make sure it was clear. He took the small black container of Hoppe's 9 from where Anna had left it. A few small dabs on the cleaning cloth filled his nose with the familiar scent, a mix of root beer and diesel. He pulled the slide forward and off, setting it perpendicular to the magazine. He still took apart his gun like he was in boot camp, under the eagle eye of his instructor. He put the gun back together, then cleaned it again. The feel of the cool metal against his hands was comforting. A tool he could use. A puzzle he could solve without thinking.

The seventh or eighth time he reassembled his gun he saw Navy entering the restaurant across the street. Anna walked past the entrance, looking down at the phone in her hand as if she were texting. In the time since they'd landed, Anna had already learned the body language of the town, a hurried shuffle with bent shoulders. She was a shadow in plain sight. At least Navy had a good team behind her.

Jackson hurried downstairs. Martin and Kevin were bent over a hand-drawn map of Dragomir's headquarters, using broken bits of corn chips as markers for people.

Anna's voice came out of a speaker on the table. "She wasn't followed to the restaurant. And the big boss is there. Just like you wanted." Kevin chose the restaurant because Dragomir regularly ate there. The plan was for Dragomir to spot Navy, and get Dragomir to initiate contact.

"Good," Kevin said into his headset. "Let me know if anything changes."

Jackson couldn't hear the audio from Navy's bug; it must be going to Kevin's headset.

Kevin gathered the papers scattered on the table into a folder. Martin took the hint and went upstairs.

"It's still kind of crowded in here," Kevin said.

"Can I listen?" Jackson asked. He tried not to look too eager.

Kevin narrowed his eyes. "Promise to be good?"

It was a promise Jackson wasn't sure he could keep. "Promise."

"You seem calm enough." Kevin studied him before he flipped a switch on the equipment on the table and took the headset off. Now Navy's and Anna's audio feeds would come over the speakers.

The faint hiss of background noise came over the tinny speakers. Navy's only protection was a phone barely larger than a box of cigarettes.

"Salut," Navy said. *Hello.* Part of Kevin's training had included a crash course in conversational Romanian. There was a scratching sound and a thump and the background noise got louder. The phone being taken out of her pocket, probably. The curtains on the first floor were closed – and would stay closed. The sidewalk was too busy to leave them open. The flowerpot that would signal when Navy could leave the restaurant was still hidden behind the curtains.

"Do you speak English?" she asked in Romanian.

"Nu," said a man's voice.

Navy cleared her throat. Was she nervous or was she just playing the role of a tourist trying out the language? "I would like the sausage and potatoes. Please." Ice clinked in a glass. Then the sharp creases of a piece of paper unfolding or folding. Jackson stared in frustration at the curtains blocking his view.

"If you want to see her, you'll have to go upstairs," Kevin said. The curtains on the second-floor windows could stay open – the windows were smaller and there weren't many nearby buildings with a second floor. Jackson had to choose between the view and the soundtrack. He chose the soundtrack – that way he would be closer to the door.

A plate was set down and she thanked the waiter. The restaurant seemed too quiet, but he knew the bug was designed to minimize background noise. There were other people in the restaurant with her. And Dragomir wouldn't do anything with so many witnesses. Of course, if everything went to plan she would end up in Dragomir's headquarters. A place with no witnesses and only one way in or out.

Kevin waited another ten minutes while Jackson fidgeted. The curtains opened briefly when Kevin set the flowerpot in the window. He saw Navy for a split second, calmly reading a guidebook and consulting a map. He heard money exchanging hands, more awkward Romanian from Navy, and a chair scraping across the floor. The phone went back in her pocket. He heard her footsteps on the sidewalk, then the cobblestone, then the concrete alley.

He was at the back door when Navy opened it.

The awkwardness from the morning evaporated as he buried his nose in her hair. He heard Kevin approach. Navy gave Jackson a peck on the cheek.

"Hello, Auntie," she said.

"I knew I was going to regret this," Kevin muttered.

Jackson slid his hands down to her waist and pushed her away gently. Kevin wasn't above sending him home.

The door opened again, and Anna entered. She read Kevin's discomfort and Jackson's embarrassment in a split second, then grinned and breezed by them.

The modest living room could barely accommodate all six of them. Kevin took the last seat. Navy stretched out on the floor and Jackson sat cross-legged next to her.

"Did Dragomir notice her?" Kevin asked Anna.

"Right away," Anna said. "I saw him make a call just after she came in."

"Excellent. Tell me what you're doing tomorrow morning, Navy."

"Going to the coffee shop where Dragomir takes his morning meetings."

"I want you there by 7 a.m. If all goes well, we'll have you recruited by dinner time."

With jet lag, she wouldn't get much sleep tonight.

"If Dragomir knew my face, won't someone else?" Navy asked. "What if I get another offer?"

Jackson hoped she wouldn't get any offers at all. Outside the restaurant a man leaned against the brick wall and lit a cigarette, closely watching the alley.

"Pretend to consider it," Kevin said. "Dragomir's the big dog in town – if word gets out he wants something, most people will get out of his way."

"How long do I wait for Dragomir to approach me?"

"Twenty minutes or so. Make sure you don't look like you're waiting for anyone."

She nodded. "And then back to the apartment."

"You'll have Anna, Martin, and Byron following you the whole day, even if you don't see them. Dragomir will probably start having you tailed tomorrow. If you spot any of his men, don't let on that you notice. You're not supposed to know what they look like."

If any of the directions rattled her, she didn't show it.

"That's it, then? Morning coffee with a botnet operator and arms dealer and then back to the apartment."

"Don't forget ch—" Martin was cut off by Kevin's upraised hand.

Child pornographer was what Martin had been about to say. The second floor of Dragomir's headquarters, which hopefully Navy would never see, had two large rooms used for production. Kevin had given strict orders to the support team that Navy wasn't to know. If she did, she might take risks she shouldn't take. Jackson already had to keep so many secrets from her, he hated to add another one. But Kevin was probably right.

"We should probably go," Martin said smoothly. The man outside the restaurant lit his third cigarette.

Kevin scanned the street and spotted the same man Jackson had. Navy followed Kevin's eyes and spotted the man, too. His face was in shadow and the glowing cherry of his cigarette shook a little every time he shivered in the cool summer night.

Worry knit Navy's eyebrows. "Is that—"

"Your first tail," Kevin said. "Congratulations. Dragomir already wants to know what you're doing. Martin, take Navy back to her apartment the long way. Make sure Lung Cancer there doesn't see either of you."

Navy stood up and brushed off her jeans. The familiar gesture tugged at Jackson's heart. It was her way of steadying herself. Her deep breath was loud to him, but nobody else seemed to notice.

Martin picked up a long cylinder – the kind an artist uses to carry sketches. Jackson knew it didn't hold artist's supplies. The cylinder held a disassembled sniper rifle complete with a night vision scope. Kevin had rented the office just across from Navy's apartment. The office would serve as the guard post. The sniper rifle's scope would let Martin see details, even from the second-story window.

Kevin's look warned Jackson not to follow Navy downstairs. Jackson didn't relax until fifteen minutes had passed and Navy's tail was still outside the restaurant. Navy would already be back at her apartment. She didn't belong to Dragomir yet.

Chapter 16

Navy shrugged into her coat and set out for Dragomir's morning coffee shop. Most old European cities were full of interesting contradictions: ancient chapels wired with modern lights, bank ATMs set in the marble of historic buildings, streets built for horse-drawn buggies clogged with metal steeds that sputtered and purred. Hackerville had all those things, plus one more. There were lots of ways to spend money in Hackerville, but on paper there were few ways to make it.

As she drove in yesterday, she had noticed the luxury car dealership on the edge of town. A gleaming temple of glass built for the benefit of Hackerville's most successful inhabitants. Men like Dragomir. Today, on her short walk to the coffee shop, she had passed two Western Unions and noted the lines at the counters. Wire transfers were a popular way to transfer money from victims. Email a thousand people claiming to be their grandson trapped overseas because all his credit cards had been stolen, and generally one would reply. If that didn't work, you could always email a million. The success rate didn't have to be high. Email was cheap.

Doubtless some of the money came from unwitting money mules all over the world who had answered an ad for a job "processing payments." The victim would receive a check for a large sum of money and then be asked to wire the money—minus their cut, of course—to someone else. By the time the victims realized the large check they'd received wouldn't clear, they had already emptied their bank account.

Only the barista was in the coffee shop when Navy arrived. Except for the techno with lyrics she couldn't follow, it could have been an upscale coffee shop in Des Moines. She ordered and took her seat at one of the circular tables, barely wide enough to extend past her knees. The chair was a hard, modern contraption designed to impress the eye more than the sitter.

Arrive by 7 a.m., Kevin had said. So here she was, alone with her coffee and her jet lag. The barista set a small tray on her table with cream and sugar and her coffee. If the double shot of espresso in its haughty white cup wasn't going to wake her up, the tempo of the music certainly would. She added cream from the metal pitcher and watched it billow into swirling clouds. Her hands felt clumsy around the tiny espresso spoon. She wondered if she was capable of defending herself right now. She hadn't slept well.

It was frightening how quickly Dragomir had picked her out at the restaurant last night. One quick dart of his eyes, and Dragomir was on his phone. One phone call and, magically, a man smoking at the end of alley waiting for her.

She checked her text messages. Nothing from Kevin. No easy excuse to run to base and skip this meeting. She took a sip of coffee and let it burn her tongue. The barista eyed her warily and made a call. Jackson was less than fifty yards away. The whole team was. Paradise. One word—three syllables—would call them. One word and she could end the mission. All the ghosts that had pushed her here stirred and held her tongue.

If she was going to keep her cover, she should do something besides stare out the window. She took out her guidebook and pretended to read, wondering how long it would take for twenty minutes to pass. A sip of coffee tickled the burn on her tongue. She was about to unfold the map in her book when Dragomir entered.

His suit was meticulously cut to hide a round stomach. His polished leather shoes reflected the slanting rays of the sun. She turned a page and tried to look busy. At the edge of her vision, she saw Anna riding by, in her ruse as bike messenger.

"You're Navy Trent."

She cursed herself for not seeing the man approach. The gravelly voice belonged to a stout man with a scarred eyebrow, peppered dark hair, and a beard that climbed high on his cheeks. It took her a second to place him. Nicolae Sas, Dragomir's main lieutenant. In the surveillance photo, Nicolae had been clean-shaven. The beard didn't soften him.

Dragomir remained at his seat a few tables away. She would be having morning coffee with Dragomir's favorite enforcer.

"I get that a lot," she said. Kevin had told her to play coy.

"No, you are Navy Trent." He took the seat across from her and his legs crowded hers under the table. "You are quite famous, you know."

She picked up her bag and phone, as if to leave. Part of

her really did want to leave. "I'm afraid you have me confused with someone else."

An iron hand closed around her knee. She fell back into her chair.

"Sit, please. I insist." His accent hardened the consonants and made the vowels musical. A hard object pressed against her leg. The nub of the sight told her it was the barrel of a gun. "The man I work for is interested to know why Navy Trent, who works for the CIA, is in our little town."

Nicolae dug his fingers into her knee joint and the pain made her gasp.

"Vampire tourism," she said. Looking into Nicolae's eyes was like falling down a well.

"Or a working vacation."

"If you know who I am, then you know I'm not a field officer." Navy imagined Jackson listening, wishing it were true.

"Some other business, then."

The painful hold on her knee hadn't lessened. From the angle of the barrel against her inner thigh, she calculated the shot would sever her femoral artery. A practical choice, not a perverse one. Only rapid medical care would keep her from bleeding out. Aside from the barb in Nicolae's smile, a passerby could easily mistake his forward posture for the eagerness of a suitor.

Paradise. One word. Three syllables.

She gripped her phone, her lifeline. "I already told you why I'm here. I'm a tourist."

He dug his thumb in deeper and she gritted her teeth.

"Fine. I'm here on my own business. Nothing you need to be concerned about."

His hand loosened, but the gun didn't waver. "Last night we watched you. You went down that alley behind me and you never came out. Who were you meeting?"

"I'm not here for you, that's all you need to know."

Nicolae held up his free hand. Three men came into the coffee shop. They had fingers like Nicolae's—too meaty to hold dainty white cups. Dragomir left. The barista left too, leaving the door into the kitchen swinging. Navy would be dead if she couldn't sell her cover story.

"I went to see a fortune teller. The cards say I'm going to come into some money soon."

Nicolae lowered his gun while he considered her statement.

She tried not to breathe a sigh of relief.

"You are selling something valuable," Nicolae said.

"Valuable enough."

"Convince me this isn't official business."

"You want a letter from the CIA saying they don't know about my side business?" Her cup clinked twice in the saucer from the tremor of her hand. "How likely is that?"

"What do you sell?" he demanded.

"If I told you, my merchandise would be less valuable."

"If you don't tell me, you're out of business."

She had played coy long enough. She needed to make sure Nicolae knew her motivation. "My job gives me access to information. I sell that information to get what I want."

"And what does Navy Trent want?"

To kill you, she thought. The violence of the thought surprised her. Had she accepted Byron's offer just to have an excuse to take another life? Nicolae's image wavered and for a second she saw an old enemy. A man she'd killed. Obviously not well enough. "I want what everyone wants," she said. "Payback. And a pile of money to buy myself a white-sand beach where I can enjoy my revenge."

"Your government betrayed you and now you betray them."

"That's how revenge works."

"Who's your buyer?"

She shook her head. "That's not any of your business."

"What if I could give you a better fortune than your fortune teller?"

Navy the officer would know who Nicolae worked for; Navy the traitor wouldn't. "If you had enough money to talk, I'd know you."

Nicolae's face darkened at the insult. "I work for Dragomir Pirvu. You must know him. He has money." Then, as an afterthought. "I have money."

It couldn't be this simple, she thought. Less than twenty-four hours after she'd landed and already she was being offered a deal. "All right. I'm listening."

Leather creaked as Nicolae's gun slid back into his holster. One flick of his fingers and the men forming a triangle around her left. The barista returned to the counter. But Dragomir didn't come back.

She tensed when Nicolae reached into his pocket, but he pulled out only a pen. He scrawled an address on a napkin and pushed it toward her. "Tonight. Six o'clock. Dragomir would like to meet you." His smile was wide and unfriendly. "It would be bad luck not to come." He left quietly for such a large man. Anna rode by the window again, risking a longer look.

Navy's coffee was still half-full but she didn't trust her hands not to shake. It was a puzzle. When she was threatened, her resolve hardened. She could think of the right sequence of moves, the right words. When the threat was gone, there was nothing left to hold her together. She dropped a few bills on the table. She wondered what the appropriate tip was for a barista who would help with an execution. She didn't know if Kevin wanted her to stay longer, and she didn't care. She needed to be outside – where she could see the summer sky.

She put the phone in her pocket and gripped the square tightly. Even in the bright day she felt shadows behind her. She would be tailed from now until she left Romania. Her toe caught on a cobblestone and almost pitched her forward, but she kept walking. The uneven cobblestones massaged her feet, reminding her of Jackson's thumbs against her soles. A memory that belonged to another place.

Is that what Erin had meant when she told Navy to leave herself behind? That while she was undercover her real life should feel distant and irrelevant. Navy suspected that she had left herself behind in the room with the bodies of her kidnappers.

Three more blocks to her apartment. And then what? A long afternoon in a strange apartment remembering the nub of Nicolae's sight against her leg. She slowed her steps and went into the next shop. Brightly colored scarves embroidered with pastoral designs floated from hooks on the ceiling. One corner of the shop held vampire figurines stamped Made in China. She was far from Transylvania. Navy picked up a vampire bust with dripping red fangs. The color was too dull. Real blood was a deep, scarlet red with a shimmer that caught the light. It smelled like rusty nails and when it dried it clung like jam.

The faces of her attackers swam in the glass. The man with the smile of a crocodile who had ordered her rape and execution. The leering eyes of the man with the drooping left eyelid who would carry out the order. And the cropped military hair of the enforcer – the man sent to punish her for telling the story. She couldn't run from them. She understood now. She carried them with her.

Navy set the figurine down. Across the street, a man with a brown coat draped over his arm browsed a newspaper stand. One of Dragomir's men? No, he moved down the street after buying his paper. She picked up a postcard showing the profile of mountains and held it up as if to study it. The man perusing the menu outside the café next door? Yes, there it was. A sidelong glance to make sure she was still there. Fear straightened her spine.

She wanted to run. But to where? The apartment that

wasn't hers. The base where Jackson waited. Or better yet, one word. Her escape hatch. All there would be left to endure was Kevin's disappointment.

No. If she ran away Clara's blood would be on her hands too.

She nodded to the shopkeeper and stumbled back into the street. Every time she neared the apartment her steps veered away, leading her in twisted squares. Eventually her bruised soles and tired legs forced her back home.

The apartment was darker than she left it, even though the sun had come up. Someone had pulled the shades. She had left them open. From the doorway she could see a pair of legs stretching out from the only chair. The lanky frame was fast becoming familiar to her. "Hello, Auntie."

"I wish you'd stop calling me that."

"I know." Her shoulders relaxed. Kevin would protect her if only to keep his reputation. "How did I do?"

"B minus."

"Ouch." She locked the door, then wondered how Kevin had gotten in without the key. There were no tool marks on the lock. "Aren't you going to tell me why?"

"First, you pissed off Nicolae."

"I'm supposed to be friends with him?"

"No. Just don't make yourself a target. Don't you remember his history from the briefing?"

All she could recall was a body count. "He's Dragomir's enforcer."

"Not just an enforcer. Last year he killed his wife's lover and the man's entire family. Just to prove a point."

"Oh."

"And don't strangle the phone when you're holding it. I can't hear what's going on with your hand blocking the mic."

Would Kevin guess that she'd been gripping it so hard because she had been shaken by her meeting with Nicolae? "Is that it?" She'd been tired before the meeting with Nicolae, and Kevin wasn't improving her mood.

"No. You didn't tell me where the meet was. Did it occur to you when we need to scout the address before you go there?"

She pulled the napkin out of her pocket. She hadn't even read the address yet. "Nicolae was right there. I couldn't just read the napkin to you."

"If the handwriting is messy, repeat the address like you can't read it. Use a landmark for reference. Is that the park near the bell tower? That famous restaurant? Or, since you decided to tour the city on your way home, use other people. Ask for directions. Ask a taxi how much the fare would be. Or if you're feeling shy, find an alley or a bathroom where you can talk to yourself. Pretend you're on your phone and—"

"I get it." She dropped onto the bed. The springs squeaked like mice.

"Also, try to stay away from the topic of white-sand beaches. It's too close to your distress word and Jackson's a little jumpy."

116

She would give anything to see Jackson right this second, even if it meant he wanted to talk. "Did he give you a message?"

"I'm not here to play Cupid."

For the first time, she wondered why he was there.

"Tell me why it took all morning to walk the three blocks home. Is there something I should know? Something that happened when you saw Nicolae this morning?"

She hadn't figured out how she felt about this morning's meeting and she certainly didn't want to talk it over with Kevin. "I wanted to practice looking for tails."

"People are the worst liars when they're upset."

"I'm not." She tried to compose herself. "Upset."

"Bullshit."

The thin blanket bunched in her hands as she gripped the edge of the bed. There was nowhere to hide in the studio apartment, even if Kevin would let her. A peculiar ache, like a knotted muscle, pressed against her ribs. She couldn't breathe around it. "I'm not as fragile as people think," she snapped. "I have a body count too."

Five men, dead at her hands. Even if they had deserved it, she had been scarred by it. She was a killer. She didn't want to be.

"No one thinks you're weak." Kevin spoke the words slowly and precisely.

He seemed sincere. But she couldn't escape the feeling that even his kindness was strategic.

"Your job is to concentrate on the small things — how to get the beacon code in place, how to stay alive. My job is to keep track of the big picture. If I'm going to do that, I need you to be completely honest with me. While you're here, pretend I'm your BFF."

Navy laughed before she could stop herself. "Are we braiding each other's hair tonight?"

"You've been hanging around Jackson too long. I don't know how that boy made it through the army without being written up for insubordination."

"He can hear us?"

"Since I told him not to listen, it's a safe bet he is. Tell me what happened with Nicolae."

"He pulled a gun on me under the table."

Kevin swore under his breath. "You should have said something."

"He's a criminal. Criminals have guns. It rattled me a little, that's all."

"I would have pulled your support team in closer. If you're so smart, tell me why Nicolae was ready to shoot you on sight."

"Aren't criminals generally suspicious of law enforcement?"

Kevin had the same expression Jackson did when he wasn't sure how much to tell her. "Criminals hide their actions from law enforcement. Unless they think they're under investigation already. Then they start threatening people.

118

Understand?"

"Oh." Another mistake. She waited for Kevin to break the uncomfortable silence.

"Dragomir shouldn't have any reason to be suspicious of us. We don't normally target men like him."

"So there's been a leak about the operation?" Navy thought Kevin should be more upset about the possibility.

"Unlikely. One of the bugs we had in Dragomir's headquarters went offline a couple weeks ago. I figured the battery had died. I guess they found it. Dragomir's suspicion is going to make this cover harder to sell. Are you up for it?"

His expression was neutral. Any answer was correct. She kicked at the carpet and watched the dust swirl in the beams of light that escaped the drawn curtains.

"You still haven't told me why you agreed to do this operation."

Wanted wasn't the right word. Called. Compelled. Obligated. But it wasn't her obligation to Byron that made her want to stay. Or even her desire to help Clara.

Kevin tilted his head to study her. "You don't know, do you?"

She did know. But she hadn't known until this afternoon. She couldn't have admitted the reasons to herself in DC, where she felt Jackson's presence so strongly even when he wasn't home. He protected her too well. He had taken responsibility for her recovery, and telling him she wasn't okay was almost an insult, a sign of failure on his part. She was glad that Jackson could hear and glad that he wasn't with her.

"The men I killed are in my head." Her voice was close to a whisper. She closed her eyes to keep the room from spinning. "Every night I fight them." Even when she didn't remember her dreams, she woke tired. In some ways, she preferred the nightmares. Then, at least, she knew whom she had been fighting. "Sometimes I win. Sometimes I lose." She felt a curious warmth behind her eyes. It could have been anger or hatred or a desire for revenge. "I'm tired of losing."

She found understanding in Kevin's eyes. Not Jackson's compassionate sort of understanding, but recognition. Like her story was familiar to Kevin. Maybe the man without an accent did have a past.

"We can work with that," he said. "Toss me your phone." He caught it with a precise flick of his wrist. "Jackson, if you're listening, stay where you are. I'll be with Navy until tomorrow morning."

Navy looked around the apartment. There was one bed, one chair, one desk, a small stove, and a refrigerator.

"I'll take the floor," Kevin said. "Right now we need to prep for your meeting."

He took out his own phone and made a call. "Anna, what are they saying on the bug we have left in his headquarters?" He nodded. "Good, good." He read aloud the address on the napkin and handed it back to Navy. "I need you to scope out the meeting site. Find a good spot for you and your sniper rifle to cover Navy from above. And find three spots for Byron, Martin, and me on the ground. I want Byron and Martin set up early to watch the perimeter. I need a spot where I can see what's going on so I can read Dragomir."

He listened for a minute and then rolled his eyes. "Well, hog-tie him if you have to. Jackson will just get in the way."

Chapter 17

Early evening shadows stretched long across the garbage that littered the alley. Jackson had chosen this spot because he knew it was on the shortest path between Navy's apartment and the meet. The only thing to keep him at base had been Kevin's threats. Anna was perched on a rooftop overlooking the park. Martin and Byron were circling the perimeter, watching for Dragomir's men. And here he was hiding behind a dumpster that stunk like rotten garlic and potatoes, waiting for a man who would not be happy to see him.

He shifted his weight and grit scratched underneath his shoes. Footsteps approached. The fast cadence and soft tread told him they were Kevin's. When Jackson stepped out of the shadows, Kevin wasn't surprised to see him. Kevin wore a set of headphones; the wire led into his pocket where the monitor for Navy's bug would be. To anyone else, Kevin looked like a man listening to music. Jackson knew the headphones had a small mic on them that would let Kevin communicate with the team if he held down a button.

"I told you to stay at base," Kevin said.

Jackson had tried. "Yeah, I know."

"I knew you were going to be a pain in the ass."

They were four blocks from the square where Navy would meet Dragomir. If Jackson wanted to start an argument, now would be the time. Before loud voices would attract the attention of Dragomir's men. "We need to talk."

Kevin pressed his lips together. "Not now." Kevin took a step forward; Jackson blocked his path. Kevin's eyes turned a flinty blue.

"Dragomir is already suspicious," Jackson said. "It's too dangerous. We should abort the mission." He almost choked on his next words. "She'll listen to you." He couldn't stop to think about why she wouldn't listen to him and what that meant. Navy could call him whatever names she wanted when they were back home. When she was safe.

"I let you come as a favor." Kevin's tone could have cut glass. "That favor can be rescinded."

Following orders wasn't generally Jackson's strong point, but listening to Kevin was second nature. Jackson wavered but held his ground. "I don't care what she thinks she's going to accomplish here. It's too dangerous."

"She was pretty good this morning."

Jackson didn't want to admit it, but it was true. "You told her she got a B minus."

"I don't want her to get overconfident." It was a classic Kevin maneuver—threaten, then distract.

"Send her home."

"I worked with her all afternoon. She's prepared. If I don't think Dragomir's convinced, we go home tonight."

It wasn't a concession. It was the same plan Kevin had formulated earlier. Jackson didn't move.

"You're going to help her by making me late?" Kevin

asked. "Anna shouldn't be the only pair of eyes on her."

"Navy's good at hiding her wounds. You don't know her like I do." Jackson hoped.

"I think I see why you two work," Kevin said. "She's almost as damaged as you are."

Jackson would have punched anyone else. "What the hell does that mean?"

"She needs this operation as much as you need this career. If you're upset she didn't share that with you, you need to settle it with her later."

The years between the end of his army career and the present fell away. The shadows of the alley were exchanged for a bright street in Bosnia and the mournful gongs of a church bell. His entire body tensed exactly as it had then, not because he had been about to fight but because he couldn't. Kevin was right.

"Get out of my way, Jackson." Kevin's expression told him their continued friendship depended on his cooperation.

Jackson fell into step beside Kevin's long strides. His throat finally opened up enough to speak at the next block. "You're not going to order me back to base?"

"Would you go if I did?"

It would be the smart thing to do. He wasn't much good to Navy in his current mood, and it was torture watching her. "No."

"You know I have no desire to see Navy hurt."

Jackson nodded. "Yeah, I know."

"You haven't told her about Bosnia, have you?"

"She doesn't need any more horror stories." The lie sounded thin even to him.

"Christ, I thought my relationships were dysfunctional."

It was annoying how often Kevin was right about things he had no business understanding. "When's the last time you had anything that resembled a relationship?"

Kevin thought hard. "Delia. Last year."

"Two dates isn't a relationship."

"She used my toothbrush once. I'd say it counts."

They fell silent by mutual agreement. They were too close to the meeting place to risk talking. Jackson followed Kevin to the spot Anna had picked out – between an unruly stack of produce boxes taller than Jackson and another stinking dumpster in an alley off the park. It was narrower than most, just a strip of asphalt a few feet wide to keep the grass from growing between the buildings. Some artful arranging of the boxes on Anna's part left an open square where the park could be seen clearly.

The park Dragomir had chosen was the size of a small block, a square of green among the buildings crammed together like impatient people. A sidewalk bordered the edges and crossed through the middle in the shape of an X. The only advantage it offered Navy was its public location. Still, it wasn't a busy place. Few storefronts faced the square and the residential buildings were all run-down apartments. For Dragomir, who knew every nook and cranny of the city, it would be easy to find a place to hide a man or escape in a hurry—with or without Navy.

Nicolae arrived early. He surveyed the park then took up

residence in the telephone booth. A rectangle of dirt on the glass showed where the phone had been mounted. For ten minutes Jackson sweated and waited in the cramped hiding spot. The sweet decay of rotting fruit seeped into his clothes.

Navy arrived on time and chose the bench facing the alley, per Anna's orders. The break in her stride told Jackson she had noticed Nicolae, whose phone booth was a few yards away. Jackson focused his binoculars on her tight expression. Why didn't Navy want him to know about how often her nightmares came? Rejecting a set of keys was one thing, hiding her problems from him was another. After a year, she still didn't trust him.

A tap on his shoulder broke Jackson's concentration. Kevin waved him away from the viewing hole. The hiding spot had only been prepared for one occupant. Jackson spotted another, smaller hole closer to the ground. He squatted, trying not to focus on the small brown objects rolling away from the toes of his shoes.

Nicolae looked around the park and made a call on his phone.

A strand of Navy's light blond hair twisted in the breeze. She tucked it behind her ear as Dragomir approached. Despite the warm day, Dragomir wore a suit. His only concession to the weather was an unbuttoned collar. Jackson knew a suit could be used to intimidate as well as provide more places to hide weapons. He fixed his feet to the concrete. If Navy wanted to be rescued by him, she would have stayed home.

Kevin tapped Jackson's shoulder and held out another

pair of headphones and a monitor. These didn't have a mic—
Jackson wouldn't be able to speak to Navy or the team, but he
could hear them all. He put the headphones in his ears before
Kevin changed his mind.

"Nicolae explained our dilemma to you," Dragomir said.

"About whether or not to kill me? Yeah, he was pretty
clear on that." She shifted her weight on the bench. "Frankly, I
don't see how this is any concern of yours. I didn't make a deal
with you."

Jackson hadn't expected her to be this good. Her body
language had perfect pitch. She kept throwing glances back at
Nicolae, as if she didn't have any sort of protection. Hunched
over just enough to show tension, not enough to show weakness.
Mimicking Nicolae's surveys of the park as if she had to worry
about being watched too.

"Anything that happens in my town is my business,"
Dragomir said. "You might be giving one of my competitors an
advantage over me."

"My buyer wasn't local. This was just a place to meet."

"Wasn't?"

"I broke off the deal. So it's really no business of yours
anymore."

"I'm not convinced you don't work for the CIA,"
Dragomir said.

She shrugged without interrupting her slow scan of the
surroundings. "You can think what you like." Dragomir's hand
drifted toward his pocket. Had she seen? "But you don't need to

bother killing me. I'm flying home tonight. It'll save you the trouble of dumping my body."

"You haven't told me what you're selling."

Kevin's murmur of approval made Jackson's stomach turn. Navy might just pull this off.

"It doesn't matter. We're not doing business."

Dragomir's expression changed from suspicious to angry. "I decide if we're doing business or not."

"Now play the investigation card," Kevin said softly. Navy couldn't hear him—Kevin had decided it was too risky to put an earpiece on her.

"Look, I made some calls." She pulled her hands out of her pockets and set them on her lap. To the untrained eye, it looked like fidgeting. But Jackson knew she was freeing her arms in case she had to fight. "The CIA is watching you. They have plans to bug your office. Even this meeting is dangerous for me. I don't need the attention."

She started to get up but Dragomir dropped a thick arm around her shoulders, reaching into his pocket at the same time.

Kevin's hand closed like a vise around Jackson's arm. He had taken a step forward without realizing it, nearly ruining their fragile camouflage.

Navy was faster than Dragomir. She slammed her elbow into Dragomir's throat and the back of her fist into his nose. Nicolae pulled his gun and ran to the bench. Dragomir's knife clattered to the sidewalk and Navy, standing now, kicked it to the curb. Dragomir's guttural coughing filled Jackson's ears. A red trickle of blood reached Dragomir's lip. The knife balanced, teetered, on the edge of the curb before it clanged dully into the sewer. Dragomir was doubled over, still coughing, his eyes tearing. Why wasn't Navy walking away?

Because Nicolae had his gun trained on her.

"I have the shot," Anna said in Jackson's headphones.

"Not yet," Kevin said. "But take out Dragomir if you take out Nicolae." Kevin's hand was still clamped around Jackson's arm.

Navy was a statue except for the rise and fall of her chest. She held Nicolae's gaze with an outward calm that unnerved Jackson.

"Have you resolved your dilemma?" she asked.

"No dilemma," Nicolae said with a sick smile.

"Ta—" Kevin started to tell Anna to take the shot, but Dragomir waved Nicolae away.

"Business before pleasure," Dragomir managed hoarsely. He must have wiped the blood from his nose on his sleeve because his face was clear. "She can be useful to us." He coughed a couple more times, then gestured for Navy to sit.

She didn't.

"You sell secrets," Dragomir said. "Access to information about CIA operations."

"No, I sell exploits. Zero-day exploits found by CIA bug hunters. Exploits no one else knows about. Guaranteed to get your malware on fully patched Windows machines if you can get the user to click on a link."

"What's your price?"

"I can't do business with you. You're too exposed."

"You should accept my offer while money is still on the table."

Nicolae, on cue, raised his gun again. Navy's expression betrayed a hint of her nerves, but it could have been contrived. Jackson heard Kevin's voice the first time he'd coached Jackson for a meeting. "They'll know you're a professional if you act too cool," Kevin had said.

"You'll pay a premium," Navy said. "For the extra risk, you understand."

Dragomir glanced at Nicolae. "Your life is not premium enough, then."

"I have more than a few enemies in Washington, Mr. Pirvu. My life was worth little to them last year. It'll be worth less if I'm a traitor." Her gaze skipped over Jackson and he felt a tug on his heart. "If I do this for you, I'm cashing out."

Suicidal was the first word that came to Jackson's mind. No, not suicidal. He had been in similar situations many times. She was doing the same thing he did every operation: daring the universe to prove he deserved to survive. He heard church bells again, felt a bright warm sun, and pushed the memories away. He should have stayed home.

"Five hundred thousand American dollars," Dragomir said quietly. "For that, I want information on my case and your exploits. And you will stay here to help us put the exploits into the crime pack."

Navy pretended to consider the offer. "I can't stay. The programming will take two weeks and I need to disappear before then."

"Five hundred and fifty thousand," Dragomir countered.

She nodded slowly. "The price is right." She wrote an account number of a piece of paper and gave it to Dragomir. "Wire half the money to this account by tomorrow morning. If I see the money, I start Monday."

"No, you start tomorrow."

Kevin had given her strict orders to start Monday.

"I have arrangements to make. I'm cashing out, remember?"

"Fine," Dragomir snapped. "Monday, then."

Navy nodded to Dragomir and then to Nicolae before walking back the way she came. Behind her back, Nicolae gestured to a man who had been sitting on another bench. The man got up to follow her.

"Nicely done, everyone," Kevin said. "I think we're in business. Byron, Martin—make sure Navy gets back to the apartment safely. I'll meet her there."

Navy had orders to take the long way home so Kevin could arrive first.

Kevin turned to Jackson. "Do you still think we need to go home?"

Jackson knew the question was rhetorical.

"Good answer. I think you've earned yourself a visit," Kevin said. "A good talk would help you two—I'll arrange it for

131

tomorrow morning. You need to go back to base. For real this time."

"Yeah," Jackson muttered. "I know." Martin or Byron would spot him if he got close to Navy anyway.

"She did well tonight, Jackson. And we'll be double-guarding her tonight just in case Dragomir changes his mind."

"Would you tell her—"

Kevin cocked his head, impatient to get back to Navy's apartment.

"Shit. I don't know."

"I'll tell her you behaved yourself."

Jackson took a meandering route back to base. The windows on the first floor were dark. In the living room, he found Anna and Byron playing poker and eating sandwiches. For poker chips, they were using olives of different colors.

"You look unscathed," Anna said. "No spankings for breaking curfew?"

"Kevin likes to keep his victims in suspense," Jackson said. It was, sadly, true.

"You want in on poker?" Byron asked.

The gesture was as close to sympathy as he would get from this crowd. "Sure," Jackson said.

Byron dealt and Anna exchanged two cards.

"Where have you been hiding Navy?" Anna asked. "That girl has style. Nicolae hadn't even pulled his gun before she had Dragomir coughing up a lung."

Jackson didn't want to think about how close Navy had

132

come to being shot today. Twice. "Can we talk about something else?"

Byron ate one green olive and added one to the betting plate. "Your move, Jackson."

***

Panic, Navy's old friend, was absent for the moment. Her hands weren't shaking. Her heart wasn't pounding, despite Dragomir's shadowy tails. What she felt wasn't happiness exactly, it was more like satisfaction. Her knuckles throbbed a little where they had connected with Dragomir's nose. She could still feel the rhythm of the attack, a double beat, resonating in her shoulder.

She wanted to tell Jackson everything. But who knew when Kevin would let her see him again.

"Welcome home," Kevin said as she closed the door. He was stretched out on her bed.

It wasn't her first choice for tonight's companion, but at least she wouldn't be alone. "So, let's hear it. What's my grade?"

"An improvement over this morning. Let's say A minus."

"A compliment from you? I'm hon—"

"Don't get cocky."

"I think I deserve full points. I followed your directions to the letter." Navy held up a hand to count each item. "I threatened to walk away. I didn't accept his first price. I start on Monday. And I used nonlethal force only."

"Nonlethal?" Kevin sat up and crossed his legs. "If

133

you'd elbowed him a little harder you would have collapsed his airway. And that bit about not having to dump your body was a little overdramatic, don't you think?"

She smiled at him again. "Guess I'll have to go for extra credit."

In the kitchen she found a box of cereal from a previous tenant. It didn't taste too stale. "For dinner I have cereal or cereal. You want?"

"Yeah," Kevin said. "Anything's fine."

"Well, I found one thing you're not picky about."

Kevin ignored her jab and wolfed down the cereal like it was candy. She had to force herself to finish it. The flakes weren't sweet enough and the clusters were too hard. If she'd stayed home she could be having eggs and hash browns and pancakes at Giraldi's. She realized she was imagining Jackson's apartment as home. She wasn't sure he would have her after all this was over. Kevin waved a hand in front of her face.

"Anything you want to tell your best friend?"

"What do you think the best flavor of ice cream is after a breakup? Cookie dough or peanut butter cup?"

"I'll take that as a no."

Now that her hunger was partially satisfied, fatigue presented itself. The sun had barely set, but she hadn't slept much the night before. Tonight she would have someone standing guard. She wondered when she'd started trusting Kevin.

"So, tomorrow." Kevin launched into a lecture about plans for the next day.

All she heard was that she would get to see Jackson in the morning. She couldn't hide her yawns. "You should probably tell me this again in the morning."

He might have smiled, sometimes she couldn't tell with him.

A few minutes later she had changed into her pajamas and was drifting off to sleep on the lumpy mattress.

"Do I at least get one of the pillows?" Kevin asked.

Even with all three anemic pillows, her head felt like it was sinking. She pretended not to hear him.

"You're right. We can't sleep until we settle this ice cream issue. If it was just a few dates, I'd go for strawberry cheesecake. But if it was a longer relationship, definitely caramel swirl."

Navy pressed a thin pillow to each ear and tried to tune him out.

"But it's a hard choice because there's always moose tracks, which has peanut butter cups and fudge."

"You're going to keep talking all night, aren't you?"

"I'm nothing if not supportive."

She aimed a pillow at his smug smile. He caught the pillow before it connected with his head.

"Good night, Navy."

"Good night, Auntie."

Chapter 18

Jackson watched from the upstairs window while a sleepy figure in an apron put out a sign with flowers drawn in chalk. Only shopkeepers and bakers were up this early. He knew Navy had left her apartment with Kevin half an hour ago. Normally the walk to base would take ten minutes, but they would have to take the long way to make sure she wasn't tailed. The long wait didn't mean something had gone wrong, he reminded himself.

Kevin had ordered everyone else away from base to do reconnaissance on Dragomir's headquarters. Maps and surveillance photos couldn't show everything. They needed to pick out the best places to do surveillance and the best routes to storm the building—if it came to that.

Jackson was alone with his nerves and his embarrassment. This wasn't exactly the shining moment of his career. He'd been as clumsy as a rookie when he wasn't stalking the base like a caged animal. At least he had a reputation to fall back on.

Relief at being able to see Navy was only one of the emotions swirling inside him. She was still recovering from her kidnapping last year and she hadn't told him. For months, he'd been trying to get her to see a therapist. He'd even compiled a short list of the best therapists in DC—his work often put him in contact with combat veterans who had similar psychological and emotional wounds.

When that failed, he had tried talking to her. About whether she felt safe or how much the nightmares interfered with her sleep.

He'd just been trying to help, and somehow he'd driven her to hide her problems instead.

The door opened downstairs, signaling Navy's arrival, and he leapt out of his chair. Better not let Kevin see he was so eager. He forced himself to walk normally toward the stairs.

Kevin was an out-of-focus blur behind Navy. She wore the same casual clothes she wore every weekend at home. What had he expected? A secret agent outfit? No, the changes he saw now weren't superficial. The tension she carried in her gait. The wariness she hid with jokes and smiles. She was damaged, like Kevin had said. Jackson hadn't wanted to see.

"One hour," Kevin said. "I'll be napping upstairs."

"Take this upstairs with you," Navy said, tossing Kevin her phone. Kevin seemed disappointed.

Jackson listened to him climb the stairs to the third floor. When the creaking floors stopped protesting, there was only the whir of the fans on the electronics cluttering the kitchen table.

Navy found Jackson's eyes but her gaze was uncertain, searching. He wondered which part of his affections she doubted. Resentment kept him from crossing the few feet that separated them.

"You're angry with me," she said.

"You haven't been honest with me." Anger sharpened

his words. He was angry at himself too. He hadn't realized how serious her problems were. "When you were talking with Kevin, you said you have nightmares every night. Why didn't you tell me?"

She hung her coat on a hook and walked past him. "As if you don't keep secrets from me."

"Not about what's important. I've never lied to you about how I feel. You've been hiding your symptoms when I'm at home."

"No," she said emphatically.

"But you told Kevin—"

"Things are better when you're home, all right?"

He wondered what bothered her more, the fact he finally knew she was having problems or the fact that he was a comfort to her. "Christ, Navy. We've been together a year." A year of cozy weekends at his apartments or hers. A year of long dinners and lingering breakfasts and eager homecomings. "Doesn't that mean something to you?"

"It means—look—I don't know what it means." She held her hands up, as if he had threatened her. "I always told you I make a better one-night stand than a girlfriend."

"Would you have been happy with that?"

She shook her head, an unconscious gesture. "I tried to talk to you," she said. "I did. But every time, you got that look."

"What look?" he demanded. He cursed his insecurities and tried again. "I never meant to . . ." A burnt spot on the scarred linoleum stared back at him. Finally, he raised his head.

138

"Tell me. Please. What look?"

"That look you have right now. Like I'm one of your patients from the refugee center. Just another project for the great Jackson Fletcher."

He'd never thought of her as a patient. Had he treated her like one without realizing? "You think you're a patient I sleep with." It sounded even uglier when he said it.

"Am I?" Her voice was soft but defiant. A tear leaked from her eye, then hung like a crystal near the tip of her chin. He hadn't seen her cry before. She'd never allowed it.

He rubbed the back of his neck. "You're not a patient. You never were."

"In Amsterdam I was."

"I said *never*."

"You called them counseling sessions. To help me recover."

The lie had been unavoidable at the time. "It was an excuse to spend time with you. We're—uh—not supposed to get involved with assets."

A cold anger settled on her features. "I'm an asset to you."

"Were. I mean, not really. Just—technically you and I met when . . ." He kicked at the dirty rug. If he didn't think of the right thing to say soon she was going to give up on him entirely. "You know I love you."

She flinched at the word love. "I don't need your pity."

"Not pity."

"Then what?" she demanded. "I've seen the way other women look at you when we go out. You could have plenty of women on easier terms."

"I'm not interested in finding hookups on Tinder."

"I didn't mean that. I mean women who come without nightmares and scars and commitment issues."

He hadn't seriously considered another woman since he'd met Navy. He hadn't thought to make comparisons. "I don't care about those things. I don't want other women. I'm trying to help because I lo—"

"Then convince me I'm not another one of your projects. That you're not with me just to have something you can put back together."

He shook his head, bewildered. "You don't really believe that."

"I'm not the smartest or the prettiest or the funniest. Why me?"

"You underestimate yourself." She always had.

"And you're dodging the question."

He was. She must feel this exposed when he pressed her to declare her feelings. He'd never stopped to think about why he was attracted to her. She was kind, strong and smart. She was vicious to her enemies and generous with her friends. The answer was so simple it startled him. She had never treated him as her bodyguard. She had protected him as much as he protected her. On the nights he woke screaming from his own demons, she didn't expect him to hide his pain. She didn't ask for

140

explanations. He didn't have to be anything but himself when he was with her. He couldn't tell her any of these things, any more than she could say the words he wanted to hear.

"Lake Superior," he said. He risked a look at her face and saw her expression soften. "My parents have this cabin in the Upper Peninsula. They have this little dock." It was a wooden dock—out of fashion now with all the new metal ones. The boards were all different colors because of how many times it had been repaired. "I like to sit down there and listen to the waves. It makes me forget for a little while how easily things can go wrong. Being with you is like that."

"I help you?" Her surprise was genuine.

"You didn't know?"

"Well." She laughed a little. "You never told me."

Her arms were still crossed, defensive. He locked her in a tight hug, not caring that her elbows dug into his stomach.

She rested her head against where his heart beat too fast. "Kevin says I should ask you about Bosnia."

"Kevin talks too much."

The kitchen was cluttered with monitoring equipment, laptops, and dirty dishes. "Should we sit upstairs? It's more comfortable there."

Her left arm brushed his on the stairs and the touch left him tingling. Like when they had first met. She stopped in the doorway, eyes widening as she studied the disarray in the living room. It took him a second to see the mess. Clothes were scattered on the floor and draped over the furniture. Dirty dishes were piled near the top of the stairs in the hope someone would carry them down. Boxes of ammunition crowded one corner next to a digital SLR with a telephoto lens. Empty beer bottles formed a line next to the couch.

"It's like a frat house with war games," she said.

"It's crowded quarters," Jackson said. He and Byron had stayed up late retelling war stories. "And the boss was away."

"I don't think Kevin slept much," she said. "He just peeked out the windows. In rotation. It was like trying to sleep with a cougar circling."

"It's a good sign that things were quiet." He wondered if he could risk a compliment without sounding patronizing. "You were . . . impressive yesterday."

She smiled. "That's something, coming from you."

He caught her nervous hands. "You should rest. It's going to be a long day." The couch was too short to lie on. He cleared a spot on the floor and balled up one of his sweatshirts for a pillow. She curled up next to him, her head a comforting weight on his chest.

Her finger absently traced the lines of his scars hidden under his shirt. "Tell me about Bosnia." She smoothed the tension gathering in his chest with an open hand. "Please?"

He studied the silhouettes of dead flies in the glass dome of the light fixture. Kevin couldn't have been less subtle. He thought Navy should know why Jackson left the army and joined the agency. Jackson wasn't sure what good would come of telling Navy the details. So Navy would know he didn't win all his

142

fights? She had seen his scars. "Navy, I—"

Damaged, that's what Kevin had called him. Was he damaged in the same way she was? His nightmares were rarer now, but not so rare they had ceased to feel routine. The memories that fed them were stuck like clots in his brain. On his weaker days, a stray similarity could trigger them. A stab of sunlight in his eyes as a car backfired. Hearing a church bell when he was in a crowd with bodies pushing against his chest.

"There's so much you can't tell me about what you do," Navy said. "So much I can't tell you." Jackson felt Navy's laugh, bitter and short, against his chest. "I was nearly murdered for *national security* and we still respect it. We keep secrets from each other. We have to."

Navy knew when his ghosts came to him. She would use a touch, a kiss, the right word to push them away. She didn't need to know the rest. No, Jackson was lying to himself. Navy thought she was his patient and his lover because Jackson had never shared his demons with her. "You think we should have fewer secrets between us," Jackson said.

"Isn't that what you told me earlier? Isn't that what you always want from me?"

She was right again. If Jackson wanted Navy to feel like his partner, she should know what had driven him to work in deception and shadows. Still, he couldn't make his voice any louder than a whisper when he spoke.

"I was still in the army when I went to Bosnia. My squad was deployed as part of a UN peacekeeping mission. We were under strict orders not to engage."

He remembered feeling hunted—a sheep in wolf's clothing—breathing in the dust of the streets until his lungs felt as heavy as the gun he wasn't allowed to use. Men with rabid, mocking eyes and blood-spattered clothing passed him. Their smiles told him about their crimes. He had radioed multiple times to beg for permission to engage and was denied.

"I was a sergeant. I led five men. We'd just moved into Srebrenica and genocide was still happening out in the open. We heard screams close by and a church bell ringing."

The church bell had broken him. All day they'd been running toward screams. All day they had let the perpetrators run away. But the bell was a call for help—a call to his humanity—that he couldn't ignore.

"When we got to the church, we found a man in a Serbian uniform ringing the bell." It hadn't been a call for help; it had been a call to slaughter.

"There was a unit of ten, fifteen hostiles at the church. There were only six of us."

His arm tightened around Navy and she shifted. He loosened his grip and took a few deep breaths.

"We fired at anyone who didn't have a human shield." The blood had been a smell more than a sight. Blood absorbed into dark circles in the dry, sandy soil. Blood mixed with gunpowder oozing from the holes in the back of victims' heads. He buried his nose in Navy's hair. Peaches and ginger. Peaches and ginger and kisses and gentle fingers that made any injury less

144

painful. "All six of us made it into the church somehow. I can't even remember. But there were more enemy soldiers in there."

And all through it, that infernal bell ringing. Even after he shot the man pulling the rope. Inside the church, he had seen a man move in rhythm to the bell tones with a woman beneath him, her eyes glazed over, nearly dead.

"We lost, of course. They cornered us and shot everyone, piled us behind one of the pews. I was underneath two of my men."

He had killed his squad by starting a fight they couldn't win. His soldiers wouldn't have chosen differently but their widows might have.

"I was shot just shy of my heart. Everyone else was killed." Later, the medics told him it was the pressure of the bodies piled on top of him that kept him from bleeding out. "I had to lie there and listen while they raped, tortured, and killed every civilian in that church."

He knew being shot had saved him. He would have kept fighting. It would have been worth it to kill just one more of them.

"Kevin recruited me from the hospital." He remembered the crisp white sheets, streaked with the dirt from underneath his fingernails. "Kevin said I could save more lives as a spy than a soldier."

Kevin was probably right, but it didn't always feel that way. Jackson missed the simplicity of the decisions he'd faced as a soldier. To shoot or not to shoot. On his operations now, he had to choose when to intervene and when to watch. The watching never got easier.

"You think you're going to find closure by winning another fight." He kissed the top of her head, held her tighter. "I've saved more people than were lost that day. I've killed more people than I faced that day. It's never enough. And now it's all I know how to do."

He swiped at his eyes and dried his hand on his shirt.

"Thank you," Navy said.

He could only nod.

Navy lifted her head to kiss him lightly on the cheek. "Now you should rest. I don't think you slept well either."

He hadn't. He could feel Navy's heartbeat against his ribs, like waves lapping at a shore. Jackson closed his eyes, but sleep came slowly. Their newfound intimacy felt raw and fragile, and Jackson wondered how long it would last.

***

"I give you one hour and you choose to fall asleep together?" Kevin's voice pulled Jackson out of a dreamless sleep. Kevin was standing over them, amused.

"Good morning, Auntie." Navy pushed herself up.

Jackson felt too cold without her warmth, too light without her weight against his chest.

"Tell me about your assignment today," Kevin said.

"Wander around town and act like I'm gathering supplies for my stay here."

"Because?"

146

"You want to find the people Dragomir has assigned to tail me."

"Good. Remember to do plenty of window shopping, you can use the reflections. It'd be good if you can recognize your tails too. I'll stop by your apartment tonight to debrief you."

Jealousy stabbed at Jackson.

"I'll even give you a gold star for every tail you can spot," Kevin said.

Navy squeezed Jackson's hand. "No lollipops?"

Kevin ignored her. "You and me, Jackson. In the surveillance van. I'd tell you to stay here but I don't trust you."

"That's probably wise," Jackson said.

The surveillance van was black and the sun was high. Jackson took a sip of his water, but the relief was temporary. Kevin had stripped down to a thin T-shirt, Jackson too. After several hours in the tiny van, they both badly needed a shower.

"You're shaking the equipment," Kevin said. "Stop fidgeting."

The long bouts of near-silence were maddening. Just the rustle of fabric as the phone slipped around in her pocket, fragments of conversations overheard as she passed people on the sidewalk, and the rumblings of cars on the street. Navy was following Kevin's directions to the letter, moving slowly and stopping often to force her tails to slow down with her. A door opened and a small bell rang—another shop, another greeting in Romanian.

"Red shirt, jeans, knife at his ankle," Anna said. "He's

hanging around outside at the corner. Martin, can you confirm?”

“Yeah,” Martin said. “He was at the café where she ate lunch.”

Knife at his ankle. Jackson heard a clinking again, his foot shaking the equipment. Kevin gave him a hard look. Jackson eased off the stool and tried to stretch out on the dirty floor. The air was marginally cooler.

“Are you looking for something special?” the shopkeeper asked in heavily accented English.

There was a scraping sound, a drawer opening. “A gift for a friend,” Navy said. She was half a mile away but her voice was right next to him. Jackson reminded himself that Anna, Martin, and Byron were following closely.

“A special friend?” asked the shopkeeper.

“You could say that,” Navy said. “He works for a church in Bosnia.”

Jackson hit his head on a toolbox, startled. “You had to tell her,” he muttered.

Kevin’s smile told Jackson that everything had worked out exactly as Kevin intended. “I didn’t tell her any specifics. You must have. After you told her I talk too much.”

“You were listening,” Jackson said.

“It’s nice that you two got to swap hospital stories from your past.”

“Swap?”

Kevin seemed surprised, but Jackson didn’t have a chance to ask why.

"A religious man," said the shopkeeper. "I have the perfect gift." A key ring rattled and a lock turned. "This watch— very manly. See the design? A cross, for faith. A dove, for peace. Thorns, for redemption."

"Redemption," Navy murmured. "You're right. It's perfect."

"I liked that little speech about the lake and the waves," Kevin said. "Very Hallmark-special."

"Were you listening the whole time?"

"Up until you got quiet. I nearly shed a tear or two."

Jackson pulled his sweaty T-shirt off to use as a pillow. "I'm glad we could entertain you."

A cash register opened and closed on Navy's mic. "Mulţumesc," she said. *Thank you.*

"I had to, you know," Kevin said.

"Had to what?" Jackson asked.

"Make sure you two had a good talk."

The hot, enclosed van wasn't helping with Jackson's temper. "What the hell does that mean?"

"Your pouting was distracting her. You were either going to talk it out or I was going to send you home."

Jackson had considered the possibility he might put himself in danger by doing something stupid. He hadn't considered the possibility that his presence would make things worse for her.

"You can stop feeling guilty," Kevin said. "I expect things will be better now."

Jackson had to admit that he'd made more progress in his relationship with Navy that morning than over the past six months. But he certainly wasn't going to give Kevin any more satisfaction by asking what hospital story from her past Kevin had referred to earlier.

Instead, he tried to imagine the video to the soundtrack playing in his ear. The wind would push tendrils of Navy's hair into unruly tangles. She would be hunched over, like when she was nervous. And there would be that single line between her eyebrows that showed up when she was thinking hard. He could hear the crinkle of the plastic bag bouncing against her leg, holding the gift she'd bought for her "special friend." Navy, carrying his redemption down a bright street, followed by thugs.

"Blue jacket with the swoop logo," said Martin. "His jacket is too warm for this weather. Gun in his waistband."

"Confirmed," Byron said. "I saw him outside the museum earlier."

Jackson didn't need redemption. He needed faith.

Chapter 19

Navy assembled breakfast from the groceries she managed to find at the corner store Sunday night: gritty instant coffee, a candy bar with some sort of crunchy wafers, and a green banana so unripe it tasted dusty. She spent each bite pondering the unfairness; Kevin could meddle in her relationships but he couldn't find the time to buy a few groceries for her. Not even with the two hundred and seventy-five thousand dollars Dragomir had wired to her account.

When Navy had seen the number appear on the screen, it felt like a trap door closing. Friday, Dragomir had spotted her eating dinner at his favorite restaurant. Saturday, he had held her at gunpoint. Sunday, he had satisfied the first half of their verbal contract.

Her confidence had faded after a night alone in the apartment. Yes, Navy had managed to get Dragomir to agree to exactly the deal she wanted. But Dragomir had been no less confident walking away from that meeting. She kept replaying Saturday's encounter in her head, reanalyzing every move. Was the curl in Dragomir's lip after he agreed to her price the surliness of a man used to getting his way? Or the momentary slip of a man luring her into a trap. Was the glint in Nicolae's eye as he put away his gun the annoyance of a lieutenant being told to stand down? Or a promise to follow through on his threat at the first opportunity.

Now would be the time to back out. Aborting the operation would be as simple as not showing up for work. Maybe Jackson was right about not finding closure just by picking a fight. Navy probed her determination, like testing a bruise, and found it had not faded. Her nerves were a reason to stay; she couldn't leave the question posed by the operation unanswered. She had to make one last foray into the mouth of hell to prove she wouldn't be burned alive.

Navy tucked Jackson's new watch into her pocket and walked out the door. She would see him tonight at the base. Her orders for the day were to memorize everything about Dragomir's headquarters so she could regurgitate it later. Who let her in, whether she was allowed to walk freely, the layout of the floors, what the rooms were used for, what the security was like, how many guards were inside . . . and more questions she had already forgotten.

The front door of her apartment building creaked open and scraped shut—it was cockeyed in the frame. Thin, gray clouds hid a bright sun. Navy recognized one of her tails from yesterday browsing a newsstand.

As she walked toward Dragomir's headquarters, the corner of her laptop bounced against her leg. Navy had configured the laptop so it would always run, even when closed. The programs it ran were designed to build a map of wireless networks. To boost the signal, she had fashioned an antenna and concealed it in the lining of the bag. Wireless would be the easiest way into Dragomir's network. One of the containers at base was filled with toys for her, toys Navy couldn't risk keeping in an apartment Dragomir knew about. Small devices that looked like power strips, or laptop power adapters, or even mouse traps, that would extend the range of Dragomir's wireless network. Or, if that didn't work, she could plug them into an ethernet jack and create her own wireless network. Or none of them would work and Navy might have to do everything the old-fashioned way.

Rumor had it Dragomir was paranoid.

As she got closer, she spotted Byron in the park seemingly engrossed in a chess game with an old man. Byron looked old too. Navy tried to fit the image of Byron, smiling at a barbecue in his backyard, with the hunched over man in the black wool coat. Like the rest of the team, he seemed to have chameleon powers. It wasn't fancy spy gadgets that let them hide in plain sight. It was discovering the unspoken language of a place—the posture, the clothes, the walk, whether or not to nod when passing a stranger.

Navy was grateful her cover didn't require that talent. Even before she opened her mouth and her accented Romanian came out, the locals knew she didn't belong. She crossed the square, feeling the eyes at the chess tables on her, and reached for the door knocker.

Before her hand touched the metal, the door opened. Nicolae's bulky frame filled the space. "In." More a grunt than a word. The door clicked shut just as Navy was thrown against the wall, knocking all the wind out of her lungs. He was punishing her for Saturday. She held herself still even as she imagined a duck-punch-kick combination that would leave him laid out on the floor moaning in pain. He pushed her arms up roughly and ran his hands down every seam of her clothing.

The violation was hard to bear even though Kevin had told her to expect it. It was the reason she wasn't allowed to carry a gun or a knife. One of the pens from her bag might do in a pinch, but hardly her first choice.

"Finished?" Navy hoped she sounded calm.

Nicolae stuck his meaty fingers in her pocket and pulled out her phone. "Why do you need this?"

Kevin had prepped her for this too.

"I have a trigger in our database in case anyone starts looking up my name or Dragomir's. The texts go to this number."

He put the phone in her pocket—his hands close to her flesh again—grabbed her shoulder and spun her around. "Don't try anything. I hit back."

And there it was. The thick vise of fear around Navy's stomach she hadn't felt since her last real fight. Since last year. Her blood roared in her ears and her heart jumped in her chest. She welcomed the challenge. "Good morning to you too."

He glared at her. "We have desk for you. Follow me."

The hallway resembled an entrance to a prison more than an office building. Scuff marks littered the walls and the dusty light fixtures made the already narrow hallway seem narrower. Next to the front door was a guard's room, occupied by a bored man wearing a gold ring on each finger. There was a set of eight monitors, each with a grainy black-and-white video feed.

154

Some of the camera locations were easy to identify. One feed showed the square—that would be the front door. Another screen showed a dumpster, probably in the alley behind the building. The largest screen showed several empty rooms, coded by floor and room number, and a garage with four cramped stalls. Each stall held a van with tinted windows.

"Eyes ahead," Nicolae barked.

Navy wondered which business of Dragomir's required vans with tinted windows. They passed two doors before reaching a set of stairs that went down to a basement and up to a second floor. Narrate your day, Kevin had said. "Will I be upstairs or downstairs?"

Nicolae looked more annoyed than suspicious. "This floor." He used a key to unlock a door into another hallway. The door locked from both sides.

She only hesitated a second before following. "Will I get a key to the hallway?"

"No. I escort. When you arrive and when you leave."

He hurried her past a closed door that hummed with clicking keyboards and overly polite voices talking all at once. The perfect American accents were jarring.

"Of course we can get you signed up for our antivirus. All I need is your credit card number."

"In order to get your files back, you'll need to pay the ransom in bitcoin. I can help you get your wallet set up."

"I'm calling from Microsoft, we've noticed a security problem with your computer. If you could just download the program at this link . . ."

Nicolae led her to a room at the end of the hall. Navy recognized Andrei from one of his surveillance photos. He was thinner now but he had the same handsome jawline and piercing eyes. Everything in the mission briefing said Andrei had been hired. Except he looked like anything but an eager employee. He had dark bags under his eyes and the same pained expression she'd seen in the photo of Andrei entering Dragomir's headquarters.

There was a glint of recognition, but he didn't introduce himself.

"Andrei, this is Navy Trent," Nicolae said in English.

Andrei nodded as if he didn't recognize her. As if she had imagined the glint of recognition earlier.

"She has new exploits for the crime pack. You show her where to put them."

"Okay," Andrei said. He waited for his next order like a trained dog.

"We want the new version ready in two weeks."

"I'll try. With all the other improvements you want in the zombie code—"

"Try hard." Nicolae's eyes swung to the only happy object in the room, a bright 5" x 7" photo of a young boy on a swing, leaning forward, laughing.

Leverage, Navy thought. The surveillance photos had caught Andrei worrying not about something, but someone.

Nicolae gave them both a humorless smile. "We are

156

impatient."

Andrei looked between Nicolae and her. The expression on Andrei's face passed so quickly she wasn't sure if the flicker of hope was her imagination or not. "Two weeks," Andrei said.

Navy took the desk next to Andrei's. If not for the thug and the captive, the room looked like many offices where she had worked. The desks were covered in laminate that had seen better days and the roller chairs wobbled a little. Tall, plastic towers hummed noisily next to dusty monitors. Schemas and papers with doodles of the program architecture were taped to the wall.

Nicolae settled into a chair behind Navy and Andrei, where he could see their screens. Navy had a sinking feeling. Planting any sort of network surveillance device was going to be difficult with Nicolae watching her every second of the day.

"What kind of exploits do you have?" Andrei asked.

"Javascript, PDF, Flash—some of all three."

"Let's start with the Javascript ones."

She nodded, still scanning the room. There were no spare ethernet ports and no clutter on the floor to hide any of her toys. An employee would get to work. Navy pulled out her laptop. Maybe if she offered to transfer the files to a server on their network she could get some credentials that would give her a starting point for breaking in later.

A heavy hand landed on her shoulder. Nicolae moved fast for such a large man. Navy's arm twitched and she resisted the urge to fight. She had beaten larger men.

"Our equipment only," Nicolae said.

Navy let go of her laptop and it slid back into her bag. "Is a thumb drive okay?" She had two in her bag, one had the exploits plus a virus she had written just for Dragomir's network. One had only the exploits.

Nicolae's hand didn't move from her shoulder.

"I can't memorize obfuscated Javascript. Do you want these exploits or not?"

He nodded slowly and returned to his chair. Navy pulled out the noninfected thumb drive from her bag. She needed to get the lay of the land before she knew whether she could risk using her virus. She found herself moving slowly, but not out of caution. The thumb drive didn't have nuclear secrets or bomber designs, but exploits were weapons nonetheless. Bits of code smaller than the ones Navy was giving away had done plenty of damage.

The tools she was giving Dragomir would be used to infect computers all over the world. Any computer with an internet connection was vulnerable. An infected machine would become part of Dragomir's botnet—a swarm of machines ready to take orders from a central server, Attila. Attila was her target. In the meantime, Navy would be adding to the ranks of compromised machines that might be used for password cracking or sending spam or blackmailing a business with a denial-of-service attack. The swarm of tiny electronic thugs would do whatever Dragomir's customers hired them to do. Most of the owners would never even know their machines were accomplices in a crime.

Navy plugged in the thumb drive and decrypted the first few exploits to the desktop in front of her. Kevin's orders were to dispense a few of the exploits at a time, as if she were an employee afraid to be double-crossed.

"We have a directory for the Javascript exploits that go into our fake ads," Andrei said. "And some configuration files that tell the ad generator which exploits to use where."

As they worked, Andrei watched Nicolae carefully. Nicolae didn't seem to notice. When Nicolae's attention drifted to a magazine, Andrei stopped typing almost entirely. She was concentrating on the intel she could glean from the configuration files when a message popped up on her terminal.

```
Message from randrei@andrei_machine on
ttys001 at 08:21. . .
                do you want to play a game?
```

He was using the old Unix "write" command. The command wasn't normally used for chatting. It wasn't normally used directly at all. Navy risked a look at Andrei. He frowned and began moving his mouse quickly, abandoning typing entirely. He was cutting and pasting characters from a text file.

There was only one reason to use such a complicated maneuver, a keylogger installed on Andrei's machine that recorded everything he typed. Only basic keyloggers restricted themselves to keystrokes. These days, most keyloggers recorded clipboard activity and some even recorded where users clicked. Their intel said Andrei was smart enough to know what a modern keylogger could do.

Another message appeared on her screen, answering the question Navy hadn't asked.

```
write commands safe if no type
too much to watch cut/paste bc of code
```

He meant the logs would be too cluttered with code if the keylogger recorded cut-and-paste actions. A trained analyst would be able to work around that with some effort. She wondered if Andrei was wrong about being safe. Her curiosity got the better of her. Kevin would want to know Andrei's angle too. She could always say she went along to see if Andrei was a CIA informant.

```
game faster to talk
```

Navy opened a new terminal window to answer him.

```
OK
```

```
close windows now
```

She closed both windows, erasing the evidence of their conversation. A new window appeared on her screen made up of jittery, blinking graphics. The game was called "ToppleWords." Players took turns selecting their words from randomly chosen tiles. Instead of a board, each word was placed on top of the word the last player made. Like Scrabble, some letters were worth more points than others. The more points a letter was worth the more it weighed. If the tower became too unbalanced, it would topple.

"I think this Javascript exploit would work well in this game," Andrei said.

The directions faded and a tropical background replaced

them, asking if Navy wanted to accept a game. She clicked yes, and a bunch of coconuts fell from the trees, bouncing around the edges of the window. A monkey sat on one of the branches, grinning. "Feed me!" said a speech bubble.

Navy clicked on a banana and dragged it into the monkey's hand. He jumped up and down. "Cheat code accepted!" Thankfully, the game was silent. A new set of directions popped up. "Choose your letters from the full alphabet along the side of the screen! Unlimited tiles! Each player must hold the 'c' key to stay in cheat mode. But you only have three minutes! And remember, don't let the tower fall!"

Andrei played the first word, raising his eyebrows to make it a question. UNDERCOVER.

Was Andrei threatening to expose her? Blackmail her? Was this some sort of elaborate test set up by Dragomir? Navy glanced at Nicolae, still reading his magazine. Perhaps she had made the wrong decision in hearing Andrei out.

NO, Navy answered.

LIAR. Four letters wouldn't balance on two and the game ended. A new invitation popped up from Andrei.

Could she risk playing again? She looked at Andrei and saw she had no choice. He wouldn't let the matter drop.

UNDERCOVER, Andrei played again.

CRIMINAL, Navy replied.

Andrei shook his head, frustrated. HELP.

Seconds passed on the clock while Navy stared at the desperate plea in cheerful orange tiles. Navy wondered what

Kevin would want her to do. Nicolae wasn't watching and she could destroy their conversation just by lifting her hand from the keyboard. Would offering Andrei help count as the heroics Kevin had forbidden? It was Andrei's expression that made her decide to say no. He couldn't keep his expression neutral. If Navy said she would help, he would blow her cover. CANT. Her family Scrabble games were paying off.

DEAL.

Andrei didn't seem to be in a position to offer her anything. There was 1:45 left in cheat mode. Navy tried to think of a word that would keep him talking but not give her away. Even a criminal might make a deal with a coworker.

NEXT, she played.

SAVE.

NEXT.

THE.

1:37 left. He had taken them down to three letters. Navy balanced her word carefully. NEXT.

BOY.

The darling boy in the photo, with the rosy cheeks and easy smile. Dragomir was holding the boy as collateral for Andrei's cooperation. She couldn't offer help in this room. In this room, Navy was a selfish traitor. She didn't have the heart to tell him just yet. Maybe Andrei could offer something that would be of enough interest to Kevin they could make a deal. A tit for tat that would allow her to do the right thing.

TAT, she played.

162

AID, he replied. A different word for help, to distinguish it from his plea. He must mean he would aid her in the undercover investigation in return for saving the boy.

But what sort of aid? Navy would need something more convincing to get Kevin's cooperation. NEXT. The word teetered precariously on the already unstable tower.

ANY.

Anything for the boy in the photo. Choosing to accept or reject Andrei's offer wasn't a choice Navy could make without Kevin. And she still suspected giving Andrei good news would make him blow her cover. Still, Navy hesitated before replying. The game was an ingenious method of communicating. An entire conversation could be erased just by lifting her hand. The graphics were crass and overdone, perfect cover to blend in with one of the many "free" games on the internet. And it hadn't escaped her notice that the tiles along the side of the game rearranged themselves after each play, making it difficult for a keylogger to track what words were played.

The game would have required hours of coding in preparation for the one moment when Andrei had a chance to talk to someone, anyone, who might help him. Navy was about to tell a desperate man his time had been wasted.

RISKY, Navy played. The word ended the game, as she knew it would.

Andrei made a sound like a hiccup and shook his head. Perhaps Navy had miscalculated. He might make a scene whatever her answer was. Nicolae looked up, saw the empty game board and went back to flipping through his copy of *Buxom Blondes*.

Another invitation to the game appeared on her screen. She would have to be cruel to be kind.

UNDERCOVER, Andrei played again.

CRIMINAL.

UNDERCOVER. Andrei was going to get her killed.

ENOUGH.

PURPOSE, he asked.

Navy was saving both their lives, she told herself, by pretending to crush his dreams. MONEY.

Andrei's whole body tensed and he raised his fist, ready to slam it against the desk. Instead, he sent her a piercing glare and one last message. BITCH. He released the keys and the tower toppled. When Nicolae glanced up, he only saw a jumble of letters at the bottom of the window.

"No more fun," Nicolae said. "Work."

For the rest of the morning, Navy worked under Nicolae's glare and Andrei's scowl. Andrei's reputation wasn't oversold. He was brilliant, speaking as effortlessly in code as he did in speech. By noon, several of her exploits had been tested on various browsers and had already infected a few live machines. Once Andrei confirmed an exploit worked, that exploit was disabled. Zero-day exploits were valuable. Dragomir would keep them in reserve until the older exploits stopped working. Or until he found a buyer willing to pay a good price. There were enough vulnerable, unpatched machines in the world that Dragomir might not need them for years.

Andrei pulled up the dashboard for the crime pack. A color-coded map showed compromised machines in nearly every country. The brighter red the machine, the more bandwidth that machine had available. A different map showed the machines color-coded by processor power. The map of infected machines changed every second. Navy imagined what must be happening behind the flickering dots. Someone at home had just closed their laptop and gone to bed. Or maybe someone had figured out their machine was infected, and the machine would be reinstalled, only to be replaced by a newly infected machine seconds later. On that same map, blue dots showed the servers used to control the botnet. These dots flickered and changed every minute or so. To keep ahead of shutdown requests by law enforcement, new servers had to be set up as fast as old ones were taken down.

Navy was typically on the other side of these investigations, digging into the code men like Andrei wrote to find the Achille's heel. Shutting down a botnet was a complex task that required disciplined global coordination across multiple jurisdictions. Like most botnets, Andrei's used multiple domains. If you took out just one of the command servers, the botnet operator could switch to the secondary or tertiary servers to rebuild. Resilient infrastructure was just good business.

A man arrived with three greasy paper bags and three foam cups. Nicolae dropped two bags between her and Andrei then dug into his own lunch. Evidently, they weren't going to get a break. The only thing Navy had accomplished so far was to figure out Dragomir monitored his own programmer with a keylogger.

Even though Navy wasn't hungry, she forced down the sausage and onion sandwich and washed it down with watery pop. Her shoulders hurt from being hunched over a desk for so long. If Nicolae didn't loosen the leash a little, Navy wouldn't be able to accomplish anything today.

Someone banged on the door at the end of the hallway. Her exit, if Nicolae ever let her leave. Nicolae went to answer the door. Every few seconds he looked back to check on them. But he was too far away to see her typing. Andrei was deep in concentration

Finally.

She opened up another terminal window and ran a command that listed all the files from the root directory down, visually scanning for files with "Attila" in the name. She didn't want to type "Attila" and have the keylogger records trigger Nicolae's suspicions. If anyone asked, Navy could say she meant to list all the files in her directory and made a typo. Nothing. Navy ran a different search, this time looking for phrases she'd seen in the code for Attila earlier, when she and Andrei had been working together. Nothing. Navy had watched Andrei check the code into subversion ten minutes ago. She knew the right keywords. She tried to ping the IP address of the subversion server. No response. She tried to ping other servers Andrei had used that morning. No response.

Her machine was hobbled. Navy could test exploits on it

166

and transfer code to Andrei's machine, but only Andrei's machine could reach Attila. Her refusals earlier had ruined any chance of earning his trust. Before she could think through her options, Nicolae's conversation ended. She closed the window to hide her search.

"Time to go," Nicolae said.

"It's only two o'clock?" Navy asked.

"Shipment arrived early. We need this room."

Andrei glanced down the hall and disgust curled his lips.

"Would you like to stay and help?" Nicolae asked Andrei.

"No. I want to go home." Andrei's tone was submissive. As if he needed Nicolae's permission.

Nicolae herded them out the front door. The empty room she had passed earlier was no longer empty. She could see a strip of light underneath the closed door and heard the sounds of rustling inside. She thought she heard a whimper, like a dog, as she walked past. Nicolae pushed her into the bright sunlight, leaving her blinking at the cobblestone street. Andrei trudged past her, his shoulders bent into a nonexistent wind.

Her phone beeped with a message from Aunt Gertrude.

"Will have to cancel our dinner plans, I have a cold."

It was code for canceling the meeting at base tonight. The excuse meant Navy was supposed to go to her apartment and restrict herself to emergency communication for the next few hours. Had she done something wrong and tipped off Dragomir? What about the operation could keep the team busy without involving her?

She wasn't looking forward to a long afternoon and evening spent trying to guess what Kevin would complain about tomorrow.

Chapter 20

Andrei wasn't allowed to take the long way home, but he could walk slowly. Being able to spend an unexpected afternoon with Petru was the rare bright spot in Andrei's existence. If he could forget it meant a new shipment of human cargo was arriving. Sometimes he found traces of the children who had passed through his office. A pair of pants that smelled of urine stuck behind the garbage can. Initials clumsily scratched into the wall. He pushed the mountain of their suffering out of his thoughts. There was nothing he could do about it anyway.

He had failed at doing the one thing he thought he could do—rescue Petru. Andrei had been wrong. When he was told Navy Trent was coming to work for them, he assumed somehow Byron was involved. She worked for the CIA, too. And she didn't have the reputation of someone who would ally herself with a child abuser just to make some money. All the pages that had been written about Navy Trent since the scandal last year agreed on one thing: she broke the rules for a cause, not for profit. The writers had been wrong. The whole world was wrong.

Byron Macalester wasn't a CIA man. Or maybe he was and he'd found a way to keep Clara from going overseas, despite Clara's insistence she was still planning on coming. Either way, Andrei wasn't going to have a chance to offer the CIA his cooperation in return for rescuing Petru.

Petru's guard merely nodded and pointed upstairs when

Andrei entered the house. The stairs creaked loudly as he climbed to the second floor. What really made escape impossible, however, was the all-night parties Nicolae often threw downstairs. Most of the attendees passed out by three or four in the morning, but there was always one guy on uppers who was awake all night. Cocaine, Andrei guessed, from the white powder he saw sometimes on the carpet where Petru played.

Physically fighting his way out had never been a serious option. Every time Andrei tried to imagine it, he felt every bruise he'd been given since his kidnapping. He'd never been a physically imposing man, and he'd only gotten weaker. It was no wonder the guards were so much stronger; they had enough to eat and slept better at night.

He opened the door to their room quietly. Petru was so absorbed in his coloring he didn't look up. The crayons were nubs now; he had to hold them with a claw-like grip. From across the room Andrei could only see large regions of blue, green, and yellow. He wondered what made children so optimistic. Most of Petru's drawings were of his house or his yard or the little black terrier his family had loved.

"We have the afternoon, Petru," Andrei said.

Petru jumped, startled, then ran to Andrei. "I want to play checkers!"

"I'll make up the board." Andrei could barely get them to buy crayons for Petru; he didn't bother to ask about board games. But some games were pretty easy to replicate with paper. Andrei decided not to use the red and black crayons; they were almost gone. He made a grid on a piece of notebook paper and colored in half the squares with blue pen. Then he carefully folded and ripped squares from another sheet of paper for checker pieces. Since two pieces of paper stacked on top of each other didn't make for a good queen, he made a few smaller squares and drew pictures of crowns on them.

Petru won many of their games even though Andrei wasn't letting him win. Petru was that smart, and Andrei was that distracted.

"Queen me," Petru demanded. Petru played along the diagonals, just like in the games of checkers, then chess, that Andrei remembered from the long rainy afternoons stuck indoors with Afina. Petru was like her in so many ways. The way Petru's forehead folded in concentration when he was studying something. His relentless optimism. How he tried to take care of Andrei even though Andrei was supposed to take care of him.

Andrei's fragile self-control shattered. He hadn't cried for months but now he couldn't stop. The occasional beatings, the midnight searches, the abhorrent work his code supported—all these things he'd been able to bear when he had hope of escape. He grabbed a pillow from the bed to cover the sounds of his hiccuping sobs. He couldn't afford to have the guard come up to ask questions.

Petru crawled into Andrei's lap and wrapped his thin arms around his uncle's chest. Petru wasn't crying, and that made Andrei cry even harder. The grimy pillow against Andrei's face smelled like the underside of a dock from the moisture of his tears. He wouldn't be able to save Petru; he couldn't even stay strong for him.

The idea slithered into Andrei's subconscious and raised its head slowly. He wasn't stronger than the guards, but he was stronger than Petru. A few minutes with the pillow, that's all it would take.

If there was no chance of escape, why keep Petru alive? Dragomir would use Petru in one of his films someday, or Petru would be sold. Petru might survive to adulthood scarred. Or he might die an early death, wandering the streets after being discarded by his buyer. Under those circumstances, would suffocation be considered murder or mercy?

"Uncle, you're hurting me," Petru whimpered.

Andrei hadn't realized how tightly he was hugging Petru.

The question was academic. Andrei couldn't do it. He would find another way. Maybe he could gather some blackmail material and hide it in a photo he sent to one his marks. Find a way to make sure the material stayed hidden only if Petru was released. Or find an excuse for Clara to play ToppleWords with him. She would help just because she was a good person. Or he could put a logic-bomb in Dragomir's control server to cut off his income and only remove it if Petru was released. Dragomir spoke the language of greed well. Andrei forced himself not to consider the possibility Petru would be put to work before Andrei could put together a new escape plan.

He would think of Dragomir as another program. Andrei

would find the right exploit. He always did. That's what had gotten him into trouble in the first place.

Chapter 21

At dusk, Navy was finally allowed to leave Dragomir's headquarters. Yesterday she'd been thrown out early; today Nicolae had forced her and Andrei to stay late to catch up. Navy watched Andrei drag himself across the square for the second day in a row. Whatever waited for Andrei at home, he wasn't eager to get there. Warm lights spilled out of the windows of a café half a block to her left. The pink-tinged sky and her stomach reminded her how late it was. Food would have to wait. She should have been at the theater an hour ago to meet Anna.

After a day of enduring Andrei's baleful stares, she was impatient to ask Kevin if she would be allowed to help. She walked back to her apartment to collect her rental car. When her tail saw her behind the wheel, he made a call. Probably to get someone with a vehicle to follow her. She bent down as if to search for something on the floorboards.

"I'm headed to the movie theater," she spoke into her phone. She could almost hear Kevin's impatient sigh in response.

The movie she was supposed to buy tickets for was almost over. Better to choose a showing that would start soon. "One for the 7:30 showing of the *Titanic* in 3D," she told the clerk. A shadow moved at the edge of her vision. Maybe Anna heading into the dark theater to meet her. Or her new tail. A beat-up motorcycle had followed her to the theater. The driver wore jeans, a leather jacket, and gloves. The driver's black helmet and tinted face mask hid any identifying characteristics.

"Glasses are extra," the bored clerk said in English.

Navy pushed cash across the counter. At the concessions stand, she tried to figure out what would make a good dinner. The hot dog reminded her too much of the greasy sausage and onion concoction she was given at Dragomir's. She settled on popcorn and sour gummy candy. There were only two other people in the theater. She knew by their profiles and adolescent voices they weren't Dragomir's men. Before the previews had even finished, they were making out.

Ten minutes into the movie, Anna dropped into the seat next to her. "*Titanic*? Really?" she whispered. "This movie makes me gag."

"I thought you might appreciate the running time," Navy said. She would need every minute of the three hours to convince Kevin to let her rescue the boy in the photo.

"True that," Anna said. "Let's go."

"It's safe? They followed me here."

"You're going out the back door. I disabled the alarm. You'll come back in that way too. Your tail is playing arcade games by the front door. He'll never even know you left."

It took Navy a second to see how Anna had rigged the back door. A magnet had been wedged at the top. The alarm must be triggered by a break in the connection. The extra magnet would keep the alarm from even knowing the door had opened. Navy followed Anna out to a car parked behind the theater.

When Navy opened the passenger door, Anna shook her

head and pointed to the backseat.

"Lie down and cover up with the blanket," Anna said. "I should warn you, Kevin's crabby. He nearly had to hogtie Jackson when Nicolae kept you late."

Anna's driving was fast and aggressive. Navy, curled up on the floor, dug her nails into the carpet on every turn. Ten minutes later Navy heard a garage door open. She blinked at the sudden brightness when she shook the blanket off. She barely had time to stretch her cramped legs when Kevin appeared.

"You're forgiven."

"For?"

"Being late."

"Gee, thanks, Auntie."

Kevin pointed upstairs. Navy followed Anna up the staircase to the living room. Jackson sat on the couch, like a child sentenced to time out. Navy recognized the set of his jaw from the rare nights he ground his teeth in his sleep. Given Kevin's mood, the most affection she could show was to sit close to him.

"Everything's okay?" Jackson asked.

"Fine," Navy assured him. "Well, I think."

"You think?" Jackson and Kevin asked simultaneously.

Kevin held up a hand to keep Jackson quiet. "What do you mean you *think* everything is okay?"

Navy hated to admit defeat, but without Andrei's help she would have to risk planting a device in Dragomir's headquarters. Without Nicolae noticing. Or get access to Andrei's computer. Without Nicolae or Andrei noticing. And she wanted to rescue Andrei and the boy—for the boy's sake and Andrei's. She knew what it was like to be trapped by circumstances outside of her control. "I'm not sure I can reach Attila to plant the code to track Dragomir's clients."

Kevin waved her concern away, annoyed. "You've only worked there two days."

"They won't let me use my laptop so I don't have my tools. I'm watched nearly every second so I can't install anything. And they're monitoring both Andrei and me with keyloggers so every command I type is reviewed later."

"If Dragomir still suspects you, we should reconsider continuing with the mission," Martin said.

"No," Navy said. "They treat Andrei the same way they treat me." She thought of the boy on the swing with the dark eyes and easy smile. "I'm trying to tell you Dragomir's network configuration makes most of my tools useless. The machine I have access to isn't even on the same network as Attila."

"Dragomir doesn't have a wireless network?" Jackson asked.

"No. My scans haven't found anything. Not even any signals bleeding in from the surrounding buildings. They must be using special paint to block the 2.4 and 5 gigahertz ranges."

"Can't you break the encryption on the firewall or something?" Kevin asked.

Navy considered asking what movie he'd pulled that line from, but it was probably better to play nice. "Firewalls don't have—that's not how things work."

"We'll re-evaluate at the end of the week," Kevin said.

"I don't think more time will get me access to Attila. There's another way."

"Go on," Kevin said.

"Your file says Andrei is working for Dragomir voluntarily, but that's not what it looks like. There's a picture of a little boy on his desk, six years old maybe, and Nicolae is always threatening Andrei and pointing at it."

"He has a son?" Byron asked in a strangled voice.

Navy hurried on, hoping to keep attention away from Byron. "Or a cousin or a nephew, I don't know. But I think Dragomir is using the boy to force Andrei to work for them."

"I warned you about this, Navy," Kevin said. "We can't afford to take on strays."

"What about enlightened self-interest?" she asked.

"Kevin's phrase," Navy heard Jackson mutter.

"Turn Andrei," Navy said. Giving Kevin an angle was the only way she would get his help. "Recruit him to be a double-agent."

"Andrei has the access we need. And you think he'll deal," Kevin said.

"Yes and yes. He already offered."

The anger on Kevin's face was bare and cold. "Maybe you should start at the beginning."

Navy wondered if she could still convince him. "When I showed up yesterday he seemed happy to see me. When Nicolae got distracted, Andrei had this game ready for us to play so we

178

could talk in private. It's kind of like a combination of Scrabble and Jenga and—"

"Back up," Kevin said. "Andrei was happy to see you? And he had a way to communicate with you?"

She nodded slowly. "This game he wrote, called ToppleWords. He was hopeful. Like he'd been expecting I could help."

"And you think he prepared this game just for the occasion?"

"Yes. It looks like one of those silly internet games that infect your machine. But he added a cheat mode that lets players talk using any letters you want and rearranges the tiles so you can't re-create the conversation based on the mouse movements. He accused me of being undercover."

"He didn't happen to say why he thinks you're undercover or how he knew you were coming."

"Maybe Andrei's been working on the game ever since Dragomir found that bug months ago. Andrei knew we might show up and he knew he'd need a way to talk to us. The game can be played over the network too."

Kevin frowned. "Maybe. Go on."

"He offered me a deal. He'd help with the operation if we save the boy."

"You can't accept any deals without talking to me first—"

"I didn't." Navy took a deep breath and waited for her temper to cool. "I told him it was too risky. And, anyway, he wasn't exactly a model of self-control. I thought he would break down right there if I told him I could help."

"You should have mentioned this earlier."

"Last night you used the code for emergency communications only." She tried to keep the edge from her voice.

"Yeah, I did." Kevin rubbed his face. It was the first time Navy had seen him show any signs of fatigue.

Jackson rubbed her knee. "It could be a trap," he said. "A ploy to get you to break your cover."

Navy had already considered and rejected the possibility. "If you'd seen him . . . Andrei's not faking his desperation."

"If they're forcing him to code, they could be forcing him to test you," Jackson said.

"We've been monitoring the bug in Dragomir's office 24/7," Anna said. "There's no indication that Dragomir suspects Navy is undercover. And he hasn't been holding his tongue about his other business, so I don't think he knows we're listening."

"Anna's right," Kevin said. "I don't think Dragomir suspects anything. Why Andrei suspects, that's what I want to know."

"What does it matter? He'll work with us."

"Motivation *always* matters, Navy. It's pretty much the only damn thing that does." Kevin stifled a yawn.

Navy considered telling Kevin he was being more of an asshole than usual, but then she noticed the dark bags underneath everyone's eyes. "What happened last night? Why is everyone so tired?"

The five officers exchanged looks with each other. Navy knew they were keeping secrets from her. Portions of the criminal dossiers in her mission folder had been redacted. Navy had managed to steal a few glances at Jackson's mission folder. Not enough to read anything, but enough to see there were no redactions. Navy had noticed Kevin's hushed conversation with Jackson just before Jackson left and the way Kevin had cut off Martin her first day here. Maybe it had something to do with the vans with blacked-out windows she'd seen on the surveillance cameras at Dragomir's and the early shipment that had sent her home mid-afternoon yesterday.

"Oh, this is about whatever it is you don't want me to know about Dragomir's business."

Jackson looked guilty. Kevin looked surprised.

"That's fine, I don't care. But consider turning Andrei. I don't think I'll be able to get anything done without him."

"You have good instincts," Kevin said.

Navy wasn't sure if she wanted to earn Kevin's respect.

"Your ship is sinking." Anna tapped her watch. "I need to get you back."

Navy reached into her pocket for the watch she'd bought for Jackson. The soft leather band felt warm and smooth. She didn't want anyone to see her give him the watch. She slipped the watch under Jackson's leg as she stood up.

Kevin leaned in close. He was a full six inches taller than she was. "No heroics. Not even for cute children. If you get any hint that your cover is blown—"

"Kiss-my-ass City," she said. "I remember."

"We'll have to do some recon to figure out if we want to turn Andrei. Until then, you need to act the same way you have been. Even if we do turn him, we may not tell him about you. Jackson, Byron, Martin — we need to talk strategy. Reconvene in five."

Navy tried to hide her smile. Kevin's answer wasn't a yes, but it wasn't a no either.

***

The garage door opened and closed with the reluctant growls of old machinery. Jackson watched from the window as Anna turned out of the alley, carrying Navy away from him again. He fingered the watch in his pocket. He couldn't wear it until they left Romania. Navy's tail had watched her buy it and might connect her to him.

Someone yawned behind Jackson, and Jackson stifled his own yawn.

They were all tired. Anna had been up all night guarding Navy's apartment. Everyone else had been documenting the latest shipment of children to arrive at Dragomir's headquarters. Jackson had listened to the bug in Dragomir's office as each child was brought in, one by one, for casting. Byron and Martin had been taking infrared photos of the vans and building to document numbers. Whenever Dragomir brought in his shipments, he hired extra guards. Even if Kevin had pulled Anna from the post at Navy's apartment, the children were too heavily guarded to

182

intercept.

"Letting the bastards get away with it … feels shitty no matter how long I've been doing this." Martin was standing next to Jackson now.

Jackson nodded. "Even if it's a temporary reprieve."

"Kevin means to see this through?"

"There's history." Jackson thought carefully about how much he could share. "When Kevin and I were on an operation together, we crossed paths with Dragomir. Or Dragomir's money, I guess. We were undercover in a nonprofit that was next to a girl's school."

"In a place where some people didn't think girls should go to school?" Martin guessed.

"Yes. That sort of place." Jackson couldn't be any more specific about the location without giving away details he shouldn't. "Every morning when the girls arrived and every afternoon when they left, small groups of men would assemble to harass them. The girls . . ." Jackson remembered how they always walked with equal parts fear and strength. Huddled together, for protection. With their heads held high, to prove they had a right to be there. "Anyway, Kevin discovered the harassers were camera-shy."

Martin crossed his arms and stared out the window, same as Jackson. No doubt Martin was thinking of his own stories. They all had them.

"So Kevin set up this little coffee break area right outside the door. Good cover, because lots of people used it. And every morning school started, every afternoon school ended, he was out there at that table drinking coffee with his camera out in plain sight."

"I suppose that's not the end of the story," Martin said.

"A suicide bomber drove through the front door and detonated a car full of explosives in the school courtyard. Killed nearly half the students. The school closed after that. Or moved, I don't know. But it was Dragomir's money that funded the bombing. The men that didn't want the school there, they controlled the local trade routes. And Dragomir paid them handsomely to make sure his shipments got through."

"You know how people talk about bucket lists? I have a shit list I keep up here." Martin tapped his forehead. "Of all the people I've seen who don't deserve to be walking free. And when I retire, that's going to be my job. Go back and even the scales."

"Better than a condo in Florida."

Jackson turned at the sound of creaking stairs. Kevin had returned. Jackson took his spot on the couch again, next to the cold absence of Navy.

"I can't read Navy as well as I'd like," Kevin said. "Does she actually think Andrei can help? Or is she just feeling sentimental?"

Jackson's answer felt like betrayal. "I think it's both."

Kevin nodded slowly. "All right. Martin, tell me everything we know about Andrei."

"He dropped out of the University of Bucharest about a year ago and went to work for Dragomir," Martin said. "He has

184

no previous criminal contacts and had good job prospects because he won Pwn2Own two years in a row. That's pretty much it. He didn't seem important," Martin said.

"I know," Kevin said. "I was the one who told you to concentrate on Nicolae. Well, Andrei's important now. Dig up everything you can on his family life. Byron, who do you think the boy in the photo is? Andrei's a bit young to have a six-year-old son. But it could have been a teenage mistake. Maybe he was quite the player at the college dorms."

"Hard to know really," Byron managed.

If Jackson didn't know Byron so well, Jackson might have been fooled by Byron's calm.

"Yeah, if someone like Andrei were sniffing around my family, I'd be worried," Kevin continued. "I might even go to Tom in Ops and ask him to run background on the phone number of my daughter's boyfriend six months ago. Clever of you to ask Tom for your favor, knowing he was going to be embedded on a long assignment with an undercover team. I finally reached him last night."

"I assume you have some sort of punishment in mind," Byron said.

"Well, I'd ask you for an apology but I doubt you can manage it."

"I'm not sorry. I had to lie. You wouldn't have let me come."

It was the right tactic. Kevin often mistook humility for weakness.

"You're right," Kevin said. "But I would have helped you. I didn't think Navy going was a serious possibility until you told me she might volunteer. If you'd come to me before you asked Navy, I would have had more time to prepare. And I would have been able to pull some strings so we could have more than one team on the ground." With more than one team, they would have been able to sabotage last night's shipment without revealing a CIA presence.

Byron couldn't hide his surprise. "You would have helped?"

"Believe it or not, I want Dragomir more than you do."

Kevin's focus on Dragomir was as close to a vendetta as the cold-blooded man would allow himself. Kevin had been trying for years to get the resources to go after Dragomir. Jackson knew Kevin didn't like being lied to, but the missed opportunity probably bothered him more.

"Lie to me again and I'll have you working night shifts with the surveillance techs for a year," Kevin said.

Jackson believed Kevin. After all, Byron had used official agency resources for an unofficial investigation into Andrei, manipulated the operations director into adjusting the timing of Operation Atilla, and inserted himself into an operation under false pretenses.

Judging by Byron's expression, Byron believed Kevin too.

"Understood," Byron said.

"I'd like a bottle of scotch," Kevin said. "As payment

for not reporting this little infraction to my superiors. Not the cheap shit either. Actually, you and Jackson should pick out a nice bottle together. Since he helped with this charade."

Jackson was lucky Kevin hadn't asked for a second bottle.

"I'll have it delivered with a bow," Byron said.

"Do that. Now we can get back to business."

"Turning Andrei could be a good angle," Jackson said. "If Navy's right about him."

"You just want to give Dragomir another target," Kevin said.

"No." He was surprised it wasn't a lie. "If they find out Andrei's working for us, I doubt they'll see Navy's arrival as coincidence."

Kevin sighed and stretched his long arms above his head. "Someone needs to follow Andrei around for a couple of days. I can't pull anyone off Navy's support team."

"Does that mean I'm off the bench?" Jackson asked.

"Only if you promise to behave."

"Scout's honor."

"I can tell when you're lying," Kevin said.

"And I can tell when you're bluffing."

"Touché," Kevin said. "If we turn Andrei, I'll need you to run him."

Fieldwork would be a welcome distraction. "Not a problem."

"Martin, I need you to finish those sketches of

headquarters from Navy's observations. Make sure everyone gets copies."

"It'll be done in two hours," Martin said.

"I want everyone to have the layout memorized by tomorrow. I don't suppose anyone knows where Andrei goes after work."

"To a house close to the square," Byron said. He seemed glad to have something to offer. "I can just see it from my post."

One by one, the rest of the team finished their assignments and went upstairs to catch up on much-needed sleep. The thought of the bedroom's dorm style accommodations irked Jackson. He wasn't sure he could sleep with the sounds of everyone breathing around him, He took a cushion from the couch and set it down next to the window. The sky was a deep blue, even with the lights of the city. Jackson rolled the leather band of Navy's gift between his fingers. Faith. Peace. Redemption. If only he were a religious man.

Chapter 22

Jackson woke up with stiff limbs from sleeping on the floor. The deep blue of the sky had been replaced by a gray dawn. Day three of Navy's work at Dragomir's headquarters. Navy's request to turn Andrei. His assignment for the day came rushing back. He checked his watch. One hour until sunrise. He should head over to Andrei's soon, to be in place before Andrei left for work. Jackson brushed his teeth and ran a washcloth over his face before going downstairs.

Kevin was in the kitchen, headphones on, frowning.

Tension sucked in Jackson's breath. "Is something wrong with Navy?"

Kevin shook his head and unplugged the headphones. Navy's even breathing came over the speakers. "She's fine. This is what's bothering me." He tapped a pencil on the notepad in front of him.

All Jackson could decipher from Kevin's handwriting was a few dates.

"It's the timing," Kevin said.

Jackson heard the rustle of sheets over the speakers. He saw the landscape of Navy's form in his bed, the soft rise of her hips and the shadows that gathered on her curves. If she was sleeping peacefully, her hands would be folded neatly under her head.

"Has she been sleeping all right?" Jackson asked.

Kevin arched an eyebrow. "She's fine. How are *you* sleeping?"

Jackson grabbed the pot of coffee that already smelled burned and poured himself a cup. He wondered how long Kevin had been up. "What's bothering you about the timing?"

"If we are going to rescue this alleged son of Andrei's, we should have at least a week of prep to nail down the guard schedule at Andrei's house. And before that, Andrei will need a couple days to make our changes to the code."

Two days of the two weeks Navy had promised Dragomir had already passed. Jackson could see Kevin's concerns. "That doesn't leave much time to watch Andrei before we turn him."

Turning an asset was always tricky, even if the asset was willing. Some assets needed coddling, some needed distance, and some needed bullying. The only way to know what approach to take was to watch them. If he approached Andrei the wrong way, Andrei might crack in front of Nicolae. Which would cast suspicion on Navy. But all that assumed Navy was still undercover while Andrei was working for them.

"Can't we wait until Navy leaves?" Jackson asked.

"I want her there to watch him. If she's right, Andrei's been under forced labor for years. That's a long time. I'm not sure he's stable. You're the psychologist. Do you think he'd still be capable of helping us without falling apart?"

"Can't say until I meet him." Before he'd met Navy, he wouldn't have imagined an untrained civilian could escape four armed guards and out-think an assassination team. "Anyway, since when do you trust a civilian to go undercover with an asset?"

"She's hardly a civilian, Jackson. And she's not half-bad at this."

Kevin was right on both counts. "I better get to Andrei's before he leaves for work," Jackson said.

"If you get anywhere near Navy, we'll spot you."

"I'm hurt that you think I'd even try."

"Uh-huh." Kevin plugged the headphones in and frowned at his notes. "Find out some good news for me today."

Jackson shoved his hands in his pockets against the chilly morning. Byron's directions led him to a plain two-story stucco building. Cigarette butts cluttered the front step. That normally meant a house with a lot of visitors. Thick curtains covered all the windows, including the large picture window on the first floor.

An alley across the way offered convenient shadows for hiding. He leaned against the cold bricks and waited for the sun to warm the air. A light turned on downstairs, illuminating two shadows behind the curtain: a large burly man and a smaller hunched figure. The door opened soon after. Andrei stepped reluctantly into the street, half-pushed by Nicolae.

Andrei looked back at the house, his face broken with grief. It was the face of a man who had been scared for a long time. A small round face pushed under the curtains. The boy had jet-black hair, like Andrei's, and wide nervous eyes. But the child didn't have Andrei's jawline. If he was Andrei's son, he had taken after his mother. The child's mouth was set in a frown. The boy was, as Navy had said, about six.

Jackson had seen enough sad children to recognize this one's sorrow.

"You work," Nicolae said. "Or he does."

"Yeah, I know," Andrei said. The voice was so soft Jackson barely heard it.

The only question now was whether Kevin would authorize the deal with Andrei.

Andrei and Nicolae headed for the square, Nicolae looming. Andrei made no move to escape. Of course he wouldn't. Not without the boy. But Andrei's obedience didn't bode well for turning him. There was no need for Jackson to keep following them once Dragomir's headquarters were in sight.

But the prospect of sitting around base for another day, or being stuck in the surveillance van with Kevin, made Jackson circle back to Andrei's house. No, he shouldn't lie to himself. He wanted to start planning the rescue. For all the children he'd been unable to save yesterday—and all the other days.

His observation post in the alley across from the house wouldn't work for all-day surveillance. The old-fashioned, steep roofs on most of the buildings didn't offer many possibilities either. But there was the restaurant next to the alley. It was modern and the roof was flat. A fire escape would get him to the roof. The observation post struck him as a little too easy. Of course, Dragomir wouldn't suspect that Andrei's house needed

192

much defending. Keeping a small boy captive didn't require much.

Jackson felt in his bag; he had a bottle of water and three energy bars. Breakfast, lunch, and dinner, depending on when he decided to climb down.

The rusting fire escape left streaks of red on his hands. As he passed the second and third floors, he looked into dark windows cluttered with catering equipment. Three stories up gave him a good vantage point on both Andrei's house and the square where Navy would soon be arriving for work. A familiar figure entered from the northern edge of the square. He could recognize the sway of Navy's hips from any distance. Gravel dug into his elbows and stomach.

He refocused his binoculars on Navy. A shapeless bag swung against her tan coat. Her bag was nearly empty because Nicolae had ordered her to leave the laptop at home. She knocked on the door to Dragomir's headquarters; Nicolae pulled Navy in quickly. Nicolae would be searching her now. The thought of Nicolae's hands anywhere on her—

Jackson looked down and saw he was crouched, ready to run.

Navy had a team of people protecting her, he reminded himself. Jackson could see Byron, entering the park now, a bag of chess pieces tucked under his arm. And Martin, sipping at his coffee. And if Jackson strained, he could see the hood of the black van where Kevin would be listening to Navy's every move.

He stretched out on the gravel again, positioning himself

in front of the rectangular roof drain. Recruiters never talked about this part of the work.

Morning passed slowly into a warm afternoon. No one came to the house or left. They weren't changing the guard regularly. Anyone on guard for that long by himself would get lazy. Human nature. There were only two entrances, one he'd seen Andrei use that morning and one around the corner. It would be easy enough to keep people from leaving—or reinforcements from getting in.

Kevin would want a look inside to confirm, but two entrances with an assault team of five would be manageable. That was some good news.

The warm afternoon melted into evening. The rocks beneath him provided a welcome warmth as the sun fell. When that wasn't enough, he put his coat back on and nibbled at his last energy bar. Andrei returned, alone. Had Navy left Dragomir's office at the same time? Focus on Andrei, Jackson reminded himself. The door opened and Jackson could see the guard holding the little boy. When the boy saw Andrei, he wriggled free of the scowling guard and ran to Andrei. Andrei noted the guard's sour expression then pried the boy's hands away from his shoulders, forcing a smile.

Jackson tried to ignore how the scene tugged at his heart. He couldn't care too much; it would only cloud his judgment.

The guard said something Jackson couldn't hear. Andrei nodded and grasped the boy's hand, following the direction the guard pointed. Apparently, it was exercise time in the prison
194

yard. The guard followed, half-heartedly watching for anyone who might be following.

Jackson noted the route for as long as he could see them. If they took the same route every day, this time could be convenient to exchange messages with Andrei. Eventually, he lost the trio among the tangle of buildings. Ten minutes later, Andrei and the boy returned, the guard close behind. They walked slower as they approached the house. The boy still looked nervous. Andrei still looked defeated. The guard still looked mean.

Jackson's phone vibrated in his pocket. "Hello, Auntie," Jackson said softly.

"You, too?" Kevin said. "Navy's going to the movies again. She'll be at base in an hour. Can you be back by then?"

"Twenty minutes," Jackson said. The couple dining on the patio were getting their check. He could sneak down after the table was cleared. He was hungry and tired and didn't expect Andrei would be let out again until the morning. The guard looked up and down the street before closing the door. Jackson waited for the table to clear and the shadows in the alley to grow long before slipping down the fire escape.

He tried not to think about the captives he left behind.

***

When Jackson got back to base, he found Byron in the kitchen.

"Martin made some beef stew," Byron said. "Left you a bowl in the fridge."

Jackson dropped his bag on an empty chair. The thud startled him. He was more tired than he had realized. "Thanks."

Byron hovered in the doorway. "Hard day?"

"Yeah." Jackson missed Byron's friendship. "How many games of chess did you play today?"

Byron edged into the room and leaned against the wall. "Too many. My game's coming back. Even made a few bucks. What'd you see at Andrei's?"

"Evil." Jackson shook his head. "They're keeping a boy prisoner to force Andrei's cooperation. This morning Nicolae told Andrei 'You work or he does.'"

"And you know what kind of work Dragomir does with children," Byron said, finishing Jackson's thought.

"You know that thing Kevin always says? Enlightened self-interest. Logically, I get it." Jackson swallowed a spoonful of food without tasting it. "But it never feels good. Just once, I wish we could do something with pure motives."

"You know it doesn't work that way." But Byron's expression was conflicted too.

"I watched someone suffer today and did nothing. And we might not do anything at all if it's not strategic for us." Half of Jackson's stew was gone. He must have eaten it. The instinct for food. For safety. To protect the ones he loved. Those instincts never went away, even when he was trying to think about others.

"Does that mean you want to turn Andrei?"

Jackson shook his head. "I don't know. It's riskier for Navy."

"Jackson, I …" Byron uncrossed his arms and crossed them again. "Look, I'm sorry. I know this operation has been hard on you."

"We're good," Jackson said. His anger against Byron had run its course. "You were right. You didn't need my permission. Whether or not to come here, it was always Navy's decision."

Byron checked his watch. "Navy should be here soon. Meet you upstairs."

The headlights nearly blinded Jackson when Anna pulled into the garage. Navy popped up from under the blanket in the back seat, her hair mussed. Anna gave Jackson a knowing smile before disappearing into the house.

Jackson hugged Navy tightly. The boy's fear and Andrei's grief would keep him up tonight.

"Where's Kevin?" she mumbled into his shoulder.

"Busy for a couple minutes."

She braided her hands at the base of his neck. She smelled like popcorn and stale cigarette smoke. "Long day for you too, I guess."

It was nice, for once, to be able to share his assignment with Navy. "You were right. They're keeping the boy a prisoner to force Andrei's cooperation."

"I was kind of hoping I was wrong."

He kissed the top of her head. "It's that way a lot in this job." Metallic clicks from the engine as it cooled echoed in the small garage. "Oh, you don't need to keep Byron's secret anymore. Kevin figured out Byron's here because of Clara."

"Is Kevin sending Byron home?"

"We need everyone we've got. Kevin settled it with some light blackmail."

"Blackmail?"

"Kevin won't tell if Byron and I gift him a nice bottle of scotch." The gift Navy had given Jackson was still in his pocket. "Thanks for the watch, by the way."

She smiled uncertainly. "Well, I know you can't wear it until the operation is over. And it doesn't synchronize down to the millisecond or shoot missiles or anything."

"Still." He tried to catch her eye, but she looked down at the greasy floor.

"I thought it'd be good for my cover. Who goes shopping all day and doesn't buy anything?"

With Navy, moments of closeness were often followed by a chilly distance. The frustrating dance left him bewildered and hurt. He dropped his arms, holding her loosely around the waist. If she wanted to pull away, let her.

Her intense study of him scraped at his raw feelings. A sad smile curled her lips. "It's been a tiring day, that's all. I didn't make any progress. Again."

"Your technical skills aren't in doubt."

"Patience isn't my strong suit. I want to go—" she cut herself off.

"To go home?"

"To be done."

198

The door opened, and Kevin leaned through the opening.

"Christ," Kevin said. "I can't leave you two alone for a minute. Upstairs. Now."

Navy kept tight hold of Jackson's hand as they walked upstairs. It meant something that she needed him. He just didn't know what yet.

Kevin barely waited for them to settle before starting his questions. "Any progress, Navy?"

"Day three wasn't any different from the first two days. I'm not any closer to Attila."

Jackson watched Kevin calculating the next move. Recruiting Andrei would have its advantages and its complications.

"What did you find out about Andrei?" Kevin asked Jackson.

"Looks like Navy's right. There's a boy at the house and a guard. Nicolae threatened the boy in front of Andrei."

"How well is the boy guarded?" Kevin asked.

"Just one guard today. We should watch for a couple more days to make sure. And I'd like to get some bugs inside, if we can."

"One guard? That seems too easy." Kevin tapped a pencil on the notepad in his lap. "You weren't, by chance, distracted by watching headquarters?"

Jackson narrowed his eyes. "No. Andrei's not giving them much of a fight. I don't think they need to try very hard."

"What's your read on Andrei?"

Jackson thought of Andrei's face, crumpled like yesterday's newspaper, as he left the boy behind. "Broken."

"So he won't be picky about our terms?"

"I think he'll take whatever we offer as long as we rescue the child," Jackson said.

Navy pressed her lips shut. The first time Jackson had made a deal with an informant he'd been uncomfortable too. Rescuers didn't normally throw drowning men conditional lifelines. She picked at the dirty carpet with her fingers.

"This has to be your call, Navy," Kevin said.

Jackson was as surprised as everyone else. It was an extraordinary amount of trust for a rookie officer. And she wasn't even an officer, Jackson reminded himself.

Her shoulders slumped with the weight of the boy's safety. "Why is it my call?"

"If Andrei cracks, Dragomir will suspect you."

Navy bit her lip. "Then wait until I leave."

"I need eyes and ears on him. We don't have anyone else in a position to watch Andrei."

"You can't bug him like I am?"

"You said yourself he's already acting nervous. Most people can't wear a bug without letting it show."

She managed a smile. "Is that a compliment, Auntie?"

"Don't get cocky. Do we turn Andrei or not?"

A line of worry etched itself between her eyes. "I don't think we can do the operation without him."

"That's not what I asked. Operations fail all the time.

200

We can come back later."

Byron shifted in his seat. "Navy, you don't have to—"

A hand gesture from Kevin cut Byron off. Kevin leaned forward, only inches from Navy's face. "Forget about the boy. Forget about Clara."

"You know I can't." Navy's voice didn't waver.

"You're betting your life on whether Andrei can handle the pressure of playing double agent. Be sure."

Navy looked at Jackson, already apologizing for her answer. She was going to take the risk. She wouldn't be the person he loved if she decided any other way.

"He can handle it well enough," Navy said.

Kevin sighed. "I guess we're turning Andrei."

"And rescuing the boy," Navy added.

"I keep my promises." Kevin stood, frustration still evident on his face. "I don't want to tell Andrei that Navy's undercover unless we have to. Jackson, is there a way we can make contact with Andrei outside of headquarters?"

"They were allowed a walk tonight," Jackson said. "Might be a regular thing. How long do you want me to do recon before we make contact?"

"Watch him the old-fashioned way for two more days. We'll get bugs in there this weekend, and we make contact Monday."

Jackson exchanged a look with Anna and Martin. Four days was tight—barely enough time to nail down the schedule. And how was Kevin planning to plant bugs in the house without pulling people from Navy's protection detail?

"Navy, you're going away for the weekend," Kevin said. "If Dragomir asks, tell him you need to do something touristy to keep your employer from getting suspicious. Anna will follow you."

"No disrespect to Anna, but Dragomir has three men following me in rotation here," Navy said. "That doesn't seem like a fair fight."

"I don't think he'll want to send them all into the country with you. That means I can use some of your support team."

"Well, in that case, I was feeling a bit cooped up," she said.

"When you get back, I'll need you on hand for the meeting with Andrei. In case we want him to know who you are."

One quick squeeze of Navy's hand and she was gone, hurrying away with Anna to get back to the theater before the movie was over. Jackson went up to the bedroom to jot down his notes from the day. The relevant details were mundane: a description of the guard, the location of the windows and doors, the route Andrei had been allowed to walk. Irrelevant details clouded his vision: a scared boy clinging to his protector, Navy's mask-like face pushing him away while her body pulled him closer. He shook away the feeling of whiplash. Forget the distractions. Work. Concentrate on the work, he told himself. It had always saved him before.

Chapter 23

Navy looked at the unappetizing sausage and onion sandwich that had been delivered for lunch. The fourth day in a row. She had expected a lot of things from undercover work—tension, fear, sleepless nights. She hadn't expected monotony. Every day the same. Andrei moping around the office, glaring at her when Nicolae wasn't looking. The heavy, greasy lunch that made her breath stink. Nicolae alternating between scowling and playing with his knife. She was convinced Nicolae had been the kid on the block who killed neighbor's pets just for fun.

Footsteps padded down the thin carpet of the hallway toward her desk. She kept her eyes on her computer screen. Maybe another mysterious shipment had arrived and she would have to leave early.

Nicolae put a meaty hand on her shoulder, squeezing it so hard she bit back a gasp. Nicolae was happy. Not a good sign. "Dragomir wants to see you."

She hadn't seen Dragomir since their meeting in the park six days ago, She tried to decipher her fate in Nicolae's smile. "Is there a problem?"

"Dragomir will tell you."

There was no time to do anything but trust her instincts. She could always call for backup later. She followed Nicolae to the second floor. Navy could tell the rooms were larger on this floor by how the doors, all closed, were spaced farther apart.

Even the rooms with lights on held an eerie silence. Nicolae opened a door and pushed her into a gray, alien landscape. Spiked foam had been glued to the walls to deaden sound. That explained the lack of noise. Her eyes traveled to the center of the room where bright lights illuminated three walls supported by angled two-by-fours. A film set. A bedroom with two walls missing. The geometric foam, contrasting light, and cluttered bedroom scene had distracted her from the three figures on the bed.

A naked woman. No, not a woman. A pale girl so young her chest was only budding. There was no hair anywhere on her body except the raven-black hair on her head. And a boy of the same complexion, also naked, even younger. The naked man sitting between them was grotesquely hairy in comparison. The bedspread had cheerful flowers. Next to the bed, a dresser with a pink scarf draped over it. A girl's bedroom. And a camera, pointed at the trio.

The children met her stare with wide, unconcerned eyes. Her lunch rose in her throat. The whimper she'd heard on her first day. The vans with blacked-out windows. This was the secret the team had been keeping from her. This was the purpose of Kevin's rule—no heroics. Let the children suffer. Walk away. She counted her opponents—Dragomir in a director's chair, Nicolae with his burly arms, two camera men, plus the adult actor on the bed. The children might be her opponents too; they seemed in no hurry to leave. She suspected even Jackson wouldn't have taken up the challenge.

Nicolae hovered, ready to pounce on her at Dragomir's word.

Dragomir waved a hand at the scene. "You don't approve. People all over the world pay good money for this. A demonstration perhaps?"

On cue, the boy and the girl leaned over and kissed the man on the cheek. The man rested four hairy fingers on the girl's knee. Navy looked away, swallowing the bile in her throat. It burned all the way down.

Dragomir was trying to throw her off balance. To catch her in a lie.

"Not my business," she said. She held Dragomir's cold eyes, fighting the sweat in her armpits, the roiling in her belly. "You called me up here."

Dragomir pulled a small metal object from his pocket, two wires dangled from a piece of metal no larger than a pencil eraser. The last active bug they had in Dragomir's headquarters. He waved Nicolae over and handed the bug to him. "Who do you think this belongs to?" Dragomir asked Nicolae.

The performance was for her.

"This bug is from the CIA," Nicolae said. "Like the last one we found."

Dragomir turned to Navy. His calculating smile was replaced by a cold fury. "You said the CIA didn't have any bugs here yet. You lied."

Think like Navy the traitor, she reminded herself. What would a traitor be most worried about? Her own skin. Her anger, at least, didn't need to be faked. "Where did you find that?" she demanded. Stalking toward Dragomir gave her a convenient excuse to turn away from the set. "Was it in the office I've been working in?"

"No." Dragomir seemed surprised. Good. "In my office."

"Have you talked about me there? Mentioned my name?"

He smiled. "You are not as important as you think. Maybe yes, maybe no. I don't remember."

"I have to leave. Right now." She was close to puking in front of them. "I'll leave the thumb drive with you. Andrei can finish without me."

"I paid for two weeks," Dragomir objected. "You don't leave until you're done."

Her mind was still calculating what it would take to scoop up the children and fight her way out of the room. She forced herself back to her cover. Navy the traitor and businesswoman. "You've paid me half my money. I've finished nearly half my work and you'd get to keep your exploits. Seems fair to me."

Nicolae moved to block her exit. The naked children lounged at the edge of her vision, talking softly and pointing at her.

"You were supposed to find out what the CIA knows about me," Dragomir said. "I want my case file."

There might be a way she could save this operation yet.

Kevin had said the bugs installed at Dragomir's headquarters were an older model, one they had mostly phased out. If she could make Dragomir less paranoid, they might still have time to turn Andrei and finish the operation.

"Let me see the bug," she said.

Dragomir handed it over, intrigued by her request.

She pretended to examine it. "The other one was just like this?

Nicolae leaned closer. "Yes. Exactly like this. We find bugs, you show up. It is not accident."

She didn't want to confront Nicolae directly. "We haven't used this model in years," she told Dragomir. At least Nicolae's hulking form blocked her view of the set.

"I am not wrong," Nicolae said. "This is CIA. I know."

She shrugged. "I doubt it. I can see if there's anything new in your file. But this doesn't look like anything I've seen the CIA use recently."

Dragomir considered her offer. "You go downstairs and check."

She had to get out of the building so she could consult with Kevin. "I'll have to go back to my apartment."

"No, you check downstairs," Nicolae said, happy to take any opportunity to undermine her.

"I was told not to bring my laptop. I need that to log into the CIA network." Navy hoped her stony expression would hold.

"Fine," Dragomir said. "Go back to your apartment. Bring a copy of my file tomorrow and give it to Nicolae. I have a movie to finish."

Navy had been forced to piss off Nicolae by contradicting him; she couldn't risk Nicolae twisting the situation to her disadvantage. "No intermediaries," Navy said. "Meet me here tomorrow morning and I'll give the file to you."

"Tomorrow, then," Dragomir said. "Go directly to your apartment—we know where it is—we'll know if you're trying to run."

Dragomir wasn't telling her anything she didn't know. Still, she had to hold her muscles rigid to keep a shiver from running down her spine.

"Prove Nicolae wrong," Dragomir said. "Or I'll make you a star."

Navy hoped Jackson couldn't hear any of this. "Tomorrow." She turned quickly, knowing she couldn't shut her eyes to the languid forms on the bed. Nicolae nearly pushed her down the stairs and out into the street.

Her tail didn't bother to hide following her home. Somehow she managed to keep her lunch down. Somehow she managed to keep the pressure behind her eyes from bursting. Her resolve broke when she closed the apartment door behind her.

She saw Kevin's form, a blur at the edge of her vision, as she stumbled to the bathroom. Her stomach emptied itself with powerful heaves. On her third retch, she heard Kevin's footsteps. She kicked the door shut in his face.

"I'll give you a few minutes," he said, his voice muffled by the door.

208

Navy wiped her mouth with a towel and leaned against the tub. Images of the damaged children painted themselves on her eyelids. Kids so abused they were past protesting.

Kevin opened the door. He searched through the toiletries on the sink until he found a small bottle of mouthwash. The burn of the alcohol cleared the taste of vomit from her mouth, but not the smell from the room.

"Let's talk," Kevin said.

She ignored the hand he offered her. She didn't have the energy to walk into another room just to hear Kevin tell her everything she'd done wrong.

"All right," he said. "We'll talk here."

On any other day, she would have laughed at someone Kevin's height trying to fold himself into the space between the pedestal sink and the wall. She pulled her legs to her chest and lowered her head. The points of her kneecaps pressed against her forehead. The tears she had been holding back leaked down her cheeks and dripped to the floor. Maybe if she ignored Kevin for long enough, he would go away.

"I'm sorry," he said. Kevin's crystal-blue eyes looked like shattered glass. He did humble surprisingly well. "I didn't expect Dragomir to let you walk in on a filming. He keeps the pornography side of his business secret from most of his employees."

"I left them there." It was the thought that had been circling in her mind since she had been pushed out the door by Nicolae. "How could I leave them there?"

"There were more than one?" he asked.

"Two."

Kevin laced his fingers across his knees. "You had too many opponents."

"How could you know?" she snapped.

"There was Dragomir and Nicolae, right? Plus whoever was filming. And since I didn't hear the children over your mic, they were either incapacitated or not fighting."

"The latter." She didn't want to remember how well the children seemed trained to the task.

"The most dangerous thing you can do is rescue someone who doesn't want to be rescued."

"Still," she whispered.

"Do you remember your first day at Dragomir's?"

The day the mysterious shipment had arrived, ending the workday early. "It was a delivery of children for his films."

"And for sale, yes."

She counted how many times she had been close enough to Dragomir to kill him.

"I cancelled our meeting so we could document Dragomir's human trafficking operation."

"You just watched." She couldn't keep the disgust from her voice.

"I didn't have a choice."

She scratched at the tile with her nails.

"He keeps his operation heavily guarded," Kevin explained. "I don't have enough people here. As you saw, some

210

of the children have been in the business for a while. So, yes, we just watched. We would have blown the entire operation otherwise. Our information will be useful to Interpol later."

"How do you do it?"

"Infrared cameras, long distance mics . . ." He trailed off at her confused expression. "Oh, you mean how do you handle it."

She nodded.

He unlaced his fingers and leaned forward, crossing his legs. "You focus on the big picture."

"Allow a little suffering to prevent more suffering." It sounded logical when she said it, but the sentiment made her stomach turn again.

"That's the general idea."

"If you came over to make me feel better, it's not working."

A smile ghosted across his face. "Nice save, by the way. I think we can convince Dragomir the bug he found isn't ours. Just don't forget to narrate when Nicolae moves you. You didn't tell me you were headed upstairs."

"How'd you keep Jackson away?"

"He doesn't know what happened. He's watching Andrei's house to nail down the guard schedule."

"Good. I don't want him to see me like this." She wondered how it was possible to wish for the comfort of Jackson's arms and yet still be glad he wasn't here to witness her break down.

"Yeah, I figured."

"Get out of my head, Kevin."

"Not until we're stateside. Sorry."

She tried to compose her expression into something that resembled normal. "You can go. I'll be fine."

"We have business to settle. What are you going to tell Dragomir when you see him tomorrow?"

Suddenly, she felt very tired. "That my handler has no concept of privacy."

"We'll figure it out over dinner." He extricated himself from the narrow space under the sink. "I'm cooking my specialty."

"I'm not hungry."

"You will be. I'm making rice porridge. Settles the stomach."

She studied the shifting patterns in the small square tiles on the floor, watching how the patterns emerged and faded depending on her focus.

Kevin snapped his fingers twice next to her ear. "You'll eat because I can't have you fainting tomorrow."

"I hate you," she said. But she took the hand he offered. His touch was dry and firm.

"Say it with more enthusiasm and I might believe you."

Chapter 24

Jackson didn't have good news for Kevin. Hours past dark, the party on the first floor of Andrei's house was still in full swing. The parties were a regular occurrence, and that complicated any rescue plans for the young boy. When it was clear the festivities weren't winding down, Jackson decided to head back to base. He trudged past bricks damp from the afternoon's rain that had soaked him. He shivered in the cool summer night. They would have a ten-minute window to grab Andrei and the boy during their nightly walk, or they would have to break into the house and face a room full of Nicolae's friends. Either option was undesirable.

The first option required fewer people but left Navy vulnerable on her own walk home. The second option would require the whole team to breach the house, leaving Navy without any protection at all.

Jackson pushed open the door to base and dropped his bag on the floor. Behind the curtained windows, he could finally relax. Byron was at the kitchen table, reviewing the drawings of Dragomir's headquarters.

"I made spaghetti," Byron said. "Do you want some leftovers?"

Jackson moved toward the fridge to search for the container, but Byron pulled out a chair for him.

"Here, sit. Let me heat some up for you."

Jackson wondered if Byron was still feeling guilty about asking Navy to come. It hardly mattered now. Jackson accepted the chair and the plate of noodles and red sauce Byron microwaved for him.

Byron didn't speak again until Jackson's mouth was full. "I have some news to share with you," Byron said carefully. His eyes flicked to the door. "Before Kevin gets back."

Jackson managed "Why?" through the large bite of noodles.

"You're going to be angry at Kevin. You need to get it out of your system before he returns."

His half-chewed food was hard to swallow. Jackson pushed his plate away. "She's okay?"

"Yes. Shaken, but fine, I think. Kevin took the spare monitor for her bug when he left for her apartment."

Whatever had happened, Kevin wanted to discuss it with Navy without the team overhearing. "Spit it out," Jackson snapped. "My food is getting cold."

"Dragomir found the bug in his office. He called her up to one of the studios on the second floor during a filming to confront her about it."

"That was our last bug." Without it, they would only overhear what was said in front of Navy. They wouldn't know in advance if Navy's cover were blown. "How did she handle herself?"

"She did well. I imagine Kevin is massaging her story right now."

214

Jackson's back ached from lying stomach-down on the gravel roof all day. The details he'd memorized about the movement of Nicolae's men threatened to fade. "Thank you for telling me. Now I'd like to finish my dinner in peace."

"Do you want some dry clothes? I have—"

"Go." It took the last of his self-control not to yell the word.

Byron's chair scraped against the floor. Jackson listened to Byron climb the stairs with tentative steps. Jackson ate, because he knew he needed the energy. He wrote down his notes, because he knew Kevin would need them. Kevin, who hadn't called him after Navy had come close to blowing her cover. The thought pushed Jackson out of his chair. Navy needed him. If Kevin didn't want him at her apartment, too bad.

Just as Jackson put his hand on the doorknob, Kevin opened the door. He looked tired and drawn. "Evening," Kevin said.

Jackson stepped aside, cursing himself for automatically deferring to Kevin. Again.

"Something happened you should know about."

"Byron told me." Jackson shut the door harder than necessary.

"Then you know she's fine."

"She witnessed a child being abused. I wouldn't say she's fine."

"She kept her cover. Quite well, actually. We have a plan."

"I want to go see her." He shouldn't be asking Kevin for permission.

"No."

"Why—"

"Dragomir's men will catch on if we use the tunnel into her apartment building too often."

Jackson knew Kevin had chosen Navy's apartment building because someone watching the entrance to her building couldn't also watch the entrance to the neighboring building. It was a weak excuse.

"She didn't want me there," Jackson said.

"I didn't give her a choice," Kevin corrected him. "You were needed elsewhere."

"Don't dodge the question. She didn't even ask for me, did she?"

Kevin locked the deadbolt on the door. "You're being a bit melodramatic, don't you think?"

"So it's true." The pain of her rejection strangled his voice. Despite all the secrets and history they shared, she still didn't trust him. "She didn't ask for me."

Jackson watched Kevin calculating a response. As his friend or his handler, Jackson wondered. Or Navy's handler.

"She must see something in you. I don't know why she'd put up with you otherwise," Kevin said. "I meant what I said. You're needed here. Upstairs. Now."

Kevin didn't wait to make sure Jackson followed. Jackson stared at the locked door. What would he tell a patient in

216

his own situation? To cool down before storming into her apartment and risk saying something he'd regret.

He went upstairs.

Martin was dozing on the couch. Kevin dialed a number on his phone as he tapped Martin on the shoulder.

"Present," said Anna through the speaker on Kevin's phone.

"Any unusual activity at the apartment?" Kevin asked.

"They're on the usual rotation," Anna said. "Lung Cancer is arriving for his shift right now."

"Martin, tell me what you've learned about our boy, Andrei," Kevin said.

"He's a gifted exploit programmer," Martin said. "He probably attracted the attention of Dragomir's gang by winning Pwn2Own. His only family is an older sister, Afina, and her son, Petru." He consulted a sheet scrawled with notes. "Petru Yonescu."

A name to go with the round face in the window. It was always harder to walk away if they had a name.

"Petru's father died about a year ago in what the police recorded as a home invasion. My guess is that's when Petru and Andrei were kidnapped. The mother was seriously hurt. The last official record on Afina is a hospital discharge form. Interpol doesn't know where she is."

"Poor bastard," Byron said.

"Warming up to your future son-in-law?" Kevin asked.

A muscle in Byron's jaw twitched. "I wouldn't go that

far."

Kevin closed his eyes and leaned back in his chair. "Jackson, how do we make contact with Andrei?"

Jackson pushed away his uncertainties about Navy's feelings. "The nightly walk. The route is predictable, and there's only one guard with them. We won't have long. I can knock out the guard, but we'll have five minutes, ten on the outside, before someone comes looking for them."

"First good news I've heard all day." Kevin stifled a yawn. "This weekend, Anna is following Navy out to the country. The rest of you are helping me plant bugs in Andrei's house to prepare for a rescue. We turn Andrei Monday."

Navy wouldn't get a second chance if Dragomir discovered more bugs. "Are you sure planting bugs in Andrei's house is still a good idea?" Jackson asked. "Dragomir's going to be extra careful."

"He thinks we're targeting him, not Andrei. If he were really worried, he'd station more than one guard during the day. Besides, I have some new toys from Langley. One of the tech guys owed me."

Jackson imagined everyone at Langley owed Kevin something. "You're not at all worried about having only five minutes to turn Andrei."

"You've never failed me before." It was a compliment and a warning.

"When are we going to bug the house? And who's going to bluff their way inside?" Byron asked.

"Saturday afternoon." Kevin said. "And I'll be taking point when we go in."

It was the only option, really. Byron and Martin were in plain sight around Dragomir's headquarters every day. They were too exposed to make themselves memorable to Nicolae. Jackson was out for much the same reason. Running Andrei might put Jackson in the same place as Nicolae at the same time.

"Byron, I want you in the square playing chess as usual, but pick a spot where you're facing Andrei's house." Kevin continued. "Close enough you can be a lookout. Martin, you're on lookout duty too. You're having lunch at the restaurant on the first floor of the building across from the house. Jackson, you'll be team leader for a couple hours. I want you on the roof with a sniper rifle."

Inwardly, Jackson groaned. Carrying that sort of equipment attracted attention. Jackson would have to leave early and climb to his post before most of the city had woken up.

"Questions? No? Good." Kevin ended the meeting and went downstairs. Jackson could hear the high-pitched whine of the portable printer from the kitchen.

Martin and Byron shuffled upstairs to the bedroom, both looking weary. Jackson followed reluctantly.

Rest wouldn't come, no matter how he arranged his body. What did Kevin mean when he said Navy had handled it well? Well for a rookie? Well for an officer? Not well at all, but Jackson wasn't supposed to know? When Kevin came up to the bedroom an hour later, Jackson was still staring at the sagging board of the upper bunk, counting the knots in the wood.

Kevin dropped a manila envelope on his chest. "Take this to Navy."

Byron and Martin stirred, then turned away.

"You're letting me go to her apartment?"

"I need to sleep. You don't seem to be sleeping."

Jackson got up before Kevin could reconsider. "When should I be back?"

Kevin crawled into the lower bunk with his clothes on, curling up to keep his feet from hanging over the edge. "Be at Andrei's house before he leaves for work." There was a smile in his voice. "And make sure Navy's not late for work either."

Jackson forced himself to walk at a normal pace to Navy's apartment building, careful to approach from a direction where Navy's tail wouldn't see him enter the neighboring building. Kevin had chosen Navy's apartment building for two reasons. The first was the glut of empty office space in the building across the street. They had rented one of the offices on a six-month lease under the auspices of an accountant. Accountants could work late without attracting attention. The second reason Kevin chose the building was the tunnel that connected the neighboring apartment building to Navy's. It was an old tunnel, left over from an underground smuggling route that had long since fallen out of use.

He let himself into the neighboring building using a key they had stolen. Getting to the tunnel required using the key again for the maintenance closet in the basement. The entrance was

220

hidden behind a shelf. He pulled off the metal grate—the bolts were just for show. Streaks in the dust along the floor showed where Kevin had crawled earlier.

Jackson emerged from another maintenance closet in Navy's building. He listened carefully for sounds of anyone coming before he crawled out. He had to take the creaking stairs slowly to minimize the noise he made. A second key let him into Navy's apartment.

"Navy?" he called softly. He didn't want to startle her.

He stepped closer to the bed where Navy was sleeping. Her long breaths were deep and even. She was undercover; she shouldn't be sleeping this well. But he was glad she hadn't forgotten how. The only time he slept without dreams was when he slept next to her. He sat down on the bed, waiting for his eyes to adjust to the dark room. Her face was undisturbed by the tension of the day.

"Navy," he said again.

Her eyes fluttered open. After a second of confusion, she recognized him. She launched herself into his arms so hard he almost fell off the bed.

"Did you miss me?" she asked.

He had never held on so tightly. "Not at all."

"Am I harboring a fugitive? Wait, don't answer that. That way, I can plead ignorance."

Jackson felt the hard rectangle of the manila envelope in his jacket pressed between them. He reluctantly loosened their embrace to retrieve it. "Kevin wanted me to bring you this."

"The fake investigation file." She held it for a second, turned it over in her hands, then set it on the nightstand. "I was wondering how Kevin was going to deliver. Did you read it?"

"No, I hurried over here before Kevin changed his mind. Should I have?"

"Kevin said I'm supposed to look it over before I go to Dragomir's tomorrow." She snuggled closer and he found a place to rest his back against the headboard.

"You want me to do your homework for you?" he asked, smiling. He was glad to see her in good spirits, and safe.

"Pretty please with a cherry on top?"

He laughed and pulled her closer. "I'm not wasting our time tonight on homework." He pressed his nose into the hollow of her collarbone. Beneath the musty smell of the room and the aroma of cigarettes from Dragomir's, he could smell the remnants of sweat. It could have been his imagination, but it wasn't the same smell she had after a good day at the gym. There was an acrid undertone, the smell of fear.

"Maybe you should let a girl brush her teeth," she murmured.

He kissed her instead. Their passions seemed equally matched, but it wasn't enough to erase the nagging doubts from his conversation with Kevin.

She pulled away from him. "What is it?"

"What is what?"

"You're distracted."

She could always read him too well. "It's nothing."
222

Saying he was worried about her and that he was upset she hadn't asked for him that afternoon would only cause an argument.

Her fingers were interlaced behind his neck; he could feel his pulse against her palm. She leaned in, past his lips, to rest her head on his shoulder. "Tell me anyway."

The dark room seemed like a place that could keep his secrets. It helped that he couldn't see her face. "I'm worried. About how you're going to deal with what you saw. About the risks you might take now that you know what kind of monster Dragomir is. I'm worried about us."

She slipped out of his arms and sat cross-legged next to him. Close one second, distant the next. He shook off the feeling of whiplash.

"About us?" she asked.

He could smell rice porridge. Kevin only made that if an officer was too sick or too traumatized to eat anything else. "You didn't want to see me this afternoon." If he was going to start this argument, he might as well go for broke. "You didn't want my help when you were in trouble."

She crossed her arms tightly across her stomach. "Kevin told you that?"

As if Kevin was allowed to know more about her inner world than he was. "I guessed. You wanted Kevin instead of me."

She looked up from her lap, startled into anger. "I didn't want anyone. Kevin invited himself over."

He felt relieved, then guilty for it. "Oh."

"I like to deal with things alone."

"That doesn't work here."

"You're telling me you and Kevin have heart-to-heart conversations about your feelings when you're on assignment?"

They were typically laced with jibes, insults, and sarcasm, but it was true. "Yes."

She shook her head, clearly skeptical.

"If you're upset, it's hard to keep your cover. That's the whole reason Dragomir tried to shock you into a confession today."

"Are we done with the lectures for the night?"

"No. One more."

"Get it over with."

He put his hands on her knees; she brushed them away.

"If you don't make it through this alive, I'll have to kill Byron and probably Kevin."

She smiled despite herself.

"So unless you want to see me spend the rest of my life in prison, talk things out when you need to." His face turned serious. "Even if you don't want to talk them out with me." His vulnerability made him slump against the headboard. The space between Navy and him was painful, but he didn't want to be the one to close the gap.

"Hey," she said. And she was next to him again, curled up in his lap, her warm fingertips trying to smooth the worry lines on his forehead. She pulled him under the covers and traced the line of his jaw. His stubble was fast becoming a beard. "You need to sleep. You haven't had a good night's sleep since we landed, have you?"

"I slept fine last night," he lied.

"Don't."

"Don't what?"

"Don't lie to me," she said softly. "I can tell."

He stopped her roving fingers, holding them tightly in his hand. Jackson Fletcher's tell would fetch a good price in certain areas of the world. "How?"

She opened his hand and kissed the fingers one by one. She moved her lips to a spot on his jawline, just past his earlobe. "This muscle," she whispered. "It tenses when you lie to me. Like when we're in bed after you get home from assignment and I ask you how you were injured and you make up some story about banging your arm on the airplane tray."

"How is it you know me so well?" When I don't seem to know you at all, he thought.

Her face was so near that in the dimness her features shifted like shadows. "You want more from me." The thought seemed to make her sad, as if wanting to be close to her was a weakness. "What we are, this is all I can give you. Don't ask me to explain. Please?"

Jackson wondered if Byron was right—if there was more haunting her than last year's traumas. Whatever roadblocks she had, whatever his frustrations, his feelings for her had never wavered. He had the same choice he'd always had, the same unvarnished deal they'd made the first time he declared his feelings. Take it or leave it. "You can't get rid of me that easily."

She punched him lightly on the arm. "I thought I told you to go to sleep."

"Hanging out with Kevin is making you bossy." Still, with her back warm against his chest and her head nestled against his arm, sleep was creeping up on him. Exhaustion pulled him down into a deep, dreamless sleep that lasted until the first fingers of dawn.

Chapter 25

"Wake up, Navy," said a soft voice. Navy was hearing Jackson's voice. Next to her. He kissed her lightly, then brushed the hair from her face. "It's time to get up."

No, not her bed, Navy remembered as she pushed herself up. She was on the used-up mattress in the bare apartment Navy the traitor had rented. A sane person would never have chosen a dangerous vacation over another lazy weekend in Jackson's apartment. "Ugh." She stretched and her limbs protested. "It's too early."

"I promised Kevin I would wake you up in time to review the file before you went to work."

"Well, *I* didn't promise Kevin anything." She tried to pull Jackson back into bed, but he rolled away and stood up. The drawn curtains kept the room dim, even with the dawn breaking outside. Still, there was enough light to enjoy the well-defined muscles of his chest and arms. "Spoilsport."

His tense expression told her he didn't share her mood. "Be careful with Nicolae today. Try not to piss him off. He might be just muscle, but he can make things difficult for you."

She yawned deliberately. She barely tolerated coaching from Kevin; she certainly didn't appreciate it from her boyfriend. "You think I don't know that?"

Jackson narrowed his eyes. "I have to get to my post before Andrei leaves for work."

She should apologize, reach for him, say something. But before she could act, Jackson went into the bathroom. She heard him brush his teeth and splash cold water on his face, three splashes exactly. Just like every morning when he was home. She tiptoed to the bathroom and eased the door open a crack. He cut a good profile, even with the stubble on his chin and the dark moons under his eyes. Dark moons caused by worrying over her.

He should give her more credit. She knew his favorite music, jazz. She knew how he always took his coffee, black. She knew his favorite drink with dinner, orange juice. She knew how he slept best, next to her. She knew he spent his free time between assignments learning languages. She knew he volunteered at the refugee center as a penance for the tasks his job sometimes required of him. She wondered if he knew that she noticed all these things.

Maybe he did know and it didn't matter. Maybe all that mattered to him was the way her throat closed over the magic word he wanted to hear. She had used the word once in Cedar City. A week before she spent the night in the hospital, thanks to a broken cheekbone. Jackson wasn't that man, she told herself. He would never be that man. And yet her superstition held her.

"Number one rule of surveillance," he said.

She jumped at the sound of his voice. Jackson was standing in front of her, smiling, water still dripping from his face.

"Don't let your target sneak up on you." He opened the door the rest of the way and pulled her into the bathroom. He

228

never seemed to hold onto his anger for long enough to finish an argument. His kiss was hard to argue with. "Shower with me." That was even harder to argue with.

He undressed first, deliberately and slowly, watching her watch him. She lifted her t-shirt over her head and dropped her boxers on the floor. His eyes didn't leave her face. He offered her a hand, a courtly gesture, and she stepped into the steam. When she tried to kiss him again, he gently kept her an arm's length away. The hot needles of the shower massaged her back. Just the temperature she liked. He picked up the threadbare washcloth and reached over her shoulder to soak it in the stream of water. His chest hair tickled her shoulder, but he never completely closed the distance between them. Even in the steam, even with the scented soap, she could smell his spiced, citrus musk.

She stood in the deliciously hot water while he washed her from head to toe. He never touched her with more than the tips of his fingers, even when he shampooed her hair.

He handed her the washcloth. She reciprocated with the same light touch. It was hard to be so close to him and settle for so little. It forced her to notice things she had never noticed about his body before. How the hair on his upper arms stopped where his tan line did. The mole between his shoulder blades, small as a pencil eraser and flat as a pancake.

He tapped his wrist to say they were out of time. The silence was deafening after he turned off the shower. She found herself shivering, not from cold, but from the intimacy. More intimate than any sexual experience they'd had. He dried himself quickly with the singular towel, then handed it to her.

She watched him leave the bathroom, his skin still spattered with water, and heard him dress. For reasons she would not name, she stood in the bathroom with her feet chilled against the tiles and her hair dripping on her shoulders until she heard him leave the apartment.

Crawling back into bed was tempting. She had an hour before she was supposed to be at work. But Jackson had leaned the folder on the lamp, highlighting Kevin's order written in large black letters, "Read me."

First, breakfast. She heated up the leftovers from last night's dinner in one of the mismatched bowls from the cupboard. He'd called it congee, a rice porridge popular in Asia. It was surprisingly good. Thick and a little sweet, with a gentle weight that satisfied her hunger.

A note fell out of the folder when she took out the sheaf of pages. Kevin's handwriting was as precise as his spoken syllables.

"You're welcome for the visit," the note read. "I figured you had enough time to fix your makeup. P.S. Burn after reading."

She burned the note with pleasure. Kevin couldn't possibly have known Jackson would be in such a hurry he wouldn't read the file. Or that seeing Jackson, even with all their complications, would calm her.

The file was too big to memorize in forty-five minutes. Most of the information she had seen before. It was all

230

background. She saw the story Kevin was trying to tell. According to the file, all the information the CIA had collected on Dragomir was secondhand. Interpol records, news clippings, Romanian police reports — nothing directly from CIA officers or surveillance. There was vague talk of a source, code-named Red Fox, they wanted to develop within Dragomir's operation. The description could have fit any male in Romania.

Kevin had helpfully included a clean folder. She recognized the brand from the corner store close to her rented apartment. She slipped the pages into their new folder and swung her bag over her shoulder. It was time to go to work.

She paused in the hallway. Her worries about dealing with Dragomir were second in her mind. It was what she hadn't told Jackson that unsettled her. Did he know how much better it was to wake up to his voice in her ear and his fingers brushing her hair?

Tonight, as ordered, Navy would be leaving for a country getaway weekend. Anna would follow Navy, though Navy wouldn't ever see her. Navy wouldn't see Jackson again until Monday when they tried to turn Andrei.

She and her tail made the walk to Dragomir's in good time. It wouldn't do to be late today. Nicolae greeted her with a scowl, as usual. He noticed how heavy her bag hung on her shoulder and grabbed the strap.

"I told you—no laptop," he said.

She had to remind herself to let go of the bag instead of strangling him with it. He found the thick file and flipped through the pages, weighed them in his hands. Satisfied, he shoved the file and the bag against her chest. The force made her stumble against the wall. Thinking of Jackson's advice, she bit her lip to keep her temper from sparking.

Navy climbed the stairs to the second floor again. Thankfully, this time she was led to Dragomir's office and not one of the film studios.

Dragomir, sitting at his desk, waved them in with a cigarette in hand. Nicolae took a post behind Navy, blocking her exit.

Before smoke and time had yellowed them, the walls might have been white. Piles of photographs and stacks of paper teetered on every surface. In the corner, a filing cabinet with an open, overstuffed top drawer threatened to tip. She wondered how Dragomir found anything in his office, much less a bug. She was careful to keep her eyes from focusing on any of the pictures.

When she handed him the file, Dragomir leaned over eagerly, nearly toppling a pile of papers. She hoped she could witness the moment when Dragomir realized he'd been had. Even pretending to be an ally of this man made her skin crawl. Ash dropped from his cigarette onto a picture of—no, look away, she reminded herself.

Dragomir's heavy breaths punctuated the flip of the pages. Nicolae's stare made the back of Navy's neck tingle. If Dragomir ever gave Nicolae the green light, it would be a hard fight. She kept her hands free and her eyes unfocused.

There was no clock in the room. It could have been ten

232

minutes or two minutes before Dragomir looked up. "This is all you have?"

There were at least forty pages of material there. "Yes. An official investigation would have a thicker file. They're just collecting information about you from other sources right now. As I said yesterday, the bug you found wasn't CIA."

"Then who?" Nicolae demanded. He had stepped so close she could smell his breath—coffee and whiskey—by her ear.

"How should I know?" Her tone was too combative. "You have rivals, right? Enemies? It must be someone who's interested in your business."

An absent-minded wave of Dragomir's hand sent Nicolae back to the door, Navy's neck back to tingling. Dragomir flipped through the file again, frowning. "This informant they're talking about, who is it?"

"You have the file. You know as much as I do."

He spread the pages on his desk, bent over in concentration. Without looking up, he ordered Nicolae to take Navy downstairs.

Navy's quick thinking and Kevin's documentation had rescued the mission. Navy should feel elated. Instead, she was daunted by the work in front of her. Another day in the cramped office downstairs with Nicolae and the sulking Andrei. Andrei looked up when she entered the room. Something sparked in his broken eyes.

"You know what they do now," Andrei said. "And you

still come back."

There was no defending herself. Andrei might always think of her as the woman who refused to help rescue his nephew and aided a child abuser.

"She is a good soldier," Nicolae answered for her. "Knows her place."

She wondered how Jackson coped with letting people think he was scum to keep a cover. "I show up to get paid."

Andrei looked at the photo on his desk and swallowed whatever he'd been about to say. The spark in his eyes was gone. "You have more exploits," he said dully. "Nicolae says we only have one more week."

Nicolae's affirming smile only made her feel more hollow.

Chapter 26

Jackson lay on the restaurant's gravel roof across the street from Andrei's prison. Again. The rocks were still hot from the afternoon sun, even as pink on the horizon heralded the sunset. At least today Navy was further from Dragomir's reach. Navy wouldn't be back until Sunday afternoon. Kevin's instincts had been right. When Navy left town Friday evening, Dragomir sent only one man to follow her.

With Anna protecting Navy, that left Byron, Martin, Kevin, and himself to do recon for the probable rescue mission. A rescue from the house wouldn't be Jackson's first choice, but after they interrupted Andrei's nightly walk Monday, it might be the only one. The immediate task was to get Andrei's house bugged, so they weren't entering blind.

Jackson had attached two optical bugs to the ledge hours ago. The first beam was aimed at the downstairs window. He could hear the soccer match on the TV in the living room. The second was currently aimed at an upstairs window. The sing-song rhythms of a child's song overlaid the sports announcers from the soccer game. Earlier, Jackson had heard Andrei and Petru playing.

Soon Kevin would be approaching. Jackson adjusted the second beam to scan the other windows in turn and heard no other sounds of people, not even snoring. He had been checking all morning, watching the house gradually empty from last night's party.

The optical bugs were mostly insurance for the bugs Kevin was about to plant. The advantages of the optical bugs were twofold: planting them didn't require entering the target and people searching for listening devices didn't often search neighboring rooftops. The main disadvantage was their easy detectability. Some minor surgery on any cheap camera to remove the RF filter and the beam would show clearly in the image.

Once they had bugs inside the house, they would be able to track daily patterns. To know where Petru was likely to be, given the time of day. To know which rooms the guards partied in at night.

On Monday, they would stage a mugging to make contact during Andrei and Petru's nightly walk. After that, their walking privileges might very well be revoked.

"Are we good to go, team leader?" Kevin asked through the mic in Jackson's ear. With Kevin playing field officer for the afternoon, someone had to be team leader.

Jackson aimed the scope of his rifle at the door of Andrei's house. Jackson could easily read the numbers just above the silver knocker. "You have Andrei and Petru upstairs," Jackson said. "And Nicolae and another hostile downstairs. That's likely it." Audio surveillance wasn't an exact art.

"Two hostiles isn't bad odds," Kevin said. "Let's get this over with."

"Martin, Byron, are you in position?" asked Jackson.

236

"Ready," they said in unison.

Kevin approached the house with quick, angry strides. His panting breaths were loud in Jackson's mic. Through the scope, Jackson watched the door shake on its hinges as Kevin pounded two fists on it.

"Open up!" Kevin yelled. "I know my wife is in there!"

Over the optical bug, Jackson heard stirring in the living room. Nicolae and the guard spoke in Romanian to each other.

"What the hell?" Jackson recognized Nicolae's voice from Navy's mic. Thanks to Jackson's various surveillance duties, he knew how to swear in several languages.

The curtains parted briefly as one of Andrei's guards sized up Kevin. "Is he talking about one of the women who partied here last night?" the guard asked.

Kevin continued to pound on the door. "Let me in!"

The curtains parted again. "People are looking, boss."

A can was set down on a table. "I'll take care of him," Nicolae said.

"Nicolae's coming," Jackson said.

When the door started to open, Kevin grabbed it with one hand and threw it open the rest of the way. He took advantage of Nicolae's surprise and pushed himself into the house. Now Jackson could see Nicolae and Kevin only from the waist down. Unless Nicolae stepped in front of the window, the best Jackson would be able to manage was a disabling shot to the knee. Once they left the living room, he'd have no shots at all.

"Where's your friend?" Kevin demanded.

There were sounds of a scuffle but no solid blows landed. Nicolae wouldn't be much of a challenge to Kevin in a fair fight, but in order to keep up the ruse, he would have to downplay his fighting skills without allowing Nicolae to get in any serious blows. It was a skill accomplished only by acquiring some bruises. Behind the curtain, all Jackson could see was a rolling shadow the size of two grown men.

"C'mon, Kevin," Jackson said. "Don't make me shoot you."

The two shadows separated, panting. "Where's your friend?" Kevin demanded. "The valet? The one fucking my wife?"

"Your wife is not here," Nicolae said. There was some joy in his voice. Maybe the thought of anyone in pain amused him. Kevin's voice dropped in volume, then rose as Kevin turned away from the window then back. Kevin would be surveying the room, looking for the best place to plant the bugs hiding in the device secreted in Kevin's sleeve. It was much like a Pez dispenser, except smaller. One click and a tiny bug, the size of a grain of rice, would fall into Kevin's hand. Releasing the bug from the dispenser would activate it. The bugs were known affectionately around headquarters as termites.

The first termite came online, thrown down in the living room. Jackson heard Kevin's footsteps out of time with themselves—the optical bug and termite slightly out of sync. The shadows behind the living room drapes disappeared and Kevin's voice echoed in another room.

238

Be quick, thought Jackson. Kevin was a good fighter but two against one was never good odds.

"There is no woman here," Nicolae said, catching up to Kevin.

A door slammed open. Another termite down. "Maybe in here then?" Kevin snarled. "Or here?" Another slam. Another termite down.

"There is no woman here," Nicolae said again, his tone was harder, despite the panting. Kevin would have a minute, maybe two, before Nicolae lost patience with the ruse.

"Three bugs transmitting," Jackson said. "You can leave now."

"How about upstairs?" Kevin asked. Three sets of feet ran upstairs, Kevin's lighter steps followed by Nicolae and the guard. Another door thrown open.

"Who are—" It was Andrei's voice, surprised. A fourth termite came online.

Andrei and Petru's conversation now competed with Kevin's examination of the house. Petru was asking about the strange man. Andrei was assuring him everything would be fine.

A fifth bug came online and Nicolae's voice blasted in Jackson's ear. "Your wife is not here!"

Three sets of steps came downstairs, this time running.

"Get your hands off me!" Kevin yelled.

Jackson's grip tightened on his rifle. Kevin hadn't used his distress word yet. The sounds of the scuffle continued, this time with a couple grunts from blows well-landed. Jackson couldn't tell if it was Kevin who had landed them or taken them.

Jackson was relieved when Kevin appeared, held by the guard and Nicolae. They threw him down the steps. Kevin faked a stumble to put himself in a fighting roll. His only visible injuries were a bloody lip and a black eye. He kept up the angry man persona until he was well out of Jackson's sight.

"And that, folks, is how it's done," Kevin said.

Jackson couldn't help but smile. Kevin could afford to be cocky. He really was that good.

Chapter 27

Navy knew the walk from Dragomir's headquarters to her apartment by heart now. It felt long anyway. The end of her second Monday at Dragomir's. After nine hours of helping a child abuser give his clients anonymous downloads, her day wasn't even done. They would turn Andrei tonight, hopefully, and Kevin wanted her on hand for the meeting.

Anna was waiting on Navy's bed, flipping through a magazine.

"Took you long enough," Anna said. "We're going to be late."

Navy wasn't eager to rush to a meeting where, in all likelihood, she'd spend the entire time hiding in the shadows. Kevin had made it clear he didn't want Andrei to know she was undercover unless it was necessary.

"Are you ready?" Anna asked.

"I guess so."

Navy followed Anna to a maintenance closet in the basement. Anna opened the door with a key from her pocket. A rusty metal grate covered the entrance to a tunnel. The tunnel Kevin had mentioned when he told her about the apartment building. The bolts were just for decoration, when Anna pulled, the grate came off easily.

"It's an old smuggling route," Anna said, flashing a smile. "Used for smuggling Jews out of Axis territory during

WWII. Rookies first.”

The tunnel was barely wide enough to crawl in, but clear of spiderwebs.

Dust stirred with the vibrations of Anna’s voice. “It’s why Kevin chose the building.”

The tunnel ended a few feet later in another maintenance closet. They hadn’t crawled for long, so it must be a building close to hers. Anna’s car was parked on the street. By now, Navy knew the drill. She went to the backseat and covered herself with the scratchy blanket.

The ride to base was short. Before the car had even stopped, the door opened and the blanket was pulled off, crackling Navy’s hair to attention.

Kevin waved her out of the car impatiently. “No time for pleasantries.” He slipped a small piece of plastic in Navy’s ear. “This is your earpiece. Everyone will be able to hear you. You’ll be able to hear everyone. Don’t talk unless you need to. Martin will take you to your position. If you and Martin are separated, find a safe place to hide and wait for us to find you. Got it?”

She nodded, hoping her nerves weren’t showing.

“Andrei and Petru are leaving the house,” Navy heard Byron say. She automatically looked around the garage for him, but Byron wasn’t there. Anna had already left.

“You have five minutes to get to the meet,” Kevin said. “Go.” He pushed Navy into Martin, who grabbed her arm and pulled her quickly under the garage door that was already closing. She followed Martin into a dark, cramped alley. They

242

crisscrossed avenues and alleys, avoiding the larger streets. Navy stopped trying to keep track of where they were and simply followed Martin's lithe, small form on his byzantine path. They crossed a large street and played hopscotch with the alleys again.

When they stopped, Navy was surprised to find herself near the square, close to Dragomir's headquarters. She checked her watch; only four minutes had passed since Anna had dropped her off.

The shadow of Jackson's profile detached itself from the wall at the end of the alley, twenty yards from Navy. Martin pulled her down a set of stairs. A weathered green door with a bell was at the bottom. "The shop is closed," Martin whispered. "We wait here."

Navy peeked over the front step. Martin didn't stop her. This Jackson was different from the one she knew. Navy couldn't say exactly how—it could have been the predatory tilt of his head or the grim set of his shoulders. Footsteps became audible in the distance. Then Andrei's voice, speaking Romanian. There was the voice of a small boy, too. The one they believed was Petru. She saw why Jackson had chosen this spot. Construction had blocked the sidewalk opposite the alley; anyone approaching Jackson's position would be unable to see around the corner where he waited.

Andrei and Petru passed the alley first. Navy saw Jackson's arm swing and the punch caught the guard in the stomach, knocking the air out of him. She saw the meager light glimmer in the moistness of the guard's open mouth, but his call for help came out as a gurgle as Jackson locked the crook of his elbow around the guard's throat. The only sounds in the alley were the guard's shoes, kicking at the gritty pavement until he passed out. The display comforted and frightened Navy. The pair of hands that had delivered the man to unconsciousness were very different from the ones that gently stroked her hair.

"In the alley, please," Anna said. Her gun was trained on Andrei. Petru held tightly onto his uncle's hand. Andrei picked up the boy and backed into the alley. Jackson was kneeling by the guard, injecting something just behind his ear.

Navy looked at Martin.

"We call it red pill, blue pill," Martin said. "One injection to sleep, one injection to wake up."

Jackson stood up to face Andrei and pointed at the guard. "Proof of our good faith. We just want to talk."

"You can put the gun away," Andrei said tiredly. "We won't run."

"He's all yours," Anna told Jackson. "I'll keep watch." She disappeared around the corner.

Jackson held out his hand to Andrei. "Chuck Redding. CIA."

Andrei adjusted Petru so he could accept the handshake. "You're not Clara's father."

Navy was dumbfounded. Byron made strangled noises over the mic.

"I guess he didn't come," Andrei continued. "Honestly, I thought you guys would be here sooner."

244

"I don't know any Clara," Jackson said.

Andrei set the boy down and murmured something to him in Romanian. The boy walked a short distance away and sat, hugging his knees tightly, against the wall. "It's not important. You're here now."

It was hard to concentrate on Andrei and Jackson with the conversation running over the mic competing for Navy's attention. Kevin was grilling Byron on how Andrei could possibly know that Clara was Byron's daughter.

"If you were expecting us, you must have a deal in mind," Jackson said.

"Dragomir helps your enemies," Andrei said. "I'd like to be your friend."

"Four minutes," Kevin warned.

"We want an electronic trail to track his clients," Jackson said. "Make his business dry up. Can you do that?"

Andrei stared at the small figure that sat too calmly against the stone wall. "The boy's name is Petru. He's my nephew. If you get Petru away from Dragomir, I'll do whatever you ask."

"Add the code to Attila so we can track Dragomir's clients. Let us know how the tracking works. Then we help you two disappear."

Heartless. Cruel. Cold. That's how Jackson seemed to Navy. Or was that how Navy seemed to herself? They were forcing a starving man to dance for his bread.

"And find Petru's mother," Andrei said. "If she's still

alive."

Jackson paused.

"Fine," Kevin said in Navy's ear.

Jackson nodded. "We haven't been able to track her down yet. But if we find her, she can go with you."

Andrei looked at the guard. "What do I tell him when he wakes up? How do I contact you?"

"This is for you," Jackson pulled a phone out of his pocket. "My number is programmed in the contacts. Text me when the tracking code is in place."

Andrei backed away from the phone as if it were radioactive. "I can't. I'm not allowed to have any sort of phone. They search my room when I'm at work and my office when I'm at home."

"This Clara girl, how do you talk to her?"

"Skype," Andrei said. "But they think she's a mark."

"A mark!" Byron said.

Navy's knees ached from kneeling on the step, so she switched to a crouch, unwilling to give up her view. Martin lounged on the steps below her.

"A mark for what?" Jackson asked.

"When I'm not programming for them, I'm supposed to run broken-heart scams. Find lonely women to seduce and ask them for money. It starts with small requests, like a deposit for an apartment maybe, or a small medical bill. Then bigger requests, until they catch on or they run out of money. Lots of people here run similar scams."

246

Byron was swearing a blue streak over his mic. Jackson pressed his finger to his ear.

"Shut up, Byron," Kevin said.

"I'll create a fake dating profile on whatever site you want," Jackson said. "Give me a name you'll remember. You can pretend I'm a mark and email me."

"They're good at picking out fake profiles, they're always looking for agents posing as minors."

"I won't pose as a minor."

Andrei shook his head and paced the width of the cramped alley. It was hard to believe the man unraveling in front of Navy was the same man who had carefully prepared ToppleWords for when the CIA finally made contact.

"I'm so close, I'm so close," Andrei said. "I can't risk it. I won't get a second chance."

"You can leave notes for us then." Jackson's voice was losing patience. "Under the flower pot on the back steps."

"But what if I need to reach you faster? If I think Dragomir knows? It's too slow." Andrei pressed his hands against his jeans, swiped at his lips. "We need something else." His hands fluttered in the air as he ticked off possibilities on his fingers, muttering under his breath, rejecting each one. Petru watched his uncle carefully, worry creasing his small face.

There was an unmistakable sigh in her ear. Kevin. "He's going to be a nervous one. I hate running the nervous ones."

"We're watching very closely," Jackson said to Andrei's pacing figure. "If it looks like something's about to happen, we can step in.”

“A code with Clara!” Andrei stopped, twirling on the ball of his foot. “They’ll let me make that call from work. I’ll ask her for money. I haven’t asked her for money yet and then you’ll know.”

“I told you, I don’t know any Clara. You’ll have to settle for the flower pot.”

Involving Clara meant exposing her to retribution if the escape didn’t work. Andrei had already risked Clara’s life by planning a visit with her. If Dragomir figured out that Clara’s father was a CIA man, she would either be a valuable bargaining piece or an unwanted liability. Byron was swearing with such venom Navy thought the earpiece might melt.

“No, no, no.” Andrei returned to pacing. “It won’t work, it won’t work at all.”

“Byron,” Kevin hissed. “*Shut. Up.* We’re going to have to use Navy. Jackson, call Navy over.”

Jackson’s eyes flicked between the unraveling man and the vulnerable child, mouth pressed into a grim line.

“Jackson, you heard me,” Kevin said. “Call Navy over.”

Jackson shook his head. “Jackson.” Kevin’s voice was sharp as tacks.

Navy looked at Martin for permission to approach. Martin nodded. The sudden influx of blood to her legs left her walking on pins and needles. If Andrei was this nervous without Nicolae around, she wasn’t looking forward to tomorrow. “I can be your contact, Andrei.”

Andrei looked up, startled. "You're with them? I mean, at first I thought you were, but then you . . ."

Jackson's tense posture told Navy he was as worried about tomorrow as Navy was. Every extra risk Navy took weighed on him. Andrei had relaxed a little, however. Navy felt a twinge of hope. For the first time since the operation had started, she felt like she'd done some good. Petru watched Navy through wide, dark eyes, like he was trying to figure out if she was a friend or an enemy.

"We've talked for too long," Jackson said. "You have your contact. Give me your wallet."

"What?" Andrei said.

"The three of you were mugged." Jackson took the guard's watch and money. "When the guard wakes up, you should be on the ground too."

"I don't have a wallet. They keep everything of mine, including my ID."

"Two men leaving Andrei's house," Byron said. "Headed your way."

"Fine," Jackson said. "We have to go." He held a syringe next to the guard's ear.

"Wait—"

Jackson struggled not to glare at the poor man. "What."

"Would you explain to Clara why we can't talk anymore?"

"Whoever this Clara is—"

"You do know her. You're here because of Clara's

father."

"Nicolae's men are on their way," Jackson said. "We don't have time for this."

"Clara told me her father was gone a lot when she was younger. Now she says he is a librarian that works late often. I looked through our databases, the information we buy from crooked Interpol agents. I figured out he works for the CIA. The kind of man who might notice if his daughter was going to visit a man like me."

"That son of a—" Byron sputtered. Navy couldn't concentrate on all the conversations around her. Kevin telling Byron to be quiet, Andrei still talking to Jackson, Anna reporting that she could hear Nicolae's men.

Jackson looked down the street. Resignation flickered across his face. "Fine. I'll tell Clara goodbye for you."

"You like her," Navy said softly. In another life, Andrei and Clara's story might have had a happy ending.

"Does a drowning man like the branch he clings to?"

Navy shoved her hands in her pocket, chilled by the deep whirlpools in Andrei's eyes.

"Petru's father died when we were taken. I watched them slit his throat because he refused to let go of his son." There was an unfamiliar strength in Andrei's voice. "My sister, his mother, I don't know. One broken heart for a boy's life. It's a small trade. I can't think about Clara anymore," Andrei said. "Save Petru. I don't care what happens to me."

Jackson injected the antidote behind the guard's ear. "On

the ground. Tell Petru."

Andrei said something to Petru in Romanian. The boy lay down, pretending to be unconscious. Andrei followed suit. Martin joined Jackson and Navy. Navy noticed that Martin was careful to keep his back to Andrei, so Andrei couldn't identify him.

"Remember," Jackson said to the prone forms. "You were mugged."

Navy could hear more footsteps now. Jackson, Navy and Martin ran.

"Do you want me to delay them?" Anna asked.

"No," Jackson said between pants. "We're done."

As Navy rounded the corner at the end of the alley, the guard moaned softly. They ran for several blocks on another serpentine route Navy couldn't hope to repeat. When they stopped, everyone's faces shone with sweat.

"Get her back to base," Martin said. "I'll wait here in case Nicolae's men come this way."

Navy followed Jackson down more alleys, walking in the shadows whenever they could. Above them, lit windows with pulled curtains jarred her with their normalcy.

"There are two men passing me and headed toward you, Jackson" Martin said. "Should I delay them?"

Jackson stopped and held up a hand. Navy could hear shouts in Romanian from behind them and in front of them.

"No," Jackson answered quietly. "They're in front of us too. We have to hide." Jackson led the way to a narrow shed behind a small house. The lock was rusted open.

The inside of the shed was pitch-black. Navy's tentative steps found the corners of boxes, the tines of rakes, and rubber tires. There was barely room for the two of them to stand. She didn't mind.

"How many, Anna?" Jackson whispered.

"Nicolae sent a team of five from Andrei's," Anna said. "They separated and fanned out. Two of them headed in the direction of your escape route."

"Byron, if you think you can manage it, count the men as they come back to Andrei's house," Kevin said.

"I can manage it," Byron snapped.

"Jackson, where are you?" Kevin asked.

"In the alley that runs east-west between Lipscani and Calea Victoriei," Jackson answered. "Inside a shed."

"Anna, I want you close to their position in case they need backup. Martin, find a post near Dragomir's headquarters. Watch for reinforcements. Everyone, keep your posts until I give the all clear. No unnecessary chatter, please. I'm going to be listening to Andrei's house to see if Nicolae buys the mugging story."

Jackson ran his fingers along the side of Navy's face, the inside of her ears. He found the mic inside her left ear and spoke softly into her right. "It'll only be a few minutes." Jackson's voice didn't echo. Kevin couldn't hear them. Navy felt cool metal brush her hand. Jackson had pulled out his gun. "Get behind me."

Navy pulled out her cell phone and used the screen to
252

illuminate the mess around her. Something in here had to be useful. In the small circle of light, all she could see was fishing poles and a scratched tacklebox. Once you caught a fish, you had to clean it. Gently, slowly, she opened the rusting clip. Navy's phone went dark and she turned the screen on again. Only hooks and fishing line. She turned in a small circle. The best thing she could reach without upsetting the delicate balance of the piles around her was a pair of hedge clippers. The ends of the blades were pointed, at least.

They stood together, facing the door, straining to triangulate the voices echoing off the brick buildings around them. Tomorrow she would find out if she was wrong about whether Andrei could handle being a double agent. She had serious doubts after his performance tonight. Still, she couldn't give up on the operation now.

It wasn't just her ghosts pushing her on. It was the image of Petru, curled up against a cold stone wall while Andrei bargained his life for the boy's. It was the little girl and boy she'd seen in the studio on the second floor. At least Clara was safe now. Navy couldn't imagine what Byron must be feeling, knowing he was responsible for Clara being in danger in the first place.

A man stopped near the shed, speaking rapid Romanian.

"We need a distraction, Anna," Navy whispered into Jackson's mic.

"On it," Anna said.

The man said something else, then his voice grew

distant. Navy could hear someone running, leading Nicolae's man away.

Navy and Jackson stood, weapons in hand, ready to fight, surrounded by the smell of oil and turpentine while the voices faded, then disappeared.

"Lost him," Anna said, still breathing fast.

Another long train of minutes passed.

"Fifth man is back at Andrei's," Byron said.

"Navy, Jackson," Kevin said. "Hang tight a bit longer. Listening to the house. I want to make sure they're not sending out anyone else."

Navy shivered while they waited. She couldn't remember exactly which hook she'd pulled the hedge clippers from. She wondered if the owner would notice if she didn't put them back in the same place. If places could hold emotions the way they held objects. Tonight, the world didn't seem that compassionate. Tomorrow, someone else would pass through this alley without knowing that Dragomir's men had hunted Navy here.

Tomorrow, Navy would show up for work again and Andrei might or might not get her killed. And either way, the world would move on.

"We're clear," Kevin said. "Get back to base."

Jackson secreted his gun in the shoulder holster under his coat. Navy put her makeshift weapon back on an empty hook.

Even the alley seemed bright after the pitch-black of the shed. Navy was thoroughly lost, but Jackson led them confidently

254

back to base.

Martin nodded from the kitchen table when they entered, a phone cradled against his shoulder. "Afina Yonescu. I know you said she moved. Anything you have on her would be appreciated."

"I need a few minutes with Navy before Anna takes her back," Kevin said.

Navy squeezed Jackson's hand, then followed Kevin upstairs. She could never tell whether Kevin was about to scold, congratulate, or apologize to her. "Was I wrong about Andrei?"

"It's hard to say for sure, but I think he'll do whatever it takes. He managed to get our attention without alerting Dragomir so far. I just wouldn't depend on him to be graceful."

"Graceful?" She associated the word with ballet dancers and acrobats, not undercover work.

"He's going to cling to you tomorrow. You'll have to cover for him."

"Andrei has to know that treating me differently will tip off Nicolae."

"He's desperate. He's not thinking. Be careful that if he blows it, you don't go down with him."

She wished she were back in the shed with Jackson. "I don't understand."

"There's a failsafe in the file you gave to Dragomir. If Andrei breaks, name him as Red Fox."

The code name in the file for the contact the CIA was developing inside Dragomir's gang. That's why the description had been so vague.

"No." Killing someone who was attacking her was one thing. Sacrificing someone else's life to save hers was another.

"Promise me, or I end the operation tonight," Kevin said.

Her head was spinning with the tangle of events that led to this point. A kidnapping a thousand miles away from her life. A man desperate enough to lead a daughter on, just to bait the father. And before all that, another kidnapping. Hers. She was here because she was a killer; she wanted to kill again. But not a victim like Andrei. Someone who deserved it. Nicolae or Dragomir or the man on the bed with the children.

"If Andrei breaks, there's nothing you can do to help him. You'll have to name him as Red Fox to get out alive."

"Promise him." Jackson said. Navy turned around and saw Jackson at the top of the stairs. "I'll know if you're lying."

It was true. The only way she managed to keep secrets from Jackson was evasion. "Fine." She made the promise because it was the only way to answer the worry in Jackson's eyes.

Kevin looked at Jackson, who nodded. "Good. Anna is waiting for you downstairs."

"Maybe—"

"No, Jackson can't take you back. Don't pout. It's not a good look for you."

256

Chapter 28

Byron didn't respond the first time Kevin called him upstairs. Or the second. Byron had done a lot of questionable things in his career. But he'd never been immobilized by his own guilt. He always had a purpose. Maybe letting the informant who had double-crossed him get strangled by a rival wasn't the *civil* thing to do, but Byron's choice had protected the operation. A hotel lobby that would have exploded hadn't. He worked to defuse conflicts abroad before they hurt his country, his family. And now Byron's job had touched the people dearest to him. Over the years he'd been careful to make himself a background player. Often it meant letting someone else take the glory, but that was fine with him. Doing good work, that was the important thing.

That good work had nearly killed his daughter.

Just thinking of it made Byron want to take the sniper rifle over to Andrei's. He was out of practice, but it wasn't a hard shot from the rooftop. Andrei had tracked the dirt of Byron's work into his home. One shot to the head seemed suitable punishment. Except it wouldn't be Andrei who would suffer. The little boy would be left without his protector and no longer useful as leverage. Only Andrei would be free.

Byron heard Kevin's hurried gait on the stairs. "Your pity party can wait," Kevin said.

"I'll be right there," Byron muttered.

The drawings Martin had made of Dragomir's headquarters were spread out on the floor.

"We could move the van to this corner once the café opens," Jackson said. "It's a blind spot for their cameras once the café puts out all their tables. Means Kevin will be one minute closer."

Kevin nodded. "Do we know anything about the basement, Martin?"

"Only that it's on a different ventilation system. Our initial recon managed to photograph some HVAC diagrams in Dragomir's office. Navy hasn't been down there and the team that planted the bugs in Dragomir's office didn't have time to explore."

In the center of the drawings, Kevin's phone was open and the screen lit up. "Byron's here. We need to review the plans for breaching headquarters," Kevin said without looking up. "In case Andrei cracks tomorrow. Anna – you there?"

"I'm here all night," Anna said over the speaker of Kevin's phone.

"The second floor won't have a lot of people—mostly noncombatants." Martin pointed at each room on the map as he spoke. "The first floor has a call center. They'll fight poorly, but there's enough of them to pose a problem. Our observations indicate Nicolae keeps between eight and ten men inside headquarters at any given time. There's a guard desk at the front entrance that holds two people. There's always one person guarding Andrei and Navy. We don't know where the rest of them are during the day."

"Has to be the second floor or the basement," Byron said. "Otherwise, Navy would have seen them."

"Our biggest challenge is weaponry," Kevin said. "I can keep bigger guns in the van, but the rest of you will have only what you can carry in a backpack. Dragomir's men will be armed."

"The ventilation intakes are here and here," Martin pointed to spots in the alley. "If you crouch as you approach them, you can stay beneath the sightline of the cameras. Unfortunately, these are only the ventilation intakes for the first and second floor. We need to get on the roof to reach the intake for the basement. Dragomir designed the basement to be a fallback location where he could hold out for a while."

"Okay, step by step," Kevin said. "Time zero, Navy uses her distress word."

Byron's observation post was the closest. That meant he would be the first to go in, without backup. "T plus two minutes, I connect the gas canisters to the air intake for the first and second floors," Byron said. "T plus three minutes, I set up the cell phone jammer and cut the phone lines."

"T plus four minutes, I'm at the front door with Kevin," Anna said. "We use small charges to breach the front door."

"T plus four minutes, I'm at the back door with Byron," Martin said. "We do the same to the back door."

"And everyone has their masks on," Kevin reminded them. "Byron and Martin, your first stop when we get in is to barricade the call center door." They used quick-set foam adhesive that looked like yellow expanding insulation and smelled like superglue. One can was good for about two doors. "Anna and I will head directly for wherever Navy is. The gas will clear after ten minutes. Remember to take off your masks. They're a liability in a firefight."

Jackson cleared his throat. "What about me? You'll have better odds with one more person inside."

"You'll be watching the building to warn us if reinforcements show up."

"I can't watch both entrances." Jackson held Kevin's stare without flinching.

It wasn't a good time for Jackson to start an argument, but Byron didn't have the energy to play peacemaker today.

"Let the poor boy come," Anna said. "If Dragomir does send reinforcements, Jackson will be of more use to us inside than out."

Byron was about to separate Kevin and Jackson when Kevin spoke. "If you don't follow my directions when we're inside, I'll shoot you myself."

"Understood."

"Play nice," Anna said. The phone clicked as she disconnected.

Confrontations like these were one of the reasons Byron didn't miss fieldwork. Tension was common among officers, even during smoother operations. The combination of stressful work, cramped quarters, and lack of sleep often led to arguments.

260

There was an entire day of training devoted to conflict resolution. It was regularly mocked—and regularly used—in the field.

"Let's go downstairs, Jackson," Byron said. "You can beat me at cribbage again."

Chapter 29

Andrei waited patiently for Nicolae's men. The ground was cold against his cheek. It felt like sandpaper when he smiled. He couldn't help himself.

They came. They finally came.

He had nearly given up. Now, he dared to hope that Petru would be rescued. And maybe even him too. Andrei could almost see Petru, Afina, and himself in a little house in a Hungarian town. Or maybe even farther. Switzerland. Germany. Board games after dinner. Finally, some space to ask forgiveness of his sister for being the cause of her worries. To talk to Petru about his father's death. Andrei couldn't replace Petru's father. But an uncle was better than nothing.

He closed his eyes and wiped the smile off his face as Nicolae's voice grew louder. Nicolae rounded the corner swearing. Andrei stirred, as if Nicolae's voice had woken him.

Their guard had pushed himself up to his elbows, shaking his head to clear it.

"What the hell happened?" Nicolae demanded.

The kick to Andrei's ribs emptied his lungs.

"Get up."

Andrei scrambled over to Petru, pretending to rouse him.

"Are they gone?" Petru asked in a small voice. Such a smart boy.

"My watch," the guard said. "He took my watch and my

wallet." The CIA man's preparations were well thought out.

"You let yourself be mugged." Nicolae leaned menacingly over the guard. "They could have gotten away."

We are going to get away, thought Andrei.

The guard stumbled to his feet. "No one steals from Dragomir," the guard said. His voice was higher-pitched than usual. "Someone's making a play for his territory." It was a valiant attempt to make the attack not his fault. Andrei wondered if they would see the guard tomorrow.

"You." Three quick strides and Nicolae's hand was locked around Andrei's arm. "What happened?"

"There were three men," Andrei said. That was about right, wasn't it? One man couldn't take out three people at the same time. "They hit us over the head."

"Did they take anything from you?"

"I don't have anything to take," Andrei reminded him. It was the wrong answer. The beating was, at least, short. Petru clung to Andrei's hand while he catalogued his injuries on the short walk home. There was no creaking; Andrei's ribs were intact. He would have a black eye and a swollen cheek for a couple days. One of his teeth felt a little loose; if he was careful he might be able to keep it. The blood on his shirt seemed like a lot, but scalp wounds were always like that.

None of it mattered. He hid his smile and went back to imagining a cozy house for him and Petru and Afina. A house with a small yard and a swing. Maybe even a little black terrier, like Petru had before. Before everything had gone wrong.

Chapter 30

When Navy arrived at work Tuesday morning, Andrei's expression changed from despondent to hopeful underneath a painful-looking black eye. Nicolae noticed. Exactly as Kevin had predicted.

Worse, Andrei couldn't seem to do anything without fumbling. He dropped pens mid-gesture. He mistyped most of his commands. Normally he was a brilliant coder, but today he couldn't seem to complete a for-loop. Kevin had said to cover for him, but she wasn't feeling graceful either.

After Andrei spilled his coffee, Nicolae glanced at them again. Normally he barely looked up from his porn magazines. The brown puddle sent a tentacle toward their notes. When Navy reached for them, Andrei did too and the whole pile fluttered to the carpet.

If Navy didn't do something, Andrei wouldn't survive the morning.

Nicolae scooted his chair closer.

She helped Andrei gather up their notes. It was a mistake. Andrei hadn't seen or didn't care that Nicolae was closer and tried to whisper something to her. She cut him off in a low voice just loud enough for Nicolae to hear. "I told you, I'm not interested." Her exasperation didn't need to be faked.

Andrei looked like a young puppy who had just been disciplined. She couldn't afford to let his hurt register. She had to convince Nicolae that Andrei wasn't a threat.

"I have a boyfriend," she said in the same loud whisper.

"The church man in Bosnia," Nicolae said. Nicolae was grinning like a shark that had just caught the scent of blood in the water. Andrei's face was a deep purple-red. He had finally figured out Navy's ruse.

"You have changed your mind about our girl then?" Nicolae asked. The possessive made Navy shiver. "Or perhaps you do not have enough girlfriends already?"

Andrei slumped, hands clutching a fan of white pages. He looked like he was about to cry. Her tactic had backfired. Never mind, she told herself. Fix it. Before she had to use the words Red Fox. She might be able to distract Nicolae long enough for Andrei to compose himself. She widened her eyes and put a tremble in her voice.

"How do you know about him?" she asked.

"We watch," Nicolae answered. He leaned in closer and she fought to keep her expression fearful instead of satisfied. "To make sure you are doing as you say."

The trill of fear in her heart was a challenge to answer. She might be weaker than Nicolae, but faster and smarter could easily win over brute strength. Play to his ego, she told herself. Keep the tremble in your voice. "Then you know I'm sticking to our deal."

"It is good fortune for you," Nicolae said. His fortune teller jokes were getting old.

She turned away before her anger sparked. "The Internet

Explorer image name buffer overflow exploit," she said to Andrei. "I think it would work better with a reverse shell."

Andrei nodded. There were still patches of red in his pale skin, but resolve had hardened his expression. "When do you think we'll be done with the exploits?" The words were spoken with deliberate concentration.

He wanted to know when they were planning the rescue. She didn't know. "I leave Friday. The exploits we don't finish I leave with you."

The answer didn't satisfy him. But under Nicolae's scrutiny, nothing more could be said. After lunch, Nicolae relaxed enough for them to play Topple Words.

GRATITUDE, was the first word he played.

For last night or this morning, she wondered.

WELCOME.

HEADER.

HEADER, she echoed, not sure what he meant.

PACKETS.

He was suggesting they use the header in the IP packet as a way to track Dragomir's clients. It was a good idea. There were certain bits in the IP header that were considered reserved. No legitimate program was supposed to set them. Nothing would break if they were set; to Dragomir's clients, everything would seem perfectly normal. The modified packets would be easy to detect if you knew what you were looking for and ignored by everyone else.

RESERVE, Navy played, to see if she was right.

Andrei nodded. Then, RESCUE.

She wasn't sure if it was a question or a statement. RESCUE, she echoed.

TIMING.

UNKNOWN.

Frustration crumpled Andrei's face. TIMING, he repeated.

She shook her head, hoping Andrei could see she really didn't know. Footsteps came down the hallway, another message for Nicolae. Another shipment of victims for upstairs? She released the keys she'd been holding just as Nicolae got up. Nicolae could easily see her screen on his way to the door. The two men didn't bother to keep their voices low. She caught a few words using her rudimentary skills in Romanian. Something about two vans.

A new game popped up on her screen. What was Andrei thinking? Nicolae was standing right there. She ignored the invite. Andrei scrawled a note on a piece of paper, crumpling the page as Nicolae turned back toward Andrei. He kept the page clenched in his fist.

"Time to go," Nicolae said.

Andrei glared at him and stood up. When they reached the front hallway, Andrei swung his arm back and tried to pass Navy the note. Instead, his arm brushed Nicolae. Andrei mumbled an apology, head down. Nicolae pushed Andrei with one open palm. Andrei stumbled, landed on his knees, and dropped the note.

Navy stepped between Nicolae and the crumpled paper. *No heroics.* Kevin's directive itched at her conscience.

It wasn't heroics, she told herself, as she set her bag on the floor and dropped to one knee, pretending to search for something inside the canvas pockets. It was self-preservation. She couldn't gamble her life—and Andrei's—on the thin chance he'd been thinking clearly enough to write a note that didn't implicate them both.

"What are you doing?" Nicolae demanded.

"My SecureID fob," Navy said. "I think I left it in the office."

"Get it tomorrow."

"I need the fob to keep track of the file the CIA has on Dragomir. I can't get on the VPN without it." With the hand Nicolae could see, she continued to search through her bag. With the other, she picked up the note. "Oh, here it is. Never mind."

The same guard who had delivered the message about the shipment stuck his head in the hallway and yelled something to Nicolae.

Andrei picked himself up. "We're going already," he said in English.

Navy felt Nicolae's hands on her back as he pushed them out onto the sidewalk. The door slammed. Navy could finally take a full breath. Andrei didn't echo her relief. Outside the office, away from the pressure of Nicolae's surveillance, the only thing left on his face was fury. It was the fury of a cornered animal lashing out. A promise to follow through on a threat—

something in the note.

Andrei strode away in the same direction he always did, back to the house where Petru was held.

She would find out what Andrei wanted when she got back to her apartment. She couldn't read the note with her tails watching. Her tails had gotten progressively more obvious. Now their presence was as much for intimidation as observation.

Just three more days—Wednesday, Thursday, Friday— at that wretched office, she thought as she climbed the stairs to her apartment. Three more days and then she would be home and whatever happened to Andrei would no longer be her responsibility. She sat down on the bed and flattened the crumpled note. It was in English, written in shaky capital letters like a ransom note.

"Rescue Petru before Friday or I tell Dragomir everything."

Yes, a cornered animal. The note was reckless and ill-considered. If anyone else had found it, both she and Andrei would have been thrown on Dragomir's nonexistent mercy. Her sympathy for Andrei was reaching its limit.

She waved to her tail standing on the sidewalk before pulling the drapes on all the windows. "Kevin," she said to the empty room. "We need to talk."

Fifteen minutes later, Kevin arrived.

"Andrei gave me this today," she said.

Kevin frowned as he read it. "We were planning to attempt the rescue after you were home. I don't have enough people to rescue Petru and protect you at the same time.”

“What if I went somewhere really public Thursday night after work? Like a club?”

“Not good enough. Dragomir owns half the police force.” He read the note again and pressed his lips flat. “Do you think Andrei’s bluffing?”

Navy thought of Andrei’s wild, dangerous eyes. “No, I think he’d do it. I guess I can’t blame him for not trusting us.”

“You think we’re taking advantage of a desperate man.”

“Aren’t we?”

The thought didn’t seem to disturb Kevin. “Informants don’t usually volunteer unless they’re desperate. This was your idea, remember?”

“I thought Andrei would want to see Dragomir’s operation end as much as we do.”

Kevin studied the note. “Try to talk him out of this little tantrum if you can.”

She wondered how many games of Topple Words that would take.

“If you can’t, tell Andrei the rescue is Thursday night.”

“You have a plan? That quick?”

“If we can’t think of a plan, you don’t show up for work Friday. Jackson will accidentally on purpose out Andrei as Red Fox, the CIA informant. Andrei can tell Dragomir whatever he wants.”

“But that’s . . .”

“Cruel? It’s exactly what Andrei is threatening to do to

270

you. And if Dragomir *thinks* his entire operation is compromised, he'll have to rebuild his infrastructure. Plus, it's necessary to protect Clara."

Navy shook her head. "I don't understand."

"Andrei's contact with Clara has to end with this operation. One way or another."

There had to be rooms in Dragomir's headquarters where informants were dealt with. Andrei wouldn't be allowed to go quietly. "And Petru?" she asked.

"You think I'm heartless," Kevin said.

The thought had crossed her mind. She craved Jackson's calm strength to counter Kevin's brutal morality.

Kevin sat down on the bed, just shy of touching her. "Dragomir has business interests in the Middle East. Poppy. Oil. Guns. Humans. A bit of everything. The money he makes on films here greases palms there. Most of his business partners are our enemies. There were less complicated targets that would have achieved the same objective. I pushed for Dragomir."

She kept her eyes focused on the threadbare carpet.

"He pays local militias or tribal leaders—whoever he needs—to make sure his merchandise isn't disturbed. Some of the groups he pays bomb pilgrimages. Mosques. Schools for girls."

Outside the curtains, Navy could hear cars and people passing by. She wondered what decisions were being made underneath her windows. What to eat for dinner, perhaps. Whether or not to replace the car this year or next. "Dragomir and

Nicolae are the bastards here. They should be the only ones suffering," she said.

"This isn't my fault, Navy." Frustration was evident in his voice. "I can't save everyone."

Imagine you're a lifeguard, Jackson had said. *And you see a hundred people drowning, but you can't save them all. You have to focus on your objective. On the people you're supposed to rescue. The people you have the power to rescue.*

"Petru is one little boy. One adorable little boy. But I won't sacrifice this operation for him. If Andrei's going to force me to make a choice, I'll protect the hundreds Dragomir will murder instead."

Would she sacrifice herself to for Petru? Should she? "You make it sound like this is pro bono work for the CIA."

Kevin moved to the chair in the corner. "More like enlightened self-interest."

She couldn't think past the image of Andrei, no longer useful even as a programmer, being worked over by Nicolae's fists before being executed.

"I know about Dragomir from a couple years ago when Jackson and I were in—" Kevin stopped himself. "It doesn't matter where we were. UNICEF had opened a school there. A few of the locals were angry because the school allowed girls to enroll. Every day there would be a small group of people jeering at the girls when they arrived. They said ugly things. Things that would make most people cry."

She had been wrong. Kevin wasn't heartless.

272

"But the girls always came. They always held their heads high. They always walked by like they didn't hear. One day I'm walking by just as the kids are arriving for school and this car veers off the road, straight into the front door. The explosives took out most of the first floor. I lost a little hearing in my right ear."

So these were the sorts of memories Jackson carried home with him. "Dragomir bombed the school?

"He funded the people who did."

Kevin was harsh when he was angry, strict when he thought she wasn't listening, but she hadn't seen this. This anger was cold, focused, and implacable. The bombing wasn't just a tragedy; it was a personal affront. Navy had a feeling Kevin had more of a connection to the school than he was admitting. "Do you do this a lot?"

"Do what?" Kevin asked.

"Spend years planning and then risk your life to go after a man because he killed a group of children you walked by a few times."

He gave her a smile but kept his secrets.

"You're not so bad, Auntie."

Kevin accepted the compliment with a nod. "I need to get back."

Navy locked the door after him. She hugged herself, trying to decide how to pass the long afternoon. Open the curtains and let her tail watch as she walked from room to room. Or hide in the empty, dark apartment under the dim light fixtures in a self-imposed prison. She had memorized already how the shadows changed from afternoon to evening, like dark strings of yarn stretching over the city, a feeling like pulling a sweater over her head. Tonight, a child would be tucked into bed with a story, a kiss, and a hug. Tonight, another child would be abused at Dragomir's hands. Tonight, somewhere, two lovers were looking into each other's eyes, swearing eternal affection. Tonight, Andrei was lying to another woman to steal her life savings.

Her life or Petru's. Petru's life or the lives of hundreds of other children. A devil's bargain, either way.

Chapter 31

Another morning, another nightmare, another stuttering heartbeat in a gray room. The ghosts Navy fought in her dreams had been replaced by people. Dragomir and Nicolae and, yes, even poor Andrei. Her alarm chimed and Navy hit snooze. She hugged the blankets to herself and turned over, hoping sleep would come again. It didn't. She curled into a tight ball. The bed was warm, if not comfortable. There would be nothing for her to do if she got up this early. There was nowhere to go until it was time to leave for Dragomir's headquarters. She wasn't sure any logical arguments would cut through Andrei's desperation. If she failed to talk Andrei out of his ill-considered deadline, she would have to deliver a promise of a rescue that might or might not be a lie. She wasn't sure she could.

Navy could imagine Andrei's face, waking up on Friday morning to find Petru still there. She didn't believe in karma, but she was sure Andrei's hatred would follow her to the grave if she failed to rescue Petru.

The ping of a text message interrupted the next alarm. A message from Auntie. "No sleeping in today! We're meeting for brunch." She rolled her eyes at Kevin, wishing he could see, then hauled herself out of bed.

Milk softened the stale breakfast cereal but didn't improve the flavor. Navy swallowed each mouthful as quickly as she could. She dressed and threw her bag over her shoulder. By the time she reached the corner near Dragomir's headquarters, she was close to being late. But she couldn't face Nicolae's morning whiskey breath or Andrei's animal eyes just yet. She detoured to a newsstand in the park. She felt Byron's eyes following her from his chess game. Kevin would be seething. Every morning Navy had gone straight from her apartment to Dragomir's. Her tail would report this break in routine to Nicolae before she even reached the front door.

Navy chose the morning paper in English and a dusty can of energy drink. The brand name was in English but she'd never seen it before. On her way back across the park, she noticed Byron had left his post. Byron wouldn't abandon her. Was he in trouble? Was she in trouble?

Her foot caught on something. As she tripped, she realized it was someone else's foot, sticking out from a bench. Attacker or just an accident? She looked up from her crouch and saw Byron's face, inches from her own.

"Everything okay?" he asked in a whisper.

"Fine," she whispered. Then louder, in Romanian, "Excuse me."

"You should have seen me." His admonition was delivered gently. "Focus." Before she could answer, he mumbled a loud apology in Romanian and pushed Navy away.

She hurried now, not wanting to make Nicolae any more suspicious than he would be already. Nicolae gave her the morning pat-down with more enthusiasm than usual, examined the paper and the energy drink, then shoved Navy toward the

276

office.

"Dragomir says to make sure Andrei works today," Nicolae said. "Yesterday, he was slow."

"He's not my responsibility." She wished.

"And don't be late again."

Apologies made Nicolae see weakness. Defiance made Nicolae see red. "I didn't sleep well," she said.

"You are staying at Teofila's, no?"

Nicolae knew exactly where her apartment was; his men followed Navy home every night. Nicolae unlocked the door and they entered the hallway that led to Andrei's office.

"Her rooms are popular with men who want—" he smirked while he searched for the word. "Discretion."

She picked up the pace, even though she could see Andrei's hardened expression from the hallway. Better to face Andrei's glare than let this conversation continue.

"Maybe a good side business for you," Nicolae said, still smirking.

Navy left the insinuation unanswered and sat at her desk. Nicolae had barely opened his magazine before Andrei started the word game with her. He fed the monkey a coconut from the palm tree—a new cheat mode? The dancing monkey delivered a new set of instructions to her. In this cheat mode, each player could still choose from any letters they wanted, but instead of alternating turns between every word, each player had five seconds per turn to play as many words as they could.

Andrei went first. TIMING RESCUE.

She wasted one of her five seconds on a breath.

BEFORE FRIDAY RISKY.

Andrei's eyes narrowed. LYING.

TRUTH.

His hands hovered over the mouse while he examined her face, his face still pinched with anger. He didn't find what he wanted. NO BLUFF. The game ended, Andrei's threat hanging in the air.

She started another game before she lost Andrei entirely. She didn't want to give away too much, but she could say they were waiting for reinforcements. That was close to the truth. She tried to think of a word for "team" that had more than four letters. Five letters would have to do. GROUP SMALL MORE SOON. Two seconds left. She balanced her next words carefully. UNTIL THEN RISKY. The high value letters 'Y' and 'U' teetered but didn't fall.

RISK FOR YOU, Andrei played.

AND THE BOY.

YOU LIE NO BLUFF. He ended the game again.

They had to get some work done today to allay Dragomir's suspicions. She gave herself one more game to convince Andrei. She tapped her finger impatiently and waited for the monkey to finish his victory dance and go into cheat mode. At least it gave her time to figure out her play.

PROMISE GENUINE, she played. TRUST PLEASE HASTY RESCUE BAD FOR ALL.

She recognized the whirlpools in Andrei's eyes from

278

Monday night. He would throw her life away for Petru's. Even though she had considered the sacrifice herself, Andrei's cold insistence made him seem murderous.

NO BLUFF, he played.

He started the next game, jumping back to the cheat mode they had used the first day. One word per turn. A clear signal he didn't want long answers. TIMING.

If he wanted his answer, he should give her enough letters to spell out Thursday. Navy would have to spell out numbers instead, today was the nineteenth. TWENTY, she played.

A cautious hope flickered across his face. She kept her expression neutral. She was only buying time. Come Friday morning, she might be on a plane, with Andrei and Petru at Dragomir's mercy.

WHEN, he replied.

EVE.

TIME, he insisted.

DONE. She ended the game. "We should be able to finish the Flash exploits today," she said to Andrei. Her words, after such a long silence, caught Nicolae's attention. Just as she intended. Andrei couldn't start another game with her now.

"All of them?" Andrei asked.

If you want to save your nephew's life, Navy thought. "Dragomir wants me to get through as much as we can while I'm here."

Andrei seemed to understand, though his expression

didn't soften. She spent the day wilting under Andrei's hostility
and Nicolae's indifference.

Chapter 32

The pen dropped from Jackson's hand, clattered onto the table, and startled him out of a daze. He knew only by his watch that it was late afternoon. The curtains on the first floor at base were, as always, closed. Hours of wearing headphones made his ears ache. Even by the standards of surveillance, Andrei's house was boring. He could hear the TV in the background most of the day. The guard rarely talked to Petru, except to tell him when to go to the bathroom or eat. Or to say "We're going for a ride" when it was time for the daily afternoon trip to get cigarettes and beer.

Anna came in with her bike and propped it up by the door. She cleared Jackson's crossword puzzle from the chair to take the seat next to him.

"How's 'Days of Captivity'?" she asked.

Jackson yawned and slipped one of the headphones off. "Needs some commercial breaks. How's—"

"Navy?" Anna finished the question with a smile. "She's fine."

"Did she talk Andrei out of rushing the rescue?"

Anna shrugged. "We won't know until she gets home. They must have been using that game to talk. We just overheard tech stuff." She filled in ten down on the crossword.

He'd been working on that one for the past half hour.

"Did you figure out a way to rescue Petru on Thursday?"

she asked.

"I have an idea. But I don't think Kevin will like it."

"Try not to piss Kevin off too much. I'm bunking here tonight and Kevin grinds his teeth in his sleep when he's angry." That meant Byron would be on duty at Navy's apartment for the night.

Martin arrived. His bag had just touched the floor when Kevin came in behind him.

"Team meeting," Kevin said. "Everyone upstairs."

Jackson was grateful for the slanted sunlight drifting in the windows after staring at curtains all day. Anna chose the floor, using the space to stretch her legs from a day of biking in circles. Kevin took the good stuffed leather chair. He perched on the edge, the elbows of his long arms resting on his gangly legs.

"Navy wasn't able to convince Andrei to wait," Kevin said. "I need a brilliant rescue plan, Jackson."

Mediocre was the best Jackson could do. "Andrei and Petru aren't allowed their nightly walks anymore. We have a narrow window of opportunity just after Andrei gets home, twenty minutes maybe. There's only the guard, and maybe Nicolae. After that, Nicolae's lieutenants will be over for their nightly party."

"It takes five minutes to run from Dragomir's headquarters to Andrei's house," Anna said. "What happens if Nicolae manages to call for reinforcements?"

The same thought had been worrying Jackson. "That's why we need everyone but Navy to breach Andrei's house.

282

Otherwise, we risk getting pinned down.”

“I’m assuming you’re not proposing leaving Navy unprotected,” Kevin said.

“She needs a place to hide. I think the tunnel between her apartment building and the neighboring one would work.” He pushed away the image of Navy shivering in the dark, cobwebbed tunnel while Dragomir’s men methodically searched every floor in her building. There was nowhere else to hide her. If she left the building, even the neighboring building, she would have to be able to lose a tail. She wasn’t trained for it.

Kevin frowned. That was never good. “I don’t like it. Nicolae said something to Navy this morning about where she’s staying. He seemed familiar with the building. They may know about the tunnels. And we need to assume they’ll move on Navy after any rescue attempt. Once they realize she isn’t working alone.”

“He won’t assume Navy knows about the tunnels,” Jackson said. The argument wasn’t even convincing to him.

Kevin shook his head. “I need other ideas.”

“I vote we abort,” Anna said. “It wouldn’t be the first time an unreliable informant has forced us to scrub an operation.”

As much as Jackson wanted to see Navy safe, he couldn’t ignore what would happen to Petru and Andrei.

“Navy might be safer if she’s with us when we hit Andrei’s house,” Martin said. “If they do know about the tunnels, she’ll be trapped. And we’ll be too far away to help her.”

“No.” Jackson tried hard to think of a good reason why.

"Her tail will follow her to Andrei's and we'll lose the element of surprise."

Kevin tapped his finger on his chin. The gesture was familiar to Jackson; Kevin was working out a plan.

"Ambushing her tail with the five of us will be easy," Kevin said. "And losing contact with Navy's tail would send Dragomir's men running to wherever we plan the ambush."

"Navy's never been in combat," Anna said. Contradicting Kevin wasn't for the faint of heart. "The girl has skills, but this is a stretch."

Kevin studied the ceiling, weighing each opinion, his jaw set. Abort the mission, hide Navy, or have her fight with them. Anna didn't know how much this operation meant to Kevin. Dragomir was a personal target for him, and getting permission to target Dragomir again would be difficult. Dragomir was a pebble in the CIA's shoe. Troublesome, but not a priority.

"Do we have a spare vest and helmet?" asked Kevin.

Jackson's fists were clenched so hard his fingers hurt. "You're not seriously considering—"

"Martin's right," Kevin said. "Hiding her in the tunnel just leaves her vulnerable to retaliation. Stop thinking like her boyfriend and start thinking like a soldier."

It took all of Jackson's training to not strangle Kevin.

Kevin was unfazed. "Martin and Anna, you're with me on logistics downstairs. Jackson, you're going to Navy's apartment."

His anger dissolved into confusion. "What?"

"You're useless to me in your mood and if you're at Navy's apartment, Byron can help me with planning here. I'll even let you choose your guard post, inside Navy's apartment or behind the sniper rifle across the street."

As if Kevin didn't know which one Jackson would choose.

Kevin opened a plastic case and pulled out an earpiece. "Give her this. Tell her to leave it turned off until after she leaves work tomorrow. I'll use the earpiece to tell her what route to take for the ambush."

Jackson escaped into the early evening, eager to be away from the base and the expectant crates of weapons. The soft light of streetlamps glimmered on polished silverware at sidewalk cafés. Orange neon signs for money order businesses reflected against the damp streets. Sneaking in to see Navy was beginning to feel routine. Use the key for the neighboring building, crawl through the tunnel, then up the stairs to the third floor. The only light in the apartment came from the bathroom. He could hear the shower running. She probably hadn't heard him enter. He hesitated before calling her name.

The last time they'd been alone together for more than ten minutes, they'd argued.

He opened the bathroom door slowly. "Navy, it's me." The humidity settled on his hands, his face.

"Jackson?" She peeked around the curtain. "Close the door if you're staying. You're letting in the cold air." Her face and shoulders, glistening wet, disappeared behind the shower curtain.

He let his memory fill in the rest.

The shower turned off, the pipes creaking in protest. She stepped out and let his eyes wander before grabbing a towel. "Am I harboring a fugitive?"

"Kevin said I was useless and he wanted Byron back at base. I'm your bodyguard tonight."

"You remember what happened in that movie, right?" She dropped the towel and wrapped her arms around his neck.

Her kiss was tempting, but he was on duty. He untangled himself, holding her firmly by the shoulders. "It would be easier for me to concentrate if you would put some clothes on."

She smiled. "Your choice."

He left the bathroom to avoid changing his mind. A few minutes later she emerged, dry and dressed in pajamas. She took her phone from the nightstand and stuck it in the fridge.

"He won't like being stuck in there," Jackson said. But he didn't take the phone out. He was glad Navy wanted to have a conversation with him without Kevin overhearing. Kevin's ability to get into her head when Jackson couldn't was unnerving.

"You're here. Kevin can deal." She stretched out on the bed, one hand tucked beneath her wet hair, just like she did at his apartment. "How was work?"

He sat cross-legged on the bed next to her. "I listened to Petru color all day. You?"

"A normal day at the office. Bad coffee. Rushed lunch. A nervous coworker who can't stop sweating."

"Andrei's not doing well, then."

She rolled over to face Jackson, hair falling across her eyes. "I thought I would need a sponge."

"How are you doing?" He wondered if he could ask the question without making her angry.

She tilted her head to study him. "Who's asking? My boyfriend? Or the psychologist?"

He wasn't sure she would believe him. "Boyfriend."

"It's difficult but good." She propped herself up on her elbows. "Every time I get afraid it's like . . . inoculation. The next time, it's not so bad."

"Most people would go to therapy or keep a journal."

She laughed, stretching out on the bed again. "I don't think normal is your style."

"I wouldn't be so sure. A home-cooked meal waiting when I got home from an assignment might be nice every once in a while. And it wouldn't kill you to learn how to use an iron or—"

She tackled him to the bed. They rolled on the sagging mattress, laughing, wrestling, until his sides hurt. He trapped her in a bear hug and tried to keep a straight face while her fingers slipped under his shirt to his bare stomach. He gave up and held her wrists instead. When she wriggled free, he rolled over to pin her and he felt the earpiece dig into his thigh. He was getting distracted again.

"The plan." He reluctantly pushed her away. "I have to tell you the plan for tomorrow."

Navy's smile disappeared too quickly. "Shoot."

He dug the earpiece out of his pocket. "Hide this somewhere in your bag where Nicolae won't find it. Same kind of earpiece we used the night we knocked out Andrei's guard. When you leave work tomorrow, you'll need to find a discreet spot to establish comms. Kevin will tell you where to go. You're going to lead your tail into an ambush."

"And then?"

"You'll come with us when we breach Andrei's house for the rescue." He should have been happy she looked shocked instead of excited. "It's the least-bad choice. You'll have a vest and helmet like the rest of us. Just try to stay out of the way." A vest would protect her vital organs. The helmet would protect her head. But a shot to the neck, could nick an artery or an airway. A shot to the leg could leave her unable to crawl away from danger. "Just stay out of the way," he repeated.

"So everything I don't bring to Dragomir's tomorrow will be left behind?"

"Is there anything you don't want him to find?"

She looked around the room, her eyes settling on the laptop in the corner. "I should wipe the laptop. In case they feel motivated enough to spend the time trying to decrypt it. The wipe will take a few hours."

Her wet hair left a dark spot on the sheets when she rolled off the bed. Sitting cross-legged on the carpet, she plugged a thumb drive into her laptop and held down a key on the top row as the laptop booted. A text menu filled the screen. She was at her most graceful when she was least aware of it. Like in the middle of a sparring match, when she was no longer thinking of the moves, simply executing them. And now, when her fingers danced over the keys so quickly he couldn't follow them. Soon a scrollbar slowly crawled across the screen, tracking the progress of the data wipe.

She hid a yawn as she came back to bed.

"You should sleep," he said.

"What about you?"

"I'm standing guard tonight." This, at least, he could accomplish.

"And then up all day tomorrow listening to Andrei's house again?"

He shrugged. "It happens on a lot of missions." He could tell she didn't believe him. This time it was the truth. "I'll sleep when we're home safe. Eating cinnamon rolls."

She let him tuck her into bed. The second her eyes closed, her breaths slowed. She must have been exhausted. A clump of wet hair had fallen across her cheek. He lifted it gently and tucked it behind her ear. She didn't stir.

Jackson took the phone out of the fridge and laid it on the nightstand. If something happened and he wasn't enough, Kevin should know. He took the only chair in the apartment, hand poised on his gun, staring at the drapes, ears trained for the footsteps of dangerous men.

Chapter 33

There were a few things Andrei wanted to bring with them when they were rescued. Petru had a tattered stuffed animal, barely recognizable as a rabbit, with one ear missing. A drop of Petru's father's blood stained the ear that was left. Petru had been holding the rabbit when they were taken. Andrei should take a few of the drawings his nephew had made. The crayon stick figures might be the only pictures left of their family. Andrei studied the wall cluttered with drawings. He couldn't take too many, Nicolae would notice. He chose a picture of Andrei's house, with Petru's father drawn pushing a mower and Afina standing by the tree swing. He could take a second picture. It was hard to choose. What memories would Petru most want later? How could Andrei possibly know?

Nerves had woken Andrei earlier than usual. Nicolae wouldn't be here to take Andrei to work for another twenty minutes. Petru was still asleep in the bed they shared, tossing and turning restlessly.

Packing a bag would be too obvious, even if he had a bag to put things in. He dropped the dirty stuffed rabbit by the door. As if Petru had left it there.

Petru stirred and stretched, blinking his eyes open. Andrei folded him into a hug, then faced his nephew toward the wall of pictures.

"Petru, can you tell me which one is your favorite?"

Petru jabbed his finger into a picture of the park near their house. "This one. I miss the swings." He rubbed his eyes. "What day is it?"

"Thursday," Andrei said. *Just hold on until tonight,* Andrei thought. *Just a little longer.* He couldn't tell his nephew about the rescue. Petru was a smart boy, but he was still just a boy.

"It's my favorite too," Andrei said. He carefully took the two drawings off the wall. He folded them neatly and put them in the desk drawer closest to the door.

Nicolae opened the door without knocking. He moved quietly when he was sober. As Andrei had planned, opening the door hid the rabbit behind it.

"We're leaving," Nicolae said.

Andrei hugged Petru again. "Remember to brush your teeth after breakfast."

Nicolae yanked Andrei away. "I said we're leaving."

You're right, Andrei thought. *We're leaving tonight, bastard.*

***

Jackson poured himself another cup of coffee while he listened to Andrei tell Petru to brush his teeth. Jackson had headquarters to himself, though it no longer felt like much of a headquarters. While he was at Navy's apartment, the rest of the team had packed up most of the gear. Except for the surveillance equipment for Andrei's house, everything the team brought with them had been loaded into the van or thrown away.

A combination of adrenaline and caffeine kept Jackson awake. Eight more hours until Navy left Dragomir's. Andrei hadn't given away the rescue yet, though the questions to Petru about the drawings this morning differed from the routine.

Petru was eating breakfast; Jackson knew because Petru always hummed between bites. The rustling sounds from Andrei and Petru's room were normal. Andrei hadn't been exaggerating. Their room was searched after Andrei left for work. Often with commentary from the guards. Nicolae's men liked to read through Andrei's notebooks and make fun of the women Andrei scammed.

"What's this?" one of Nicolae's men muttered in Romanian.

Jackson tensed. More commentary about Andrei's "girlfriends"? Or had Andrei left something out of place?

Nothing else was said.

From the bug in the living room, Jackson heard the front door open and close. Also normal. The guard who normally stayed with Petru was a habitual smoker. A few minutes later, the door opened again and Jackson heard the guard return to the living room. Then a short, mechanical joker's laugh from the guard's phone. That ringtone meant a text message from Nicolae. Nicolae had his entire team set a special notification for messages from him. A few seconds later, Jackson heard the swoosh for a text message sent. Conversation between Nicolae and the guard went back and forth several times. More than usual. But they'd only placed the bugs in Andrei's house six days ago.

292

Everything was fine. Probably.

"Petru," the guard said. "We're going for a ride."

The daily run for beer and cigarettes usually happened in the afternoon.

Jackson called Kevin.

"Is Navy at the office yet?" Jackson asked.

"Nearly," Kevin said. "Why?"

"Could be nothing, but . . . there were a few oddities at the house this morning. The guard might have found something in Petru's room. And then he and Nicolae texted for a while. And now the guard is taking Petru out of the house outside of their routine." Jackson listened to the silence while Kevin weighed Jackson's words. Jackson hadn't been at his best this operation. Kevin might think Jackson was trying to abort the operation to avoid putting Navy in the middle of a shoot-out this evening.

"You think we might be compromised?" Kevin asked finally.

"I don't know," Jackson said. "All I can say is their schedule is off."

"The store where they normally take Petru, how far away is it?"

Jackson wished he had the answer. "The guard's never said the name. They always drive, and they're back in about an hour."

"Move your monitoring post to the restaurant across from Andrei's house. Let me know right away when they come back or if you hear anything in the house."

"Sure," Jackson said.

"And Jackson?"

"Yeah?"

"Be prepared to breach Dragomir's HQ."

Finally. Jackson looked at his gun and knife, lying on the table. "I'm ready."

***

Act like it's a normal day, Andrei told himself.

He walked across the square with Nicolae, just like they always did, all the time hiding a smile. He sat down at his desk in front of the ever-changing, ever-blinking map of compromised computers, just like he always did. He found his lips pursed, ready to whistle, and forced them back into a frown.

Had he given himself away?

No, Nicolae was texting. Andrei went back to his work. He was examining some assembly code when Nicolae appeared at his shoulder. Nicolae was smiling.

That wasn't good. Nicolae was happiest when his assignments were the most brutal.

"Meeting with Dragomir," Nicolae said.

Andrei never met with Dragomir. He looked at Navy's empty chair. There was no one to help him. Eight or so hours until Petru's rescue. Could Andrei handle Nicolae's cruelty for that long? He would have to. As long as Petru was still at the house. Would the CIA know if Petru had been moved? Did they have enough people to rescue Petru from the more heavily guarded headquarters?

Andrei's fears were confirmed when Nicolae headed toward the basement. The second floor was for filming. The ground floor was for working. The basement was where they made people disappear.

Each step down the stairs made Andrei's heart sink a little more. The caustic scent of bleach stung his nose. In the hallway at the bottom of the stairs, Andrei recognized a few of Nicolae's men from the parties at his house. One held Petru by the neck. The guard's blunt fingernails rested in the hollow of Petru's throat.

"No!" Andrei cried. He lunged toward Petru. His intellect knew it was useless; his instincts could do nothing else.

Nicolae yanked him back and gave him one hard punch to the ear. It left Andrei lying on the floor with his ear ringing, disoriented by the pain.

Andrei thought he'd seen Nicolae at his worst. Apparently, he hadn't.

Nicolae kicked Andrei until he struggled to his feet, then pushed Andrei through a doorway. The guard holding Petru followed. The room was tiled and brightly lit at the center, dim at the edges. Dragomir leaned against the wall in the shadows. A metal table and chair stood in the center. A pile of stuffing and worn fabric, about the size of Petru's rabbit, was on the table. Next to the dismembered toy were a few paper bills. Shit. The money. He'd forgotten about the money he hid in the rabbit. When he still had delusions of escaping on his own, he had started collecting paper money wherever he could find it. In the couch cushions or underneath furniture in the living room. Places where Nicolae's men would lose it while they were too drunk or high to remember.

"Sit," Nicolae said.

What choice did Andrei have? He sat.

Petru was sent to the corner with the best view of his uncle's interrogation.

Nicolae picked up the bills with one fist, triangles of paper sticking out from between his knuckles. "Where did you get these?"

"N-nowhere. I found them around the house."

Nicolae's fists were a blur at the edge of Andrei's vision. The blows circled his chest, tightened his breath.

"Try again," Nicolae said.

"I swear!" Andrei hated how eager he was to please. How desperate he was to avoid Nicolae's fury.

"No, the CIA is paying you. You are working for them."

Andrei watched Petru's expression. More scared than Andrei had ever seen him. And behind that, perhaps imagined, a sense of betrayal. Petru finally knew how weak Andrei was.

Nicolae's fist snapped Andrei's neck back. Andrei's head bounced against the hard floor when the chair fell. Another man quickly set the chair upright.

Dragomir emerged from the dim edge of the room with the walk of a general. "I have two clients who want a boy Petru's age. The first client wants a capable child who will cook and clean for his house. No pay, of course. He has a bit of a temper,

296

but provided Petru works well and doesn't talk back, he will be left alone. The second wants a companion. If you tell us who your CIA contact is, I will sell Petru to the first man. If you don't, I sell him to the second. You die either way."

Even if Andrei agreed to the deal, there was no way he could hold Dragomir to his word.

Andrei's denials were answered with a broken rib and another black eye. Navy should be here soon. When Andrei wasn't in the office, she would know something was wrong. She could call the rescue team, right? She had to have a way to talk to them.

"It's Navy, isn't it?" Nicolae said. His face filled Andrei's vision. "Tell me, do you like her enough to sacrifice Petru?"

Andrei would have to switch tactics; they weren't going to believe he was innocent. "Not Navy," he managed. The swelling around his eyes narrowed his vision. "Chuck Redding." Andrei had meant to make up a name, but the name slipped out. Oh well. It was probably a fake name anyway. All that mattered was keeping Navy above suspicion.

This time Dragomir spoke. "And what exactly did this Chuck Redding ask you to do?"

Despite the threat of Nicolae's fists, Andrei took his time in coming up with the answer. Navy might or might not arrive in time. Dragomir might or might not honor the promise to sell Petru into child labor instead of sexual abuse. But Navy knew Andrei planned to put the tracking code in the packet headers.

She could find the pattern.

If he could hold on to that one secret, Andrei could make sure Dragomir's business was destroyed. Andrei would have his revenge, even if it was from beyond the grave.

Chapter 34

Nicolae didn't scowl when Navy arrived. The toothy grin was more predatory than friendly. Before she could make up any excuse to leave, Nicolae pulled her inside and gave her a half-hearted pat down. The earpiece she was supposed to wear for the rescue tonight was nestled in a pack of gum, but Nicolae hadn't even searched through her bag.

A dreadful curiosity carried her down the hall to the office with Petru's picture. Andrei wasn't there. A flicker of fear, like a snake's tongue, touched her heart. Tell Kevin, she reminded herself. "Where's Andrei?" she asked. Her quickening pulse made the words seem slow.

That smile again. "Meeting with Dragomir. You work alone for a while."

Paradise. A week ago she would have used the word without hesitation. But what was the emergency exactly? That Nicolae was having a good day? That Andrei was having a meeting with Dragomir? Kevin would love that explanation. She had met with Dragomir twice, after all. The operation was nearly sewed up. They were so close. Tonight, after they rescued Andrei, she would learn the signature in the packet headers. They could start tracking Dragomir's clients. A worldwide child sexual abuse ring would be cleaned up now instead of years from now.

She did her best to look busy, but there wasn't much to do without Andrei around. She sipped the burnt coffee to keep her throat from going dry. It didn't help. She argued with herself over whether to use her distress word. Ten minutes passed like an hour.

A phone rang – not hers, Nicolae's. He answered it with a grunt. He tipped his chair to level again. Slowly, deliberately, he lifted his muscled form to standing. He approached her with that smile. No, not a smile. A promise. That Nicolae could finally do what he had wanted to do at their first meeting.

"Dragomir wants to meet with you," Nicolae said. "Now."

Yes, Navy thought. *Now is when you find out how dangerous I am.*

"Can it wait five minutes?" Navy asked. "I'm working on the graphics for a new game. Birds of Paradise."

Nicolae pulled her out of the chair. Her heartbeats sounded like a bass drum. Jackson. Kevin. Anna. Martin. Byron. This time she wasn't alone. They would all come to help her. She just had to stay alive until they got here.

Navy had been pulled all the way down the hall before she recovered her wits. "Dragomir has another office in the basement?"

Nicolae tightened his grip on her arm. "Sure. An office."

The basement smelled of bleach. And a tangy, rusty scent she hadn't smelled since her last real fight. Blood. It brought back images of pools of blood, so still they reflected her opponent's glassy, dead eyes. She felt woozy and bit her cheek. The smell was in her in mouth now too.

300

Nicolae shoved her into a large room with beige linoleum. Dragomir stood in the center, flicking a lighter at the end of a fresh cigarette. A wide smear of blood started at Dragomir's feet and led to Andrei, propped up against the wall opposite the door. If Andrei wasn't dead already, he was close. Petru huddled next to Andrei, trying to close Andrei's hand around his own. When Petru saw Navy, a spark of recognition reached the boy's eyes.

Dragomir was discussing something in rapid Romanian with Nicolae. She looked back at Petru and held one finger to her lips. Petru looked at the floor. She hardened her expression just in time.

"We have a problem." Dragomir exhaled a cloud of white smoke.

She suppressed a cough. "Beating people up isn't my specialty." Could her team still hear her or did the basement block the signal?

Tendrils of smoke curled around Dragomir's fingers as he waved his hand dismissively. "Andrei and the boy are our problem."

Navy couldn't look at Andrei's purple face without losing her composure. *Focus on where Dragomir and Nicolae are. Focus on breathing.*

"We need your help with the code. Andrei admitted to changing the code so my clients could be tracked by the CIA. Despite our best efforts at persuasion, he has refused to tell us exactly how."

She wondered if hastening someone's demise was the same as wielding the knife. "So Andrei was Red Fox." She hadn't known Andrei was done, only that he planned to put a distinctive pattern in the packet header. Andrei must have thought the CIA would back out of the deal.

"Yes," Dragomir said. "You understand this would be bad for my business. My clients appreciate their privacy."

Dragomir hadn't mentioned anything about her working for the CIA yet. Perhaps Andrei was stronger than she thought. "What can I do?"

"Find what Andrei has added and fix it." He pointed to a laptop sitting on a table. The chair next to the table was spotted with Andrei's blood.

Navy saw their plan. They were hoping in her eagerness to save her life, she would find the code too quickly and give herself away. They would have proof of her involvement with the CIA, if they didn't have it already, and get their code fixed at the same time. "I've never seen the client code. It might take awhile." Where the hell was her team?

"C-V-S." Dragomir pronounced the letters so slowly it took her a second to recognize the acronym.

"You mean the subversion server. Your version control system."

"The changes were made sometime after Monday. The code has already gone out to my clients."

"Okay." She turned the chair to face the laptop and sat down, feeling the cool dots of blood stain her clothes. There

302

should be sounds of fighting upstairs by now. But there was nothing. No sounds from a floor that normally bustled with the noise of the call center. Navy thought of the gas canisters she'd seen at base. She held on to that hope as she began to type.

Andrei coughed. Navy flinched. A thin red ribbon trickled from his mouth as his head rolled to the side. She reminded herself that Andrei had been ready to sacrifice her not that long ago. Anyway, if she wanted to help him, she had to look like she didn't care. She knew where the code should be – in the C library that built the packets for each client request. Nicolae leaned over her shoulder. The oppressive aroma of coffee and whiskey and sausage and sweat made her hands shake.

Just a few minutes more.

She typed a command that would print every change ever made to the screen, hoping Nicolae would be too ignorant to notice. One page per each hit of the space bar. She pretended to study something to placate the cloud of breath at her shoulder.

"Faster," Nicolae said.

Normally she could read code in her sleep, but the functions scrolling by might as well have been in Romanian. She pretended to study something again. Nicolae's beard tickled her ear. She kept scrolling, hoping her rescue would arrive before the code ran out.

Upstairs, there was the unmistakable sound of running. The steps got louder, echoed on the stairs to the basement. Through the open door, she saw a few of Dragomir's guards race down the hall. They stumbled into the room, panting heavily. For a split second she saw Jackson's face at the bottom of the stairs, then the guards slammed the door shut.

Nicolae pulled her from the chair and shook her so hard her teeth rattled. Somehow she managed to avoid biting her tongue. "Your friends?" he demanded. Andrei had kept her secret.

"No," Navy said. "I swear."

Nicolae threw her to the floor. She landed hard, on her hipbone. Her mouth was as dry as cardboard, her heart was a gong against her ribs, her stomach was tangled in knots. This was the demon she'd come to face. The kind of mind-numbing fear that pushed out everything but her will to survive. She was glad to find it intact.

Navy backed against the wall, forgotten while Nicolae and his men concentrated on forming a defensive semicircle around the door. There were six of them, each with a gun pointed at the door. Five people on her team. She waited for the small black tube to slip under the door, gas to quietly end the fight. She didn't want a firefight. The walls were concrete. Her team would have to concentrate on shooting through the door, and Petru was directly in the line of fire.

No gas came. She had to get Petru to move before Nicolae's twitching finger fired the first shot. She couldn't help Andrei; he was too heavy for her to move.

Navy motioned for the boy to come to her but he shook his head. She eased herself closer and motioned again. The boy refused, clinging to his uncle.

304

She heard a small explosion and saw the door hinges rattle. Her team was going to blow the door down. Dragomir's men fired indiscriminately at the door. Another small explosion outside the door separated the top hinges from the frame. Navy felt like she was right next to a fireworks display. She grabbed Petru by the waist and pulled, trying to stay low. Andrei slid down the wall without Petru to hold him up, but the boy kept a tight hold on his uncle's hand.

"Nu! Nu!" Petru's screams were barely audible over the gunfire.

Andrei stirred. His mouth was moving but the words were too soft to hear. A bullet hole appeared in the wall next to Petru's head. Navy dug into Andrei's skin to get underneath Petru's grip and finally yanked him free.

Life flickered into Andrei's limbs. He pushed his nephew away. "Du-te. Cu." Andrei took a shallow breath. "Ea." She didn't know what the words meant, but Petru stopped fighting her. She was so grateful for a second she forgot she shouldn't be able to hear Andrei whisper. A lull in gunfire. She smelled sausage and garlic. She looked up to find Nicolae staring down at her.

More gunshots erupted in the background. Nicolae ignored the chaos behind him and pointed his gun at her heart. Petru curled up against her and clamped his arms around her neck.

"Give me the boy," Nicolae said.

Navy tried to put her body between Nicolae's gun and

Petru, but Nicolae was too fast. He wrapped one arm around Petru and yanked him away. Petru's nails left burning scratches on Navy's neck. Nicolae tried to steady the gun as the boy kicked and clawed at him. She couldn't maneuver enough to get out of Nicolae's range, not backed against the wall. Closer would be better. Navy launched herself at Nicolae, feeling a shot graze her arm.

His surprise gave her a momentary advantage. She swung the barrel down, away from Petru. As she struggled with the tangle of Nicolae's fingers, the barrel drifted over her feet. Every time she focused on prying Nicolae's hand loose, he took the opportunity to pull the gun up. Better to lose a big toe than risk a shot to a vital organ. She wrapped her hand around Nicolae's and pressed the trigger down, pulling back her feet as far as she could without risking her balance.

She managed three shots before Nicolae figured out her strategy. He pressed his finger against the trigger guard, trapping her knuckle against the hard metal. The pain was exquisite. The door was at an angle, almost down; the explosive charges and carefully aimed gunfire from the hallway had done their job. .

Nicolae smiled.

She reminded herself that he had one hand busy holding Petru and she had two. She felt her way down the handle until she could feel the magazine clip. The door flew open, kicked down. Dragomir's men ducked to avoid the flying rectangle. Jackson rolled into the room. A blinding pain hit her stomach. At least Nicolae had missed her heart.

306

She released the magazine as she fell against the wall, trapping it beneath her. Without the clip, Nicolae only had one bullet left, the one in the chamber.

Nicolae raised his gun to finish the job, but a shot whizzed by his ear. It was the only clear angle Jackson had without hitting Petru. Nicolae retreated to a corner near the door—with a writhing Petru boy in his arms and one bullet. Navy pushed herself a foot or two outside the line of fire before the effort exhausted her.

Her stomach wound throbbed, one stab of pain for each breath she took. She wondered how badly she was hurt. She pressed her hands to the wound, but they slipped in the spreading circle of her blood. She was too weak.

The room rearranged as clips emptied of ammunition—a bag of popcorn almost popped. Navy felt an increasing distance between her and reality as her mind slipped closer to numbness. Kevin was in the hallway, trading shots with Dragomir. Everyone else was fighting hand to hand near the door. Their fighting styles were as distinctive as their voices. Martin was nimble and lithe, using his small size to slip away from his opponent's blows like a weasel. Anna used her long arms to dance outside her opponent's reach, a smile playing on her lips in between each contact. Byron fought like a bulldozer, absorbing every blow without expression.

Jackson fought more like a machine than a man. He was quick and strong, but also distant and mechanical. A violent man with a distaste for violence. Still, his frustration was starting to show.

No, not frustration. Desperation.

The scarlet blossom spread wider, impossibly warm. She was cold. She was going into shock.

Navy looked up and watched Anna's opponent catch Anna under the chin. Anna fell to the floor with a sickening crack and didn't move. Anna's opponent turned toward Navy.

Nicolae waited in his corner, eyeing the crowded path between him and the door.

Navy looked around to see if there was any hope of assistance for Anna or her or Petru. The boy had stopped fighting Nicolae. Dragomir aimed at Kevin again, but the gun was silent. Out of bullets, the last kernel popped. Dragomir threw it away with a curse and advanced on Kevin. Strangely, Kevin took a few steps back. He weighed his gun. Was Kevin out of bullets as well? No, he was scanning the room. Deciding something. Kevin couldn't shoot Anna's opponent, now headed for Navy, without hitting one of his own officers. He had two choices—shoot Dragomir and hope he could fight his way over to Navy in time or give her his gun and engage Dragomir hand to hand. Kevin threw his gun in an arc to her. It bounced and slid to a stop next to Andrei's body, nearly an arm's length away.

Kevin would not forgive her for dying.

She wiped her hands on her jeans and reached for the gun. *So heavy.* She aimed at her attacker, who was fifteen feet away. The team was closer now, paying for each inch with grunts and pants. They might save her yet. But Kevin had pushed Dragomir into the room, leaving Nicolae a clear path to escape

308

with Petru.

She aimed her gun at Nicolae. It was heavier now, slippery in her hand. This wouldn't be an easy shot. A head shot was her only choice, any other shot might kill Petru. Breathe through the pain, she told herself. She lined up the back of Nicolae's head in her sight. Breathe through the pain and the roar of blood in her ears and the cold traveling from her toes to her shins. She pressed the trigger. Nicolae fell.

She didn't wait to see if Petru was hurt too. Her attacker was ten feet away, nine. Her arm was shaking, losing strength. But this was an easier shot. The heart or a lung, either would do. She used the last of her strength to pull the trigger. The bullet stopped him like a wall. The room shrunk. No, it was only her vision, going black at the edges.

Petru's face appeared before her, serious and calm. He took his shirt off and she felt small, warm hands press the cloth against her wounds. Her head rolled to the side and she couldn't roll it back.

"You're shot." Kevin's voice, but too far away to be speaking to her.

"Grazed my arm, that's all." Jackson's voice. "Get out of my way."

"Mulțumesc," Kevin said as he lifted Petru. *Thank you.*

A set of hands turned her head. She saw the blur of Jackson's face before her vision went black entirely. "Navy, c'mon. Stay with me." He cupped her face and then her shoulders. "There's an ambulance on the way."

His voice seemed distant even though she could feel his hot breath on her face, still panting. Another set of hands tied something around her wound. Her head dangled from her neck when Jackson lifted her. She couldn't control the movement of it any more than she could control her moan of pain. He adjusted his arm to support her neck, pressing her nose against his sweaty shirt. Her skin was an emptied container; she was numb. She tried to hold on to the scent of Jackson, of musk and spiced oranges, but even that faded as her consciousness faltered.

It was such a small hole really. No larger than a pea or a marble. But her entire life fit through it.

***

Jackson watched Navy's eyes move restlessly as she slept in the hospital bed. The hospital was somewhere outside Bucharest. Jackson had forgotten exactly where he was and didn't much care. Navy was alive, for now. Kevin's carefully laid contingency plans had saved her.

As far as the doctors and nurses at the hospital in Hackerville knew, a nice tourist named Linda Woods had been shot while walking on the sidewalk. Unfortunate, really, but since a rival gang had tried to break into what the local police knew was Dragomir's headquarters, the tourist had simply been a victim of circumstance.

Dragomir, Nicolae, and most of Nicolae's lieutenants were assumed to be in hiding, since no one had found their bodies. The call center staff on the first floor of Dragomir's headquarters had been passed out during the whole confrontation and couldn't provide any details to the police. The filming operation on the second floor would be paused until Dragomir returned, since Dragomir had always run that himself. Other than that, most of Dragomir's business was humming along quite nicely. And would continue until the geeks at the CIA had decided Dragomir's network of terrible people was no longer useful to the CIA.

Kevin would see to it that the worst offenders on Dragomir's customer list were taken care of. Just like Kevin had organized the cleanup at Dragomir's headquarters, the cover story for the local police, the reunion between Petru and his mother, and a long list of other cleanup tasks. While Kevin had been busy with all those details, Jackson had been waiting in hospital room chairs.

Jackson had waited for two hours in the emergency room in Hackerville while Navy was in surgery. He had slept in a chair by her bed overnight. The next day Jackson had organized Navy's transfer to Bucharest, to the hospital Kevin had chosen in advance. Just in case.

And last night he had slept in another hospital chair by another hospital bed. This hospital bed. Where Navy still slept.

Byron knocked lightly, then entered the room. "Any change?"

Jackson shook his head.

"She'll wake up, Jackson."

You don't know that, Jackson thought. "The doctors don't seem sure."

"The surgeon wasn't sure she would make it through surgery," Byron said. "She did. The bleeding has stopped. There was minimal damage to internal organs. She'll wake up."

"I'd feel better if it weren't taking so long."

Byron nodded. "Yeah."

"Can you text Kevin for me? He's asking me about Navy's condition every five minutes."

"I will in a bit. I'm mostly here to check on you. You haven't slept in a real bed the past two nights. I can take a shift."

Jackson shook his head.

"Things are going to get busy when she wakes up. We lost reception in the basement. We don't know if Andrei got the tracking code in place. And she's now the resident expert on Dragomir's botnet."

"She was so calm," Jackson said.

Byron touched Jackson's shoulder briefly to reassure him.

"When she used her distress word, Nicolae had no idea she'd just called for backup. And in the basement, after she'd been shot. She still managed to take out two people before passing out."

"She's safe now, Jackson," Byron said. "No need to torture yourself with what might have happened."

"Kevin recruited me from the hospital," Jackson said. "He told me I was the rare sort of person who would fight for a hopeless cause. Alone, if I had to. He said those were exactly the kind of people he wanted on his team."

"You're afraid Kevin is going to recruit Navy," Byron said.

"And that she'll say yes."

"If that's what she wants, you'll figure out how to handle it."

"You're awfully optimistic today," Jackson grumbled.

"Let me sit with Navy for a while," Byron said. "You need a break."

Some time alone with his thoughts would probably do Jackson good, as much as he hated to admit it. Jackson could get a cup of coffee and find a quiet place away from the constant activity in the hospital halls. "If anything changes—"

"I'll let you know right away."

Jackson stood up and stretched. "I won't be gone long."

"I think you're missing the point." Byron pointedly took Jackson's chair and waved him away. "Shoo."

The hospital coffee wasn't the worst Jackson had ever had. The walking paths near the hospital were nice. Jackson might have been able to appreciate the nice weather, if Navy were awake. But she wasn't. And his worries about their future left him with a sense of shame. He had always considered himself an enlightened man. He was often in places where girls were told they didn't need school. Where women spoke of their periods in whispers and young girls were told not to ask about health issues. And Jackson could see all the damage these attitudes caused. How much it hurt women, and everyone else, to treat half the population as if they were less entitled to direct their own lives.

So why was it so hard to imagine Navy taking on the role of field officer? She put up with the uncertainty and stress of waiting for Jackson to come home. If Navy wanted to do the same work, he owed her the same consideration.

Perhaps the why didn't matter. If Navy woke up—when Navy woke up—he would tell her how he felt. That she should take any job she wanted and his feelings were his to deal with. They had made it through so much already. Surely they would make it through this.

Chapter 35

The climb back to consciousness was jarring and painful. Navy's stomach wound ached like a deep bruise. Even the soft beep of the machines was sharp in her ears. Wheels and voices clattered in the hallway. The sun assaulted her eyes when she opened them. White sheets against white walls with bright, cheerful speckles on the linoleum floor. She was alive.

The tube of an IV rested against her right hand. The weight of someone's hand pressed against her left.

She turned her head gingerly and found Jackson sprawled in the chair next to her bed. Even in sleep, worry creased his forehead. A spot of blood showed through the bandage on his upper arm.

He stirred and relief flooded his face. "Welcome back."

Navy's greeting came out as a croak. Jackson lifted a cup of water with a straw to her lips. She finished one cup and asked for another. How long had she been out? Her last minute of consciousness came back to her: Anna getting knocked out, a small child's hands trying to staunch her bleeding.

"Anna? Petru?" Her vocal cords protested.

"Anna was treated for a concussion. Petru's with his mother."

At least she had accomplished one good thing. "Andrei?"

Jackson shook his head.

The sadness Navy expected didn't come. Her grief felt secondhand, the kind of grief she might feel hearing about a stranger dying. "I should be sad."

"He nearly killed you once with that note. Twice if you count how you got here. I don't miss him."

It wasn't like Jackson to have so little compassion. Navy lightly pressed her hands against her stomach, and felt a layer of bandages underneath the hospital gown. "Did I have to have surgery?" she asked.

"You were in surgery for a couple hours. The bullet nicked an artery. You lost a lot of blood. You almost—" His hand tightened on hers. "You were so pale."

"I'm here now."

In the hall, a nurse's rapid footsteps echoed. "Sir—sir—those wheelchairs are for—"

"Patients, I know." It was Kevin's voice, calm and commanding as always. "The doctor said a short stroll would do her good."

Kevin opened the door without knocking, pushing the wheelchair in front of him.

"So much for a private room," Jackson muttered.

"Mind if I take our patient for a walk?" Kevin asked. "Please?" Even with the last word, his request was more a command than a question.

"Navy?" Jackson asked.

"I'm not sure I—" Navy was interrupted by a nurse arriving. Probably the same one who had been following Kevin.

"A little bit of fresh air would be good," the nurse said. But she stepped in front of Kevin. "As long as you'll let me help you get settled in the chair. Need to be careful with the IV."

Navy did her best to hold the hospital gown together as the nurse helped Navy into the wheelchair. Then the nurse took the blanket from the bed and tucked the fabric around Navy's lap and behind her back. Next, after adjusting the pole, the nurse hung the IV bag.

When Kevin took the handles of the wheelchair, Jackson moved to follow.

"Give us ten minutes," Kevin said. "Then you can meet us by the lake."

Navy's stomach wound flared to a sharp, stabbing pain. "I'd rather have Jackson with me."

"Technically, the operation isn't over until we're home." Kevin said. "That means you still have to listen to me. And we have a mission debrief to do."

"Kevin—"

Kevin cut Jackson off with a wave of his hand. "Ten minutes, that's all."

They didn't speak in the hallway or in the elevator or in the lobby.

It was a beautiful day. The lawn was green, the sun was warm and flowers lined the walking path. Romania had flowers. She hadn't noticed.

"Where are we?" she asked.

"Outside Bucharest. You were stabilized in Hackerville

and then we moved you here."

"So I've been out—"

"Nearly two days."

Navy couldn't have guessed how long she'd been unconscious. She couldn't remember anything between passing out as Jackson carried her away and waking up in the hospital bed with Jackson at her side.

"There's some housekeeping we need to do to wrap up the mission," Kevin said. "Most of it can wait. But I need to know if Andrei told you anything in the basement. Was he able to get the tracking code in place?"

"Andrei was out by the time they brought me down there," Navy said. "But Dragomir said Andrei had admitted during interrogation to adding code to track Dragomir's clients."

"Did Andrei tell you anything about his plans?" Kevin asked.

"He was going to use reserved bits in the packet header."

"I have no idea what that means."

Navy smiled. "I figured. Get me a laptop today and I'll email what I know to your technical contact. The code is probably in the C library for building packets."

"Now you're just rubbing it in," Kevin said.

"A little bit. It's nice to be able to focus on what I'm good at again." This whole operation she had felt like the beginner stumbling in front of the experts. Navy thought of Dragomir and Kevin's desire for revenge. "You got your wish. You got to kill Dragomir."

318

"Killing him in hand-to-hand combat was quite satisfying. A shot to the head was too good for him."

Navy didn't mind owing Jackson her life. She wasn't sure how she felt about owing Kevin. "Yeah, about that—"

"How many bullets did my gun have when I threw it to you?"

The question hadn't occurred to her. "I don't know."

"It was stupid to shoot Nicolae first." The statement was said without anger. He eased the wheelchair over a small curb to cross a driveway. "We could have tracked Petru down later. But without a second bullet, you'd be dead. You nearly died in surgery."

"Is that why Jackson seems so upset?"

Kevin's smile was indecipherable. "Yes and no. He probably thinks I'm going to recruit you." He turned the wheelchair toward a smooth lake that glittered. "I should."

As with most of her conversations with Kevin, she felt like she was several steps behind. "You don't seem impressed with my performance."

"I've never met an officer who didn't make a stupid mistake on their first operation. Including your precious Jackson."

She closed her eyes, savoring the warm sun on her skin. The memory of going into shock hadn't left her.

"You both earned a failing grade for this one."

"Jackson saved my life. That doesn't get him a few extra credit points?"

"A lucky accident. He directly disobeyed my orders—don't smile—it wasn't romantic. Your knight in shining armor nearly got himself killed."

The wound Navy had seen on Jackson's upper arm. What would the bullet have hit if it had caught him a second earlier or later? A shoulder? A kidney?

"And you would have been fine if you weren't trying to get Petru out of the way."

"If you're such a boy scout, why didn't you bring a knife as a backup to your gun?"

"Had to leave it in someone upstairs," he said. "I'm always losing them. They're like sunglasses that way. I don't buy expensive ones."

Strange that she considered him a good man, even though he talked so matter of factly about death.

"I couldn't ignore Petru," Navy said. She understood now there was something beyond the fear she'd come to face. She needed to prove to herself that even good people could kill, that she was still a good person.

Kevin frowned and nodded. "Yeah. I know."

A hospital orderly pushed a wheelchair past them, speaking cheerfully in Romanian to his elderly patient. Kevin stopped her wheelchair and took a seat on the small bench next to the water. The lake was filled with tame ducks who swam up to them, expecting food.

"If you're done giving me my grade, we can go back now."

"But it's such a nice day." He checked his watch. "And we have plenty of time."

Whatever Kevin wanted, he wouldn't take her back until he had it. She closed her eyes and imagined that the wind, the sun, the chirps of the birds were somewhere else. The top of the rock at the end of a long climb. A campsite after a long hike. She had almost succeeded when Kevin spoke again.

"You lived in Cedar City for a while?"

That chapter of her life had ended painfully. The few friends who knew why also knew better than to ask about it. "Yeah, I went to college there."

"I had a nice conversation with a friend of yours while I was doing my background research on you. You remember Officer Grant, right?"

"That police report was never filed."

"Officer Grant kept it. He said he hoped you'd change your mind."

She might not have used a wheelchair before, but she'd figure it out. Kevin saw what she was thinking and reached the brakes before she reached the wheels.

"Tell me about him," Kevin said, implacable.

"Officer Grant? He seemed nice enough."

"Not the officer. Theo."

She took a hissing breath.

"He put you in the hospital overnight with a broken cheekbone. Seems noteworthy. Why haven't you told Jackson about it?"

She imagined what Kevin would look like with scratches from her nails on his face. "Theo and I were together for eight months. He hit me. Once. I left. I'm over it."

"Obviously not."

"What the hell do you care?" The paths, the other benches, the manicured lawn were all deserted. "Take me back. Now."

"Jackson won't wait forever, you know."

Her wound ached as she slumped forward, still clutching the wheels that were frozen in place. "Wait forever for what?"

"He's a good man. Better than I am, certainly. But he can't be in a relationship by himself."

Jackson wasn't alone. The two of them worked in their own way. At least, she thought they did. She wondered what Jackson had told Kevin about her. Her throat was dry and she wished for the pitcher of water in her room.

"I meant what I said. I should recruit you."

The change of topic left her head spinning. "But?"

"Jackson would slit my throat."

She looked up to see if Kevin was kidding.

"Well, I'd lose him as an officer anyway. And he's one of my best, when he's not in the field with you."

"I don't want the job." Jackson had been right enough. She had learned she could still fight, that her blood still flowed warm. But she had collected as many ghosts as she had exorcised. The desperate Andrei, her uncertain ally, wouldn't leave her anytime soon.

322

Kevin checked his watch again. "You have no idea what that man is willing to do for you."

"You're wrong." Navy squirmed in her wheelchair. She did know. She just wasn't sure her devotion matched his.

"Oh?" Her answer didn't seem to surprise him. As if Kevin had asked the question just to hear her deny it.

"I do know." The ducks lost interest in them and swam across the lake to a family offering bread.

"He doesn't quite understand yet that you'd sacrifice just as much. God knows I tried to tell him."

She checked to see if Kevin's hand was still on the brakes. "If you're not going to let me leave, you might as well tell me what you want."

"I've known about you from the beginning."

There wasn't any question for her to answer.

"He called me for advice when you two were in Amsterdam, right after you rescued yourself. He wanted to know how best to protect you. And later, after you were both back in the states, he came to me again. You refused all his offers to help. You should have seen how upset he was."

She knew she had hurt him, but it wasn't easy to hear Kevin say it.

"I knew how you had escaped—the real version—not what Jackson put in the report. So I knew you were smart."

She kept her face turned away from Kevin. Maybe their ten minutes were almost up.

"I kept asking myself, why would a smart woman

choose to take on a government hit squad on her own?"

"It was risky. I had no right to ask."

"You didn't ask. He offered."

"Maybe we should skip ahead to the part where you tell me what you want."

"Do you know why Officer Grant remembered you?" he asked.

She shook her head, too tired to compose a reply.

"Most cases of domestic violence are tragically predictable. There's almost always drugs or alcohol or family history involved. You didn't have any of those things. Neither did Theo. No financial stress, no drinking problem—"

"Why don't you get to the point?"

"Officer Grant said Theo was a rarity. An 'overnight bastard.' One of those people who goes through life seemingly nice and normal until the day they're not."

"Fascinating. Can we go back now?"

Kevin leaned back, finally giving her space to breathe. "Whatever instinct led you to Jackson, you can trust it. What happened with Theo had nothing to do with you." The words were plain, unadorned with mockery or sarcasm.

All the fight left her muscles. She wondered if it was possible that she had sabotaged an endless series of relationships without cause. If she was about to drive away a good man because of yet another ghost, a ghost she had lived with for so long it had become invisible to her. "Do you enjoy playing psychologist?" she snapped.

324

"Answer the question. Why go it alone when Jackson was willing to go underground with you?"

She pressed her lips into a thin line. The answer was obvious. But it was none of Kevin's business.

"It's just us and the ducks." The family across the lake was gone. The dusky blue water lapped at the shore.

"Because I loved him even then," she said softly. "I knew my chances weren't good—with or without Jackson. I wasn't going to drag him down with me."

Kevin rubbed his hands together, as if he'd won some sort of prize. "Right on time."

She was confused. Again.

His smile was knowing. "Jackson should be here soon."

"Good."

"You should tell him about Theo."

Navy shook her head, unable to form a coherent objection.

"You should tell him how you feel," Kevin said.

"And that would fix everything? You have no idea what it's like to be—" Navy stopped herself. She had been about to say weak.

"Oh, honey, you think you know me." The southern lilt had crept into Kevin's voice again. "You don't. I know what it's like to be betrayed by someone who's supposed to protect you. I know what it's like to have to run away. You and I are a lot more alike than you think."

Navy couldn't decide if she hated Kevin or not.

"And I know what it's like to have a string of distant relationships. Because I don't talk about my past either. But I'm not you. I'm not Jackson. I'm better off alone."

"Maybe I am too." Navy tried to imagine a life without Jackson. Without the tangled, barbed mess of emotions their intimacy forced her to confront.

"If you really believed that, you wouldn't have stayed with Jackson this long," Kevin said.

Navy took a shaky breath. She could see Jackson approaching. "I don't know if I can talk about these things with him."

"Last year you escaped a terrorist kidnapping plot by making a shiv out of a mirror handle then taking one of their machine guns. And a few months after that you fought a special forces soldier and killed him with a crowbar. This has got to be easier."

"You'd think."

Jackson was close enough to hear them now. When he reached her, he rubbed Navy's shoulders. She took his hand.

"All done with the debrief?" Jackson asked.

"For now," Kevin said. Then, to Navy, "Just think about what I said, okay? Jackson's a friend. And you're kind of growing on me. I don't know exactly what you two are going to be, but you should at least start talking." Kevin walked away with his hands stuffed in his pockets.

Navy wondered when things between her and Jackson had become so complicated. No, they had always been

326

complicated. Her careful distance and his long absences had just allowed them to pretend. She traced the line of her cheekbone, the small bump only she could feel, where the break had knitted itself back together.

Jackson sat on the bench. He put his hand on her knee and she found she had missed his touch. "I owe you an apology."

An apology was the last thing Navy had been expecting. "For saving my life?"

"Well, not that. But I—" Jackson cleared this throat. "I haven't been fair to you. I shouldn't have tried to talk you out of going on this operation. I shouldn't have sulked around while we were here. I should have listened to you, asked more about why you wanted to come."

I wouldn't have told you, Navy thought. "Thank you. I appreciate that."

"And if something like this comes up again or if you want to become a field officer, I'll . . . I'll figure out how to deal with it."

Navy searched for the right words. Her nerves were already raw from the conversation with Kevin. "I'm happier in an office behind a keyboard," Navy said. "But you're right. You weren't being reasonable. And . . ." *Why did acknowledging forgiveness feel like losing? Why did Navy always fall back to treating relationships like combat?* "I forgive you."

"Can I ask what Kevin was referring to?"

"I—" The sentence stuck in Navy's throat. She looked beyond Jackson, to the green hills dotted with wildflowers and houses. "He exhumed a secret I thought I had buried."

"He mentioned something about you spending a night in the hospital, years ago."

Navy's whole body tensed. Telling Jackson was going to be harder than even she had expected. But, damnably, Kevin was right. And there wasn't enough time in the world to figure out what to say to Jackson, the man she desperately didn't want to lose.

"Let's try something new." Jackson squeezed her hand. "Just for today. I won't ask you any questions. You can tell me as much or as little as you want."

She liked the idea. "You won't last five minutes."

He pretended to be hurt. "What are you accusing me of?"

"See, you just asked me a question. You didn't even last thirty seconds."

It was good to hear him laugh. "A technicality. I call do-over."

A doctor walked by, a cigarette carefully balanced between her red fingernails. A couple that must have been in their seventies sat in a bench along the path. Despite his oxygen tank and her stoop, they held hands like lovers.

"I get to ask as many questions as I want, and you get to ask none?"

"Anything," he said.

Navy decided to use plain words as a sort of anesthesia for the pain the memories summoned. "When I was in college, I had a boyfriend, Theo. He was abusive. Emotionally, at first. I didn't know enough to recognize what was going on. Then later . . ."

Jackson opened his mouth, then closed it and pressed his lips together. She tried to decode the emotions flickering across his face. "Theo put you in the hospital," Jackson said.

"You're angry I didn't tell you."

"Not angry exactly. Worried. About why you didn't want to tell me."

"Surely you understand." *Please understand.* She wasn't sure she could explain.

"Understanding and not being upset are two different things. It makes me think you see something in me that reminds you of him."

"He said 'I love you' first."

Jackson pulled a hand down his face, rubbing at his temples. "You didn't tell me. I can't avoid stepping on land mines I don't know about."

"You want to listen or argue?"

"Listen."

"He said 'I love you' months before I did. We hadn't even been together that long." She remembered the day exactly. Strange how a memory she hadn't thought of in years could come back so clearly. A spring day in the park, watching the sunset. Midwestern weather being what it was, they were bundled up against the chill. *I love you. Don't you love me? Maybe, I can't say yet. I've only known you for a few weeks.* "When I finally said

'I love you' back, we had already moved in together. The change wasn't overnight, like everybody thought." She took another shaky breath. "It happened over a few weeks. It was like once I said the words, he knew he had me. He started to get possessive. Jealous. He wanted to know where I was all the time, who I was with. Then, one night . . ."

God, that night. She still didn't know what had possessed her to walk into their apartment. She knew what sort of reception she'd get; she just didn't know how bad it would be. "I was out with friends, having some drinks. I told him I would be. When I came home, he was waiting up for me." Two plates of cold dinner on a table set for two. A candle burned down to its bitter end. Dirty dishes from cooking stacked next to the sink, and a pan left on the stove. That pan. "He had cooked this big dinner for us, even though I told him I wouldn't be home until late. He accused me of cheating on him. I told him what an ass he'd been lately. We got in this yelling match so loud the neighbors called the police."

The embarrassment made her face sting. They must have sounded like an episode of *Cops*. "I guess that was a good thing, because right before they arrived was when he hit me in the face with a skillet. I heard the bone break."

"Navy—"

"I told you to listen." When she woke up on the floor, her tears had made the wound sting. She had covered her face, imagining how malformed her face must look, like a tent with a broken pole. "The worst part was he started babbling about how

330

he was sorry. Like I was supposed to forgive him right there." She carefully kept Jackson's face at the edge of her vision. "So I spent the night in the hospital, like Kevin said. Then I had a cop arrange a time for me to get my stuff from the apartment Theo and I shared. The officer went with me, just in case. I haven't seen Theo since."

"There's no shame in being overpowered. Hell, you've seen my scars."

"You don't understand. I knew something was wrong, and I still stayed with him. I let him hurt me. I was weak."

Jackson shook his head. "The one thing nobody has ever called you is weak."

"You didn't know me then. That's the real reason I've kept my distance. Once I fell for Theo, I got so wrapped up in us I couldn't leave even when I knew I should."

"And you don't trust that I won't turn into him."

Her words had been as good as an accusation, even though she hadn't meant it that way. One of many reasons she had never wanted to have this conversation with him. Compassion and hurt flickered across his face in equal parts.

"You know I would never hurt you," he said.

"*Listen.* What I'm trying to tell you is I don't trust myself. Can you understand that?"

He nodded slowly. "I think so."

"I know you're not like Theo. We were never as comfortable together as I am with you."

A cautious smile broke his somber expression. "I think

that's the most romantic thing you've ever said to me."

She reached for his wrist to check the time. He was wearing the watch she gave him. "Looks like I have seven more hours of questions in my day."

"Be gentle," he said.

Every time Navy had been physically threatened, Jackson's response had been to offer to fight on her behalf. Less than a week ago, he'd joked with her about revenge. *If you don't make it through this alive, I'll have to kill Byron and probably Kevin.* "Will you be planning some sort of a physical attack on Theo now that you know my history?"

"I'm sure you could manage it, if that's what you really wanted."

"The boy learns." This is what she had wanted all along, she realized. His protection and her independence. It hadn't occurred to her that she could have both.

Jackson smiled. "I'm slow to learn when it comes to you." He rolled her fingers between his own.

"So what happens now?"

"We stay here until the doctors say it's safe to travel."

I meant with us, Navy thought. "And then?"

"There's some operations stuff to wrap up in DC. Then some time for you to rest, at my apartment if you want. Or Des Moines."

"I meant—" Navy cursed the scars holding her words back. "What about us? Where do we go from here?"

"You tell me." Jackson was waiting for her to make the

332

next move, giving her the space she thought she wanted.

"I'm moving to DC," Navy said.

"That's good news."

"That's all you have to say?"

He grinned. "My questions have to wait until tomorrow."

"Six months ago, you said you wanted me to move in with you. Do you still?"

"That hasn't changed."

"The way we argued before the operation, I didn't know." Navy had said something wrong again; Jackson was frowning. "Say something, Jackson."

"This no questions thing is hard for me. Give me a minute," he said.

Navy watched a translucent cloud drift, pushed by a gentle wind, in the sky behind Jackson. A lump gathered in her throat. Had Kevin's advice been wrong? Had she broken everything?

"I'm not a saint," Jackson said. "Even knowing your past, it's hard for me to hear you say you don't have faith in us."

"Trusting your feelings comes so easily to you."

"Only with you."

"Don't say things like that." She felt the responsibility for someone else's happiness heavy on her shoulders. Or was that just another gift from Theo? Every awful fight had ended the same. Theo would beg, plead, apologize until she agreed to stay. *I'm sorry, I'm sorry, I'm sorry. I need you. If you leave me, I'll kill myself.*

Navy thought of all the nights she and Jackson had shared. Quiet nights. Passionate nights. The troubled nights he held her when the nightmares threatened. The nights his own demons stirred, and she had comforted him. Jackson had never tried to make her responsible for his happiness; he had simply tried to be with her. All she needed to do was the same.

"Navy? Something wrong?"

"That's another question," she said, smiling. "I knew you couldn't do it."

Jackson kissed the top of her head. "You're right. I'm a lost cause."

Navy stared at the blue diamonds on her hospital gown. "I'm a lost cause too, you know."

"I think we could be lost causes together."

It was two words instead of three, but she had a feeling that didn't matter as much anymore. "Yes. Let's."

Acknowledgements

Lately, I've been puzzling over why most writers are introverts. We are the people who hide in the corner at parties and give politely evasive answers to personal questions. And yet, here I am publishing my third novel. Dessa, one of my favorite singers, describes releasing an album as a trust fall. You can't avoid putting your psyche on the page when you write a song or a poem or a story. When you find someone who wants to read your book, it's both exhilarating and frightening.

I can't deny that all my books have been therapeutic to write, but if the goal were therapy I would have stopped after the first draft. Instead, I've spent years finding time in between my day job and personal life to rewrite, revise, and polish this book. This is not a solo process. I owe a debt to friends like Kelly Stahlberg, Christopher Gales, Bryan Zlimen and Ry4an Brase who gave me valuable, honest feedback. I also owe a debt to other writers like Carol Ervin, Katherine Lato, and Alex Sheridan who not only critiqued my work, but gave me a model to follow on the rocky, slow road to publishing. Once again, my editor Dara Syrkin has been invaluable in forcing me to polish and cut, cut, cut.

My life has been far from perfect. But I've also been lucky in a lot of ways. I'm lucky I have the resources to follow this compulsion of mine not just to write, but to publish. Not everyone gets that chance.

9 781734 759006